D0911349

ETHELDREDA

Books by Moyra Caldecott

The Tall Stones
The Temple of the Sun
Shadow on the Stones
The Silver Vortex
Hatshepsut: Daughter of Amun
Akhenaten: Son of the Sun
Tutankhamun and the Daughter of Ra
The Ghost of Akhenaten
Weapons of the Wolfhound
The Eye of Callanish
The Lily and the Bull
The Tower and the Emerald
Etheldreda
Child of the Dark Star
The Winged Man
The Waters of Sul
The Green Lady and the King of Shadows
Adventures by Leaf Light and Other Stories
The Breathless Pause
Crystal Legends
Three Celtic Tales
Women in Celtic Myth
Myths of the Sacred Tree
Mythical Journeys: Legendary Quests
Multi-dimensional Life

ETHELDREDA

Moyra Caldecott

Published by
Bladud Books

Copyright © 1987, 2000, Moyra Caldecott

Moyra Caldecott has asserted her
right under the Copyright, Designs
and Patents Act, 1988, to be identified
as the Author of this work.

First published in Great Britain
in 1987 by Arkana

This large print edition published in 2018
by Bladud Books, an imprint of Mushroom
Publishing, Bath, BA1 4EB, United Kingdom

www.bladudbooks.com

All rights reserved. No part of this
publication may be reproduced in any
form or by any means without the prior
written permission of the publisher.

ISBN 978-1-84319-454-5

Contents

Introduction

England in the seventh century was a place of violence and conflict. The seven kingdoms of the Germanic tribes were warring against each other and against the native Celts. Occasionally an uneasy peace was bought by the skilful use of the diplomatic marriage. Pagan Mercia was ruthlessly dedicated to expansion and to stamping out Christianity. Within the Christian kingdoms themselves there was the clash between the organized Roman Church and the much more individualistic Celtic form of worship from Iona and Lindisfarne.

Through all this, the four remarkable daughters of Anna, King of the East Angles, fired by the ideals of a new and revolutionary religion, managed not only to hold their own, but also to emerge head and shoulders above most of the people of their time.

One of them, Etheldreda, became Queen of Northumbria during the golden age of its power and was later declared a saint, her shrine at Ely near Cambridge the centre for miracles even into the present century.

As a young girl she felt herself called to be a nun and vowed chastity, but politics intervened and she was twice married to save her father's kingdom. Once to Prince Tondbert, ruler of the wild fen country around Cambridge, a man much older than herself, and later, at his death, to Prince Egfrid of Northumbria, a boy of fifteen. Faced with the violent deaths of those dearest to her and with upheaval and treachery on all sides, she not only endured, but ruled Northumbria with strength and wisdom for many years.

When she was in her early forties and Egfrid twenty-five, he refused to accept the arrangement he had agreed to honour when he married, and tried to force her to bed with him. She fled. He and his men gave chase. After an extraordinary journey south in which storms seemed to intervene on her behalf, she escaped at last to the Island of Ely, which had been her first husband's marriage gift to her, and there founded a religious community.

Bitterly King Egfrid gave up his claim to her, throwing her friend Bishop Wilfrid, who had supported her bid for freedom, into a dungeon and embarking on a series of punitive wars against his neighbours to the north and across the sea in Ireland. But this is not just the story of war and treachery in early England. It is about the general human struggle to comprehend the enigma of existence and to come to terms with Christ's God, faced as we are by a violent and cruel world. It is about the periods when we give up the struggle, reverting either to the darkest negativity or to superstition—and the rare but wonderful periods when we are lifted high by the inrush of spiritual certainty.

* * * *

Edwin holds a council with his chief men about accepting the Faith of Christ, AD 627:

> *'Your Majesty, when we compare the present life of man with that time of which we have no knowledge, it seems to me like the swift flight of a lone sparrow through the banqueting-hall where you sit in the winter months to dine with your thanes and counsellors. Inside there is a comforting fire to warm the room; outside, the wintry storms of snow and rain are raging. This sparrow flies swiftly in through one door of the hall, and out through another. While he is inside, he is safe from the winter storms; but after a few moments of comfort, he vanishes from sight into the darkness whence he came. Similarly, man appears on earth for a little while, but we know nothing of what went before this life, and what*

follows. Therefore if this new teaching can reveal any more certain knowledge, it seems only right that we should follow it.'

From A History of the English Church and People by Bede (Penguin Classics, translation by Leo Sherley-Price, 1955), Book II, Chapter 13.

1

War AD 640

To the defenders of Egric's dykes, Penda's warriors seemed numberless.

All day they came.

Time after time the air was filled with the high deadly whine of arrow flight, the scream of the wounded, the barbarous battle shout of the enemy. Where the dykes were most easily breached, at the point where the trade road to the south-west crossed the great ditch on ramp and wooden bridge, the fighting was hand to hand, Penda wielding his battle axe as though he were cutting the tall wheat at harvest time. The Seer he had consulted had promised him that much blood would be spilt, but that not much of it would be theirs.

The invading Mercians had few casualties. The hapless East Anglians, defending their homeland, had more than they could count.

* * * *

Before the last great dyke the Mercians paused. Evening was coming on fast, and the sun was staining the sky with a reflection of the blood that they had shed upon the earth.

Penda called back his men to rest and gather strength, intending to take the dyke at dawn. They made camp, roasting the cattle they had taken from their enemies, drinking the ale they had brought with them from their homeland.

Two young princesses of the East Anglian court, Etheldreda and Saxberga, daughters of Prince Anna, were far from home, staying with relatives. The first they knew of the Mercian invasion was the sudden arrival of terrified refugees making for the fenlands, preferring to take their chances with the ghouls and demons that inhabited those mysterious regions than be put to the sword or split by the axe. Behind the refugees the princesses could see the black smoke as village after village across the land was set on fire.

Panic-stricken, the princesses' relatives hastily packed up all they could carry of their possessions, and the girls joined them in a dash for the east. They hoped that they would reach the final dyke and be allowed over the ramps before they were closed for battle.

At the last ford before the dyke, where the crowds of hysterical people were struggling against each other in the effort to get to the other side, Saxberga was knocked off the horse she was sharing with Etheldreda and trampled under its hooves. Screaming for her sister as she saw her go under, Etheldreda flung herself after her and tried to drag her clear. The horse was instantly seized by someone else and ridden off; the two girls, separated from their friends, were left in the muddy water among the pushing, violent people.

Etheldreda was weeping and trembling, but she would not let her sister go for fear of losing her. She managed to drag her unconscious body somehow across the river and out of the path of the stampeding cattle, people, horses and carts. She called for help, but no one came to aid her. She stared in astonishment. It was only the day before that these same people had been bowing with respect to her and her sister as they rode high and fine upon their royal horses. The sun had shone on peaceful fields of yellow buttercups. Cows had grazed and chewed on the cud.

Now it was as though she and her sister were invisible. Torn and muddy and bedraggled, they were indistinguishable from the peasants and slaves who drove the farmers' cattle across the ford and, for the first time in her life, she knew that she was on her own, that her survival depended entirely on her own ingenuity. She could not even turn for help to her older sister.

She stopped crying and looked around her. A little further on to the left was a wood; this would give them hiding place and shelter. She knew that they had to get away from the terrified mob, who were almost as destructive as the invading hordes from which they were fleeing.

Little by little she half dragged, half carried her sister to the wood, and did not rest until they were deep inside and well out of sight of the crowds and the distant columns of smoke. There she carefully made Saxberga as comfortable as she could on a bed of bracken, and carried water from a tiny trickling stream in her hands to splash into her face.

Saxberga regained consciousness with a jerk, and screamed with the pain she felt in her leg. Etheldreda flung her arms around her and held her tight.

'We're safe,' she whispered, the tears she had held back for so long beginning to flow.

Saxberga's face twisted with the pain, but she tried to pull herself together for her little sister's sake.

'What is happening?' she asked. 'Where are we?' She could hardly bring the words out as she struggled to make sense of the situation.

'We're safe,' Etheldreda babbled on. 'No one will find us here, we'll wait until the fighting is over.' The tears ran through the dirt on her cheeks unnoticed.

Suddenly they heard a movement behind them and swung round, horrified to find themselves observed by a strange, rough youth clad in skins, his hair and eyes dark, a dead deer over his shoulder. Etheldreda seized a stone that was lying next to her hand and clutched it, ready to use it as a weapon if necessary.

He took a step nearer, staring at them curiously. She shrank back. Was this one of the dread heathen Mercians? He certainly was not of their own race, though he did not look as fierce and cruel as they expected. Perhaps he was one of the native people, a Celt. She moved away from Saxberga and stood up straight, like the princess she was, looking him in the eye.

'We need help,' she said, trying to keep her voice steady and cool. 'Will you help us?'

He looked her up and down. She was covered in mud from the ford and blood from her sister; her hair was matted and hanging in strings; her pale, dirty face was pinched with weariness and anxiety, but she spoke as though she expected to be obeyed like one of the hated Angles who had invaded his land and made a slave of him. He almost turned away and then his eyes fell on the girl in agony on the ground.

'Where are you hurt?' he asked gruffly, his accent strange to them, but his voice not ungentle. Etheldreda silently pointed to the bone protruding from her sister's leg and he put the carcass of the deer down in the bracken and crouched down beside them, looking thoughtfully at Saxberga's leg.

From somewhere in the distance they heard a terrible scream.

'Haven't you heard of the war?' Etheldreda asked him. 'You don't seem to be running away like everyone else.'

'Yes, I have heard of the war,' he said as though it was of no importance. Then—'You take the deer,' he said to her, and put his arms around Saxberga to lift her from the ground. 'Come.'

Etheldreda looked with horror at the animal that she was expected to carry.

'Come,' he said again, urgently, commandingly.

Etheldreda tried to swing the carcass to her shoulder, but she almost fell over with the weight.

'Can't I leave it?' she pleaded.

'No. Bring it,' he said roughly, already moving away through the wood.

Terrified of being left alone, she took a grip on the deer's antlers and dragged the body behind her, tugging and struggling as it caught on fallen branches and tough little bushes. Not once did he look back to see if she was managing to keep up with him.

When he finally stopped walking and lowered Saxberga to the ground, Etheldreda was sweating and exhausted, but determined not to cry. They were deep in the thickest part of the wood, the undergrowth of brambles making the way almost impassable. He started to bend back branches, and she discovered that an overhang of rock made a sizeable cavern behind a wall of bushes. He indicated that she should go ahead, and when she had crept and scrambled and slithered her way in, he carefully lifted her sister in after her.

Etheldreda looked around her. There was a small lamp cut out of the chalk, with a rush wick and, by the smell of it, animal oil; earthenware pots and jugs, and the blackened stones of a small hearth fire. There was also a pile of straw with furs flung over it, onto which he now lowered the older girl. He then left them for a moment to attend to the deer carcass the child had left exposed outside.

Etheldreda crouched down beside Saxberga and held her hand tightly. It was very dim in the cave, but as her eyes grew accustomed to the lack of light she noticed the grotesque figure of a heathen god staring at her from a niche in the rough wall. Seven-branched antlers grew from his head and a garland of leaves hung around his neck.

* * * *

That night as Penda tried to sleep in his tent of skins he heard a terrible sound. Only half awake he went to the entrance of his tent. The battlefield of the day before, still covered with the bodies of the slain, lay behind him. Above him the sky was swirling with dark clouds, and from the wind came a wild keening. Could he see the women of death riding the clouds, crying high and loud, calling the names of the warriors who had died and would die... and behind them the hounds, howling across the sky?

He shuddered, remembering the eyes of the Seer he had killed when she had told him he would have victory and yet no victory. She had spoken in riddles of a man who would come bearing no spear, no sword and no axe, who would rise again when he was killed.

He raised his fist and shook it at the sky.

'I vowed by Thunor's silver ring I would defeat the upstart god who challenges him,' he shouted into the wind. 'I, wielder of Thunor's avenging hammer, wearer of his belt of power and his iron gloves, swear again by the true gods, I will destroy the heathen Christ!'

The sky was ripped open by a deadly blade of lightning and his god spoke to him in the thunder.

* * * *

In the cave, Etheldreda, sleepless through the night, clutched her sister's skirt, watching the lightning flicker through the branches over the entrance, weirdly illuminating the figure of the idol. She heard the thunder and then the heavy hushing of the rain.

The youth slept soundly and seemed unaware of the storm. Saxberga slipped fitfully into a heavy state that was at times more unconsciousness than sleep. Etheldreda alone kept vigil, trembling and afraid. All the order she had known and taken for granted was gone, and it was as though she were in the swirling dark and chaos of the first Creation. Within her she fought the fear of the void, the fear of becoming nothing.

As the lightning flashed she caught the eye of the stone god, and almost screamed aloud with the shock of feeling that it was watching her. It seemed so real she cried out to it for help. But in the next flash of lightning she saw the god's eyes were hollow and sightless, his ears of stone. He could not see her plight, nor hear her prayer. There was no one in the cave besides herself, her sister and the youth.

Near dawn she crept out of the cave. Saxberga was lying fast asleep on the young man's straw and fur, her leg firmly and skilfully bound. The youth himself was hunched against the far wall, snoring.

The rain had stopped, but drops of water were still dripping from the canopy of leaves. At first it was quite dark but every moment it was lightening. And so were her thoughts. She could hardly believe that the dark horrors of the day before had really happened and she began to feel that it would not be difficult to find a way out of the wood and back to her family and friends. Surely there would be a village nearby where she would be able to find a horse for Saxberga to ride. She set off at once to look for one.

She had not gone far when she smelled burning and saw smoke through the trees. She began to run, joyfully sure that she would now soon be among friendly people cooking their breakfast. But something made her cautious, perhaps something she had only just learned. She slowed down and kept under cover, approaching carefully. The wood suddenly gave way to a large clearing.

She stood transfixed, staring at the scene,

as though she were above the world looking down. The fire was no hearth fire as she had hoped, but the smouldering remains of a village and, lying among the charred wood of the fallen house beams, were the mutilated bodies of the villagers. The child clapped her hand to her mouth to stifle a scream. She wanted to run, but she found she could not.

Suddenly Etheldreda felt a hand seize her shoulder and her heart jerked painfully. She felt herself pulled backwards and terror seemed to break over her like a dark and icy wave. She twisted her head and then, sick with relief, she recognised the youth who had taken her sister and her to the cave.

Her legs gave way as he lifted her in his arms. He ran with her as swift and sure as a wild animal through the woods, scarcely cracking a stick underfoot.

She put her arms around his neck and clung. She felt she had known him all her life. He had become father and mother and home and security, light and warmth and sleep. Tears poured from her eyes and ran down his neck.

He did not stop until he was outside the cave and then he lowered her to the ground. He pulled aside the branches and pushed her roughly under them. The lamp was not lit, but the light of dawn had penetrated a little and she could see Saxberga sitting bolt upright reaching out her arms to her. She fell into them sobbing.

She was aware of being scolded, of being closely held, of alternate sisterly endearments and angry accusations—but she could not stop sobbing.

Saxberga demanded to know what had happened, but Etheldreda could not tell her.

The older girl looked over her head at the youth sitting on his haunches trimming pieces of meat from the deer with his belt knife, the small hearth fire comfortably blazing. But his face was totally absorbed in what he was doing.

* * * *

The early light that crept into the cave where the two princesses were hiding brought no comfort to the thousands of men behind King Egric's last defensive dyke. Tensely they waited, crouched in the cold dawn air praying to their god, the ramps taken, the wooden bridges dismantled. All night they had watched the storm and wondered what it presaged. It had doused the enemies' fires: if only it would douse their battle spirit. Some had thought they heard the fierce ride of the women of death and had said goodbye to the fair world in their hearts, but others had seen the anger of Christ's father against the heathen in the lashing of the storm and had stubbornly clung to hope.

By the time the grey dawn came, the storm had passed though the sky still hung close to the earth, heavy and swollen with dark drops of rain.

Lying along the ridge of the dyke the East Anglian look-outs saw the earth move, its black mantle creeping forward towards them. Some made the sign of the cross, others reached for amulets of the old gods. None thought that they would live to see the sun set that day.

* * * *

Penda, the plunder-lord on his great war-horse, rode ahead with his picked men, the most feared fighting warriors of his whole force, men whose blood-curdling screams in battle were said to melt men's minds and burst their hearts before even a blow were struck. He gripped his spear. It had lain on Thunor's iron altar and would be guided with supernatural accuracy to its mark.

His eyes glinted under his beetling brows. This is what he lived for: the moment before a battle when everything depended on his signal to strike. At such a moment he felt himself possessed by his god. Penda stopped just outside arrow range and raised his spear arm.

The whole vast body of men froze where they were, the silence stretched so taut a lark's call would have shattered it.

And then, suddenly, an incredible thing happened. A man emerged from the great ditch in front of the ridge and started walking calmly forward towards Penda.

Penda frowned. This was not as it should be. Straining, he tried to see more clearly in the dim light. The figure approached steadily, head up, shoulders squared, purposive and authoritative. But as he came nearer Penda saw that he was unarmed and he remembered the Seer's words: 'No spear. No sword. No axe.' A chill came to the Mercian's heart. This had been foretold. This was his adversary.

Sigbert, the King who had given up his kingdom to become a monk, came near enough to look into Penda's eyes and, as men's lives and the fate of kingdoms hung in the balance of that tense and silent dawn, the two men faced each other, each a formidable warrior, each fighting a different war.

Penda forgot the waiting men, the blood shadow that hung above the landscape, the women of death that rode at his heels, the hounds that hunted. It was as though everything in the world had ceased to exist except this one man, and this man, though he uttered not a word, was asking him a question.

'What am I doing here?' he found himself thinking. 'Why do I want to kill these people?'

But even as he struggled for the answer an arrow came whining through the air and fell at the end of its reach just ahead of him. The spell was broken. So it had been only a trick to distract him!

He threw his spear with all his strength into the breast of the sorcerer who had made him look into his own heart. With a high and fearsome scream his men rushed forward, their arrows and their spears falling like deadly rain upon the defenders of the dyke.

* * * *

It was at Prince Ethelhere's command that the arrow had been loosed, and it was Prince Ethelhere, brother to King Egric, who shouted commands and led the defence.

With tears in his eyes King Egric knew that they had lost, but might not, had his cousin, Sigbert, been allowed to live. He remembered how they had taken him away from the peaceful fields he was ploughing and demanded that he lead them into battle. His reputation as a warrior before he gave up the world to become a monk was so formidable that they knew the people would have no fear of Penda if he were at their head. Egric could hear Ethelhere's haughty voice even now.

'Have you heard no rumours of the war, sir, in this remote place?'

And Egric could hear Sigbert's reply.

'There is always war in the souls of men.'

Ethelhere scowled. 'Real war, sir!' he snapped. 'Penda of Mercia attacks our country and kills our women and children! We come to demand that you help us to defend our land—your land!'

'Your land? My land?' Sigbert said quietly. 'Is it not God's land?'

It was he, Egric, who then spoke up.

'It is God's land, my cousin, but He has given it to us to work in His name and to defend against His enemies.'

'How can His children be His enemies?'

'Penda's wolves are not God's children,' one of Egric's thegns shouted angrily. 'They are heathen and mock Him with their idols and their blasphemous ways.'

'A man standing in a field at night looks up and sees the moon caught in the branches of a tree. If he is wise he will know this cannot be, because the moon is immeasurably higher than the tree. It only seems as though it is caught, because he is standing where he is.'

'What has this to do with us?' Ethelhere said impatiently.

'The heathen are children of our God, no less than we, but we have learned that the moon cannot be caught in the tree.'

The men looked puzzled, but Egric had understood, and wished that there was more time to discuss these deep matters with his cousin.

'Enough!' Ethelhere growled. 'While we stand and play with words, Penda marches and kills our people. We must ride against him, and when we ride, you must be at our head!'

'I will not ride to war,' Sigbert said firmly. 'I have no right to say who will live and who will die.'

'You will let your people be killed?'

'Each man is answerable for himself at the throne of God.'

'I see we have wasted our journey,' Ethelhere said bitterly. 'The Lord Sigbert will not help us. He is content to hide in safety and watch his people die.'

Sigbert looked around the table at the disappointed and hostile faces. Only Egric chose not to meet his eye.

'I will come with you,' Sigbert said. 'I will come to meet Penda. But I will not fight him with weapons, but with the power of the Lord's spirit within me.'

'You are insane!' Ethelhere muttered in disbelief.

Egric raised his head, a glimmering of hope in his eyes. Then Ethelhere took a deep breath and thought hard. He knew that with Sigbert there the men would fight, no matter if he wielded sword himself or not.

'Come and use what weapons you will,' the prince said at last, 'but come before it is too late.'

* * * *

After Sigbert's death, Egric had tried to fight, but he knew he was not a fighting man, and his heart was soon stopped with iron. On seeing both Sigbert and Egric fall, the men turned to run and no amount of shouting and commanding on Ethelhere's part would make them stay and face the Mercians. Penda's hordes poured unchecked into the ditch and up the other side, and Ethelhere was forced to flee with the rest.

* * * *

Penda was almost sorry the victory had been so easy.

He rode back to where the mysterious sorcerer had stood, still haunted by the words of the Seer: 'No spear. No sword. No axe', and the memory of how he had felt with the man's eyes boring into his, how he had momentarily wondered whether he had a right to take men's lives.

Sigbert's body had been beaten into the ground under the charge of men and horses. There was very little left of it to rise again. Penda was satisfied that this part at least of the Seer's vision was false.

* * * *

That night, installed as conqueror in the great hall at Exning, Penda called for a prisoner to be brought before him.

'One who was at the dyke,' he commanded.

This order was not easy to obey. The Mercians on the whole did not take prisoners and it was some time before a boy was found who had escaped killing.

He was flung at Penda's feet.

'You saw the sorcerer who came to trick me?' Penda growled. The boy looked bewildered and was kicked.

'The man who came out unarmed before the battle.'

In dumb terror the boy nodded.

'Who was he?'

The boy was silent, struggling to think how best to stay alive. He was kicked again.

'Who was he?' shouted Penda, his eyes of fire boring into the young lad's dimming ones.

The boy muttered something.

'What was that?'

Penda gestured impatiently for the guards to bring the prisoner nearer to him.

'Well, who was he?'

'Our king,' the lad said, and even as he said it he seemed to gain courage.

'That is a lie,' Penda snarled and nodded brusquely at one of his men. He left the tent and returned with Egric's head and flung it before the lad.

The boy tried not to gag.

'That... that is the new king,' he sobbed. 'King Sigbert gave up being king to... to become a monk.'

Penda, who had clawed his way up to kingship, its power being more important to him than anything else on earth, confronted the image of a man who had had that power, and given it away.

'You mean he gave up being king to become a priest?' he said disbelievingly.

The boy nodded. He wished he could remember a prayer he had once learned, to keep him from the harm of demons. Penda was surely demon-driven with those dark and restless eyes, those beetling brows, those knotted muscular hands closing and unclosing on the hilt of the dagger in his belt.

'Your priests, are they richer and more

powerful than the King?' Penda demanded, still trying to understand a man who would give up being king to be a priest. If he must be priest, could he not have been both?

The boy looked helpless. He had no idea how to answer this. The soldier jabbed him fiercely in the side.

'No, my lord,' he said. 'They're poor. They have nothing of their own. They even beg for food.'

Penda strode about. He could not get the eyes of the man Sigbert out of his mind. He had killed many men, but none who had disturbed him so much.

'These priests, do they know magic?'

The boy shook his head, darkness seemed to be closing in on him. He knew that he had heard a wandering monk once condemn magic as being of the devil though this had not prevented many in his village turning to it when they needed it. For his own part he could never understand why an amulet that had the power to heal was evil, when a relic of a holy man doing the same work was not. His brother, who seemed to understand these things more than the rest of them, said it was because the amulet was 'blind' power and no one knew what dark forces might work through it without your noticing, but the relic was 'seeing' power and was linked to a spirit that was known and proven to be good.

'If he was not there to fight, and he was not there to make magic, why was he there?' Penda demanded.

'King Egric and Prince Ethelhere had brought him to us to lead us into battle. He used to be a warrior. But he spoke to us of friendship with the Mercians, and said it was wrong to kill, even our enemies. He said he had taken a vow to God not to kill and he would not do it even to save his own life.'

'He vowed to his god that he would not kill?' Penda asked in amazement.

The boy nodded.

Penda grunted and rubbed his bearded chin. 'What did he hope to gain by coming up to me like that?'

The boy shrugged helplessly.

'I respect a man who keeps a vow and who honours his god. Even a god who is as foolish as this one seems to be.' The Mercian king spoke as though to himself. And then, louder, to his men, he said: 'Find this priest-king's body and let it be buried with dignity.'

But before they could leave his presence to do his bidding there was a disturbance at the entrance and a man rushed in with urgent news. The boy could not catch what was said, as there was a great deal of shouting, but he heard enough to know that the Mercians were alarmed at a sudden change in the situation. When they rushed out leaving him alone, he began to crawl towards the entrance, but fainted before he reached it.

* * * *

The news Penda had heard to change his mood so swiftly had been that the East Anglians, whom he had thought he had defeated, were rallying under the standard of a new leader.

Prince Anna, brother to both Egric and Ethelhere, had missed the battle, being at the time on a visit to the Kentish court. But he had had a dream of such horror about his country that he had set off for home even before messengers arrived with the news of Penda's invasion. And so it was that he was now already on East Anglian territory, having sailed up the Deben river while Penda's army was mostly scattered, looting in isolated villages, celebrating with the local strong ale, over confident in the extent of their victory. He and his companion rode in from the south-east, fresh from their sojourn in Kent, angry and determined to retake their land.

Penda had overreached himself and knew it. His spies had told him East Anglia would be easy taking once he had breached the dykes, and at first it had seemed that they were right. But the Seer had warned him he would have a victory that was not a victory.

He had been foolish to relax so soon and he was angry with himself. That damn sorcerer had taken his mind off things he ought to have been thinking about.

Within a few days Anna had turned the Mercians around. No matter how cruelly Penda's troops tried to stamp on the people, enough of them always seemed to get away to join their new leader.

By the coming of the Lord's day, Prince Anna could give thanks to his god for deliverance from the enemy, while Penda, angry and disappointed, had had to retreat.

* * * *

All through these terrible events Etheldreda and Saxberga lay hidden in the cave under the care of the taciturn youth. During the day he went out to forage for food and drink. At night they sat in the dark and talked long hours together, learning that the young man's name was Ovin and that he was a runaway slave of the Celtic race.

The punishment if he was caught would be certain death, and probably not by the most merciful method.

All their lives the princesses had taken slaves

for granted, assuming that they would always be there at their father's house at Exning or at Rendilsham, taking care of everything. They were not treated badly, for Anna and his wife were kind people and their slaves respected them and worked willingly. But Ovin told them that all masters were not so fair and gentle.

He started to describe the suffering and humiliations that he had endured, but had to stop because Etheldreda wept so piteously. She had been growing steadily paler as the days went by and now would scarcely eat or sleep, her eyes almost like dark holes in her head. She felt as though she had been living all her life believing that she was in a sturdy boat on a calm lake, and had suddenly found that she was on the open sea in a frail craft buffeted by winds and lashed by tremendous waves. One night as she dozed uneasily she thought she saw dry land and a beautiful country... but she could not see a way to reach it. She stretched out her arms, sobbing.

'Ssh,' hushed Saxberga, rocking her gently in her arms. 'Ssh!'

Ovin woke and crept over to them.

'She is having a bad dream,' whispered Saxberga. 'Do you think I should wake her?'

Runaway slave or not, Ovin had become for them both a strong and a comforting force, the only thing that kept them from absolute despair. He had treated Saxberga's leg with herbal concoctions to keep it from going gangrenous and he had set the bone well, probably better than the king's own physician would have done, binding it with strips of hide to a stick of wood. They had grown accustomed to his making every decision and waited patiently for the time when he thought it would be safe for them to leave the cave.

He put his hand on Etheldreda's shoulder.

'Wake up,' he said softly. 'You are safe.'

She jerked awake at once and sat bolt upright.

And for one amazing instant it seemed to her that she was not in the dark, but was seeing everything around her as clearly as though it were full daylight. But everything she saw, and everything she had ever seen, was as nothing to the fair and distant land she had glimpsed in her dream.

* * * *

The next day Ovin returned from foraging with good news.

'The Mercians have gone,' he told them. 'King Anna has driven them away.'

'King Anna?' gasped the girls.

He looked at them and smiled. 'Yes, King Anna,' he said.

2

The marriage of Saxberga

King Anna looked gravely down upon the mutilated bodies of three Mercian soldiers that had been laid proudly at his feet as he entered Garbaldisham.

'I would rather these men were alive,' he said quietly.

'My lord,' protested the young man who brought them to him, 'they killed my mother and my wife.'

The king nodded sadly.

'They kill your family, so you kill them. Their family must kill you in revenge for their death, and your kin must kill their kin in revenge for your death. And so it goes on. When will the killing stop if we do not stop it now? Why do we speak of being born again into a new life, if we do not change our ways?'

'But my lord, my wife and mother must be avenged!'

'"Vengeance is mine," said the Lord. "I will repay",' the king murmured, almost under his breath.

There was an uneasy silence among the

people gathered before him, until at last one spoke, a challenging spark in his eyes.

'Is it true, my lord, that your own daughters have been killed by the Mercians?'

A shadow passed over Anna's face and a muscle twitched in his cheek. He took a long time to answer this, and when he did his voice was full of pain.

'It is true.'

'And do you still say we must not take vengeance?'

There was another long pause. He shut his eyes and took a deep, slow, breath. Those who were near could see his knuckles white as he clenched his fists. But when he opened his eyes again, his gaze was steady and clear.

'I do,' he said simply.

The crowd murmured and shifted restlessly in front of him.

'Take these men away,' he said, straightening his shoulders and suddenly speaking in quite a different tone of voice. 'I do not believe in vengeance, but I do believe in self-defence. We have driven the Mercians from our land, but they will be back. Next time they must not penetrate the dykes. I want every man, woman and child in the country to pledge two days out of every week for digging at the dykes until I am satisfied that they are too high and strong for Penda's men to take. Those who live far from the place may work their days off in groups of ten, returning to their homes for the intervening weeks. Make this known,' he commanded, and leapt upon his horse.

After he had gone there was murmuring, some complaining about having to work on the dyke, others relieved that King Anna, though Christian like King Sigbert and willing to forgive his enemies, was shrewd enough at least to see the necessity of strong defence. They remembered also that he had delivered them from Penda.

The council of elders and priests, thegns and earls, had no hesitation in confirming Anna's claim to the crown, and people flocked to him from far and wide willing to take the oath of allegiance.

It is said that when the news of his daughters' safe return was brought to him he fell down on his knees in the mud and wept.

Later, at Rendilsham, he heard the details of their escape and was introduced to Ovin, who, only with the greatest difficulty, had been persuaded to come out of hiding and throw himself on the king's mercy. When Anna had listened to his story he sent for the man who had been Ovin's master.

That night the youth tried to run away, feeling sure that he had been betrayed, but he had gone no further than the stockade that surrounded the royal buildings when he found himself seized by the belt of his jerkin. He spun round, his fists at the ready, to find that he was looking into a child's face.

'My lady 'Dreda!' he gasped.

'You are not going to run away again?' she hissed.

'I have to,' he whispered miserably. 'Please, my lady, let me go.'

'No, I will not let you go to live in a hole in the ground again like a hunted animal, or become a wolf's-head outlaw, harrying the countryside for food. My father will not give you back to your master.'

'He has called for him.'

'He has called for him to punish him for how he has treated you. Come back with me and you will see.'

'He will give me back. He has to. It is the law.'

'He has promised me that he will pay the price for you. He will buy you. You will see how different masters can be.'

'My lady,' Ovin's voice broke slightly. 'I am grateful, but...'

'But what?' she asked sharply. The night was

dark and they were in shadow. She could see people moving, silhouetted against the house fires, the guards talking near the gate. She hoped that she could persuade Ovin to return to the slaves' quarters before he was missed.

'I can't go back to being a slave, no matter how kind the master.'

'Why not?'

Ovin shook his head in the dark.

'I can't!' he repeated vehemently—forgetting caution. Etheldreda put her hand upon his arm.

'Ssh,' she said. 'I will persuade my father to free you. But it must be done correctly or you will always live in fear.'

Ovin looked at her. Was this possible? Was the nightmare he had lived for so long finally going to end?

'Come,' she said, tugging at his arm. 'Trust me. Please! I owe you my life. Let my father give you back the one my people took from you.'

He allowed himself to be led to the slaves' quarters, but he hesitated to go in.

'It will only be for a little while,' she pleaded. 'I promise you.'

He sighed and disappeared through the low door into the darkness.

* * * *

It turned out that Ovin's master and most of his family had been killed in the fighting. Only his wife and one small child were left, and they were brought before King Anna. They were offered a good price for the slave, and accepted readily. Had the husband been alive he might have demanded Ovin's life, but his wife was destitute and preferred the money.

'You see!' cried Etheldreda joyously.

Ovin bowed his head glad that half of the promise had been kept, but he would not rejoice until he had the whole of it.

He was taken to the crossroads and there the ceremony of manumission was performed. The record of it was entered into King Anna's gospel book and witnessed by two priests and two thegns.

After the signatures, the curse was written in against anyone who would deny Ovin's freedom in the future.

'May he have the disfavour of God who at any time perverts this grant of freedom.'

It was signed by King Anna and the witnesses.

Ovin took a deep breath and looked up at the sky. He had never seen it so high and wide before, so full of splendour. He leapt into the air and ran like a young colt over the fallow field to the west.

The group at the crossroads watched him quietly, Etheldreda slipping her hand into her father's.

'It must be a terrible thing to be a slave,' she said thoughtfully. 'I hadn't thought of it before.'

'Most people are slaves, my child, in one way or another.'

'I am not!' she said fiercely.

'The strange thing is,' her father continued, ignoring her, speaking as though to himself, 'More often than not the only way we can prove we have our freedom is to give it up voluntarily.'

Ovin came running back, his eyes alight, his breath short.

'Well, my friend,' the King said. 'We are at the crossroads. You are free to go. Which way will you choose?'

Ovin looked around at the vast landscape, the fields of grain, the forests in the distance, the paths spreading out from where they stood. In every direction freedom lay.

He looked down at Etheldreda standing beside her father, still thin from her recent ordeal, but her cheeks now warm and glowing with happiness. The sunlight caught her hair and it shone like gold. Her eyes were full of caring and concern.

He suddenly flung himself on the ground and kissed the hem of her skirt.

'I ask to stay and serve the Princess Etheldreda as a free man,' he said, with a catch in his voice.

She cried out with delight and would have flung her arms around him, had her father not pulled her sharply back.

'My daughter is very young and has not yet learned fully the constrictions of her place in life. You too will find your new role confusing. If I give you permission to serve her, have I your oath that you will not abuse my trust?' He looked hard at the lad.

Ovin stood up and met his gaze, eye to eye as a free man would, then he bowed his head as a free man bows.

'You have, my lord,' he said quietly.

* * * *

Not long after this, Saxberga was called into her father's presence. The message was so formal Saxberga was alarmed, and insisted that Etheldreda accompany her.

But when they arrived they found him sitting in his favourite chair with his wife upon his knee, his head resting on her hair. They looked so happy together the two girls hesitated to draw attention to their arrival and thought to turn around and creep out. But

Anna noticed them and held out a hand to draw them close to him, encompassing all three with his arms. Tears came to Etheldreda's eyes to think that they were all together again, and the nightmare of war was over.

After a while he pushed them gently away from him and they could see that it was time to speak of the reason he had sent for Saxberga. They stood patiently in front of him, Saxberga beginning to feel a little uneasy as he gazed long and thoughtfully at her. She looked questioningly at her mother and was met with eyes half full of tears.

'What is it?' she cried, suddenly frightened.

Anna raised his hand soothingly. 'Don't be alarmed,' he said. 'I have good news for you. I hesitate only because I know at first it might seem a little...' His voice trailed away.

'What is it?' she demanded.

Anna looked appealingly at his wife and she stepped forward and took Saxberga's hands.

'My dove, your father has arranged for you to go to Kent to meet King Eorconbert,' she said.

Saxberga looked at her father suspiciously.

'Why?'

'Because he is a good man, a great man, king of the most powerful country in southern Britain, and his help in times of trouble would be invaluable.'

'What are you saying?' Saxberga almost screamed the words, knowing very well what he was saying.

'Hush, my dear. It is a great honour,' her mother said.

'What? What is a great honour? What is going on?' cried Etheldreda, bewildered.

'What is going on,' said Saxberga to her little sister, 'is that I am to be married off to a total stranger for the good of the country!'

Anna stood up. His face was no longer soft and loving, but stern.

'You are a woman and you know you must marry soon. You are a princess and you know you cannot marry whom you choose. Our country is in danger. You have seen with your own eyes what that means. Why do you pretend to protest? You know what must be, must be. The king of Kent is a fine man. You will marry him from necessity, but you will grow to love him. I promise you. There is no more to be said.' He looked at his wife and she hurried them out, Etheldreda bubbling with excited questions, Saxberga bitterly silent, her face red and angry.

They went to their special place in the woods, where they knew they could be alone. They talked for hours. In the end Saxberga was reconciled to the idea. Their own parents had not met before the betrothal vows. At least King Eorconbert was a young man, not much older than Saxberga herself. His country, Kent, had been the first of the kingdoms in the new land to be converted to Christianity. Under his grandfather's long rule it had become a strong and peaceful country, where people could travel and not be in continual fear of their lives, where the crafts that made for gracious living flourished, and the songs that were sung around the hearths were of love more often than of war. It was a fertile land, farmed intelligently according to the Frankish system, each field yielding more than an equivalent field in their own country.

The work of the Kentish weavers and of the goldsmiths was famous. When they returned home their mother showed the girls the presents Anna had brought from Kent. They held the fine cloth and pretended that it was already fashioned into clothes. Etheldreda fastened several necklaces at a time to her shoulders.

'Look! Look!' she cried, standing upon a wooden stool so that the cloth flowed down around her to the ground and she looked as tall as any grown woman. On her head she had placed a circlet of gold. 'I am to be a queen too! I am to marry a king!'

Their mother looked at them as they played at being queens, and tears came to her eyes. If only it were just a matter of wearing fine clothes! She knew that, as Anna's queen, her own days of peace and happiness with her family were over. From now on she would be continually with other people, on her guard, watching to protect her husband's interests, diplomatically helping him to keep the power he had against jealous contenders, helping him to carry out unpopular but necessary laws, smiling, talking, charming powerful foreigners to enlist their help, entertaining strangers who would be useful to her husband as friends and deadly as enemies, cultivating people because she needed them, and not because she enjoyed their company.

She sighed. The Mercian attack, and the years of Egric's indecisive reign before that, would make Anna's job more difficult.

In Kent her daughter would not have an easy time either. The peace and plenty of the reign of the great Bretwalda Ethelbert had been almost destroyed by his easy-going son Eadbald. From the moment of his father's death when he had taken his mistress, his father's second wife, to be his own wife, things had gone wrong. Heathenism, which in spite of thirty years of Christian rule was still not far from the surface, had welled up and almost overwhelmed the church Augustine had founded. Eventually Eadbald had paid lip-service to the new religion, but had never really understood it. He put away his step-mother, and married Emma, a Frankish princess, after the Archbishop of Canterbury had shown him the miraculous scourge marks received on his own back, he said, at the hands of Saint Peter for allowing the king to love so grossly and so sinfully. The child of that new union, Prince Eorconbert, grew up at a court that was unruly and licentious, watching his father and his father's friends drunk and boasting, taking women as they pleased, sometimes upon the very tables of the mead hall.

He watched, because he could not stop himself, but he secretly vowed that things would be very different when he was king.

* * * *

Saxberga had agreed to the marriage as her parents knew she must, with one stipulation, and that was that her sister Etheldreda should come with her and stay with her for the first few months. Her mother agreed gladly and Etheldreda was delighted with the prospect of her first sea voyage and her first visit to another kingdom. Their home had not been the same since Anna had become king. He and their mother seemed always to be too busy for them, and even their aunt Hereswith, King Egric's widow, who used to be so fond of Etheldreda, had left to go to France, taking with her their eldest sister Ethelberga, both to become nuns at the monastery of Faremoutier at Brie. Hereswith left her infant son, Aldwulf, born after Egric's death, for Anna's family to raise.

* * * *

In Kent the days before the wedding passed very quickly for the two princesses.

King Eorconbert's Gallic mother, Emma, was dead, but his aunt Ethelberga, once Queen of Northumbria, widow of the great Bretwalder Edwin, was there to take her place. She was a woman in her late forties, beautiful and elegant, her hair already silver-white from the sorrows she had endured.

It was her request that Paulinus, now Bishop of Rochester, should speak at the wedding ceremony after Archbishop Honorius of Canterbury. She had been through much with him since he first accompanied her, a nervous young girl, to Northumbria to marry King Edwin. It was he who had finally persuaded her pagan husband to baptism, and it was he who had protected her and her children in their flight after Edwin's defeat and death.

Paulinus was now very old and he reminded Etheldreda in some ways of a bird of prey. He was tall and very thin, his shoulders stooping, his eyes like dark and burning coals. He was originally from the Mediterranean and had a sallow complexion that contrasted very strikingly with the fairness of the young couple. Etheldreda scarcely heard a word he said though he spoke a long time. She was watching her sister who had so recently fought against the necessity of the marriage, already smiling up into the handsome young king's eyes and twining her fingers lovingly in his. She suddenly felt very much alone.

At the end of the sermon Etheldreda felt a touch on her arm and beside her she found the exiled Northumbrian princess, Eanfleda, the only surviving child of Queen Ethelberga and King Edwin. She was a girl of fourteen, so slight of build that she did not seem much older than Etheldreda, though her face had the weariness and the bitterness of a much older person.

'My mother says that we should go together to the wedding feast,' she said without enthusiasm. 'Shall we go now?'

Etheldreda was glad to leave the crowd that thronged around her sister. She looked at Eanfleda. She too looked lonely. Her face was set and worn, as though she had been weeping.

'What's the matter?' Etheldreda asked, touching her arm.

Eanfleda shook her head, and turned to move away.

Etheldreda took her hand and walked beside her.

'Tell me why you're so sad,' she insisted.

Again Eanfleda shook her head. 'You wouldn't understand,' she said. She longed to speak to someone, but Etheldreda was too young.

'I understand more than people think,' Etheldreda said.

Tears began to form in Eanfleda's blue eyes and well over to fall down her pale cheeks.

'I am ashamed to tell,' she whispered.

They were away from the crowds now, hidden from the other wedding guests by the trunk of a huge old tree.

Etheldreda squeezed her arm and looked at her with such compassion that Eanfleda broke down.

'I had hoped,' she said with a sob, 'that my cousin Eorconbert... and I...' Her voice faded away.

'You wanted to be his bride?'

'Hush, not so loud. I should not have said it.'

'Your cousin is most handsome, most brave. I am not surprised that you love him.'

Eanfleda sobbed freely now, the relief she felt for having told half her guilt encouraging her to blurt out the rest.

'Do you know what I have done?' she whispered, clutching Etheldreda's arm and staring wildly at her. Etheldreda shook her head, beginning to feel very uneasy at the intensity of the older girl's expression.

'I went to the witch woman of the pagans,' Eanfleda whispered. 'I asked for a love potion to make him come to me.'

Etheldreda gasped.

'You must tell no one. I shall be cursed as long as I live.' The Northumbrian princess gripped Etheldreda's arms tighter with her thin fingers.

Etheldreda shook her head dumbly.

'Vow,' hissed Eanfleda.

Etheldreda could not bring the words out. She continued to stare at Eanfleda, not so much shocked at what she said, but at the expression on the girl's face.

'Vow,' sobbed Eanfleda, starting to shake her, tears streaming down her cheeks.

3

The attack on Oswald AD 641

'Are you not satisfied, my lord, with the blood that you've already shed?' Cynewise, the Mercian queen, was looking angrily at the fighting men gathering, the horses riding in from the hills, the wagons being loaded.

Penda was standing with arms crossed on his broad chest, his eyes gleaming. This was more like it! No country would stand against this force. He had killed Edwin and purged his country of the false faith of the Nazarene god, but in his place had come another cursed Christian, Oswald of the Bernician royal line, brought up on Iona, an island of monks. There was surely not a good swordsman or axeman among them to have taught the prince how to fight. Northumbria was practically his.

Penda took a deep breath, almost smelling the wild places of the hills and the heather wind sweeping across the high moors. His men were happier with this type of terrain, no sticky marshland and narrow bottle-necks guarded by dykes. Wide open spaces and rocks to hide behind, heights to reach and hold.

'Did you hear me, lord?' Cynewise persisted, long years of marriage and the bearing of five children having given her confidence to speak her mind.

'I heard you woman. I heard you,' he muttered, then raised his voice and pointed with one stubby fierce finger at some boys who were struggling to load a wagon with some huge barrels.

'Take it from the other side, fools! Do you want your fathers to sleep thirsty after a day of fighting?'

He moved away and Cynewise was left alone, to be joined by her second eldest son, Wulfhere, a moment later.

'Can I go with him this time, mother? Can I?'

She looked down at his thin, fine face, eager for adventure.

'No,' she said. 'Not this time.' Not this time, her heart echoed, but soon there would be a time when she would have to let him go.

'Peada goes.'

'Peada is blooded. He has years on you, my son.'

'I am strong and my horse is faster than Peada's. His is made of lead.'

'You are needed here. If all the men go, who will guard the women?'

Wulfhere's face wrinkled with disgust and

he moved away, but he was glad she had called him a man. When all the men were mustering it was frustrating to be a child. A king's son could not afford to waste his time on childhood.

Cynewise returned to the stockade and the royal house. Penda was busy and would not return until late in the night. He would be drunk and full of fierce lusts as always before he started on one of his raids. She would need strength. She made sure no one would disturb her and told her women that she was going to sleep. Then she drew the heavy cloth over the windows of her chamber and lit a tiny iron lamp. She listened for a moment to make sure that there was no one moving in the other chamber and then pulled out from under the wooden bed that she and Penda shared, a small plain box. With trembling hands she fumbled to open it, knowing that if Penda caught her now she would be dead, though she bore him a hundred sons. The lid came away at last and inside, wrapped in silk, was a tiny golden crucifix set with pearls given to her by her father Cynegils on her last visit home to Wessex.

They had talked long into the night about his conversion to Christianity and, although she had refused baptism for fear of her husband, she had taken the cross, well hidden in her robes, to be kept secret in this box ever since. From time to time she came to it and pondered over the strange religion that it symbolised. That a god could be invisible and only show himself when he chose was not strange to her, but that he commanded that they did not slay their enemies (the Northumbrians, the East Anglians, the Celts) but only the desires in their own hearts, the secret roots of hatred deep in their own minds, was new to her. 'Fight only against yourself,' he said, 'prepare *yourself* as a temple for your god instead of building one of stone and wood. Have no blood feuds... pay no wergild... forgive all men for what they do...' She shivered. There was so much she did not understand.

Again she listened and when she heard no sound she knelt before the little cross now propped up on her clothes-chest.

'God of my father Cynegils,' she whispered, her heart pounding nervously, 'protect my sister Cyneberga and her husband King Oswald of Bernicia. Soften my lord's heart and let him be content with his own country, with his own people.' She stopped, opening her eyes a crack to see if there was anyone or anything changed in the room, but nothing had that she could see.

She rose from her knees, wrapped the cross in the silk, and returned it to its box and thence to its hiding place. She then bowed low before the small wooden statue of Thunor that stood in an alcove.

She took off her ring and laid it at his feet. 'Lord of Storm, wild warrior and defender of the gods,' she said softly, 'watch over my lord and bring him safely home.'

* * * *

King Anna and his family only heard of Oswald's defeat and death at the battle of Maserfield more than a week after it had occurred.

News of Penda's army on the move had reached them earlier, and Anna had breathed a sigh of relief that it was northward bound this time and not towards his own country. His spies in Northumbria were many, but the savagery of the fighting that followed Penda's invasion was such that none could leave until, defeated, many of the Bernicians and Deirans fled, and refugees came straggling south.

The queen and Etheldreda were so moved by the stories of the suffering of the refugees that they insisted on travelling north to see what they could do to help.

Tondbert, prince of the marshlands, gave them a lodge on the island of Ely in which to rest and ordered his men to help the women in any way they required. He himself took Etheldreda in his light reed boat ahead of the main party, impressing her with his skill at manoeuvring the craft through the reeds, finding the waterways, and avoiding the mud-banks, the water snakes and the fen demons. He was a grizzled old man in his fifties, tough and brown-skinned from continual exposure to the weather, rough in manner, having learned no courtly graces in ruling such a wild and independent bunch of fowlers and fishermen, but Etheldreda liked him. He treated her with gruff respect as though she were an equal instead of still a child.

Ovin was in the boat that closely followed them and it was he who lifted her out onto the bank when at last they reached firm land. The excitement of the journey through the marshes had brought high colour to her cheeks and her eyes were sparkling. For the moment she had forgotten the reason for their mission, but it soon came back to her as they came upon the refugee encampment. The sights that she had tried so hard to forget from Penda's attack on her own country came welling back and she turned to Ovin with a sob.

Tentatively, remembering her father's words,

he put his arms about her. 'Don't cry, lady,' he said softly against her hair. 'These people need our help, not our tears.'

She tried to pull herself together at this and look at the children with thin bones and dark-ringed eyes, the women with dirty, blood-soaked bandages, the pathetic collection of bits and pieces they had brought from their homes. She wiped her tears on his tunic, drew away from him and walked firmly towards the ragged crowd. Within minutes she was completely in control of herself and, child as she still was in body if not in spirit, she took command and with grace and dignity organised the distribution of the food that they had brought with them and the administering of herbal potions. She dressed wounds and listened with a pale but calm face to women telling of what they had seen.

But, all the time, at the back of her mind, a voice kept saying over and over again with the insistence of a drum beat: 'This is not all there is. Remember—this is not all there is.'

And then, almost as confirmation of what she was thinking, one of the refugees told her about the death of King Oswald.

'With his very last breath he prayed for the souls of his enemies. All who were near saw a light hover over the place where he fell and, as they looked at it, they felt no pain over his death nor our defeat.'

Etheldreda watched and listened intently, beginning to grasp the importance of what was being said. In realising that his enemies were, like his friends, all the sons of God, all eternal souls, she understood he had gained something more valuable than the life and lands Penda took away from him. He had won the only victory worth winning.

There were tears in her eyes as she turned suddenly to Ovin, her friend, her comforter, her rock.

'You see, there is something more,' she whispered.

He nodded, smiling broadly.

And then there was no more time to be thinking of these wonders. One of the pack-horses started to slip on the slimy mud of the riverbank and everyone had to rush to his assistance.

At the end, laughing and covered in mud, they collapsed exhausted—the immediate distracting them from the eternal. But, behind the horse's desperate floundering and their clumsy but energetic attempts to rescue it, the eternal was still there.

* * * *

On the way back they rested again at Ely

and Etheldreda, tired as she was, insisted on walking round the island.

'I love this place,' she said to Prince Tondbert. 'I feel at home here.' He could see that the cares of her recent experience were almost gone from her face.

He smiled at her. 'It's yours, my lady.'

She looked at him sharply. 'Don't tease me, my lord.'

He opened his mouth to confirm his gift, but was interrupted by the arrival of Etheldreda's mother and one of Oswald's men. They were talking of what would become of Northumbria now that Oswald was dead.

'His brother Oswy should by rights be king,' the man was saying, 'but he'll have to win his kingdom back from Penda, and there are many in his own country who hate him and wouldn't like to see him king.'

'Why is that?' the queen asked mildly. 'Wasn't he brought up by the monks of Iona in the same way as his brother Oswald?'

'Aye... but...' The man hesitated, looking at Etheldreda.

'I heard that he is a hard man to his enemies, that's for sure.' The queen frowned. Whoever became king of Northumbria affected them all. If Penda kept what he had won they would suffer most. Separate, the seven kingdoms kept a kind of balance, but if Northumbria and Mercia were united it would not be long before they were all absorbed. But if Oswy was as they hinted... what then?

4

The school at Dunwich: Oswy and Eanfleda

While Prince Oswy of Bernicia was fighting to regain his brother's throne from Penda and hold it against others of his country who wished to wrest it from him, Etheldreda was growing up. Heregyth, a girl a few years older than herself, the daughter of one of Egric's thegns who had died defending Rendilsham, was assigned to be her special maid and companion and in her company Etheldreda was sent to Dunwich to study at the famous school that had been founded by Bishop Felix during the reign of King Sigbert.

The princess at once took to the life of study, eagerly learning everything she could as fast as she could, finding in scholarship and the long hours of work the pleasure that others might find in the playful company of friends and the noisy evenings of entertainment at court. She found that by learning to read she now had a direct door into the Gospels through which she could go whenever she wished, finding things there that the priests, on whose interpretations she had been dependent before, had never shown her.

Each day had its excitement and at night when she returned to her small bare chamber, where Heregyth was waiting to comb her hair, she poured out her enthusiasms to the girl. Heregyth, who could neither read nor write, nor had any wish to do so, longed to return to Rendilsham. She had been enrolled in the embroidery school and although the work they did there was famous throughout Europe, even the Bishop of Rome wearing a cope that had been designed and worked at Dunwich, she found each day longer than the last.

Just before Michaelmas Etheldreda was allowed to start work in the scriptorium and every evening when she and Heregyth were together she talked enthusiastically about her work. The bemused girl heard about the difficulties of applying gold leaf when the resin underlying it dried too quickly or too slowly because of changeable weather, and the preciousness of ultramarine, which was one of the few pigments they could not grind themselves, but had to have sent from Rome.

'Even in Rome,' the princess told Heregyth, 'they don't know how it is made and have to import it from the East. They know its base is lapis lazuli but not one has been able to find out just what else they use. The others are easy. We use orpiment for yellow when we can't get the gold, verdigris from copper for green, woad for blue, white and red lead, ox-gall for brown, and then it is just a matter of knowing how much to mix with the egg, the gum or the vinegar.'

Heregyth combed Etheldreda's hair so that it floated out around her and became a haze of fine gold threads in the lamplight, and then she put away the comb and folded back the rugs on the bed.

'I'd be frightened that I'd make a mistake and ruin a whole page,' she said.

Etheldreda smiled.

'Even experienced scribes make mistakes. We think nothing of it,' she said airily. 'We just turn the mistake into a little animal or a flower or something. My pages are usually full of extra figures!' She laughed, and then she looked serious. 'But one day,' she said, 'one day I will write the perfect page.'

* * * *

Being a school attached to a monastery there were not many hours of the day and night that were not accounted for in duties. But sometimes Etheldreda felt the need to be by herself and she would rise before dawn and, instead of going to the chapel where the monks and nuns would already be gathered, she would slip away to the sea and walk along the beach, watching for the sunrise. The air would be fresh and clear as though newly washed, the long beach curving to the distant headland pure and deserted. She would stand right at the water's edge, her sandals abandoned further up the beach, her shift gathered up and held above her knees, the waves washing over her feet, tugging at the pebbles.

At last the sun would rise, filaments and veils of light falling from it and floating away; she at the centre.

* * * *

When Oswy had finally established himself on the throne he sent to Kent for the young princess Eanfleda. The marriage would serve a double purpose. The fact that her mother was of the Kentish royal house would help to extend his influence far to the south, but more importantly, as the last remaining offspring of the great Bretwalder Edwin, who had so effectively welded the Deiran and Bernician kingdoms together, her place on the throne beside him would strengthen his own case for doing the same. For the moment he ruled only Bernicia. Oswin, descended from Edwin's cousin, held Deira.

* * * *

Eanfleda left for Bernicia with her chaplain Romanus, as though she were going to prison instead of to marriage.

Her mother watched the brave train of thegns and women companions that accompanied her, the chests of treasure and the gifts of fine horses and Frankish weaponry, and thought of the time she too had set off for the north to marry a man she had never met. Edwin at that time was a pagan, a warrior prince who had won his kingdom fiercely and mercilessly. She had had no way of knowing then that as the years of their marriage passed she would grow to love him and that he would eventually embrace the Christian faith. Their child Eanfleda had been baptised by her priest Paulinus, as pledge that the king and all his people would accept baptism if the God of his wife would give him victory over the West Saxons.

But Oswy was a very different man.

Tears came to her eyes to think of what Eanfleda might have to face. Oswy was officially a Christian, but from the tales told of him the teachings of the Saviour had not sunk very deep. He was a man in his thirties, twice married, known to be hard natured and a womaniser, the son of her father's enemy, Ethelfrid, who had been king of Northumbria before Edwin.

Her daughter looked frail and young as she sat her horse, her cheeks pale as chalk, her eyes looking into her mother's with such desperation that Ethelberga could hardly bear to meet them. She might indeed have given in at this moment, had not Eorconbert joined her and said with calm satisfaction:

'Do not worry, lady, with this marriage we will all sleep easier in our beds. Besides—it is only fitting that she should take back her father's kingdom. It is rightfully hers.'

Ethelberga bit her lip. He was right. Eanfleda's sacrifice would win years of peace for them.

She turned back to her daughter with a speech about duty ready on her lips when she was startled to intercept a look in the girl's eyes as she gazed at Eorconbert that could only be interpreted in one way. Sharply she looked back at Eorconbert, wondering if the same emotion would be expressed in his. But he had turned away from them and was shouting orders for the train to start moving. The mother saw Eanfleda's expression turn to bitterness as he rode off.

Ethelberga crossed herself and thanked God that her daughter after all was going far away from Kent.

'May guardian angels go with her and protect

her in all that she has to face,' she whispered. 'From within and from without. Amen.'

Saxberga rode up on her chestnut horse and embraced the girl.

'I want you to have this,' she said, and held up a necklace of silver and jet with a small pendant cross. 'It was my mother's and I held it all the way to Kent. It gave me courage and, as you see, brought me good fortune.' Saxberga's smile was so warm and loving, it was clear that she had no idea of Eanfleda's secret feelings about her husband.

Ethelberga watched anxiously as the girl took the necklace. She hesitated for a long time, turning it over and over in her fingers. But at last she looked up, and met the young queen's eyes. 'Thank you,' she said in a low voice, her face expressionless.

Saxberga kissed her on the cheek and rode off to find her husband. It had not been easy to part with her mother's necklace and she had thought Eanfleda would have been more pleased to receive it.

The entourage started to move forward.

Eanfleda turned her back on her mother and her home and all that she had known and loved. She lifted her chin and set her eyes on the horizon.

So be it. It was God's will.

5

Oswin

When Etheldreda had been six years at the school at Dunwich, her studies ranging from logic and arithmetic to metaphysics, astronomy and theology, she received a message from her father requesting that she return home to take her place at court.

At first she was determined to refuse, instructing the messenger to declare that she wanted to become a nun like her eldest sister Ethelberga, her step-sister Sathryd, and her aunt Hereswith, thinking that in this way she would be allowed to pursue her studies uninterrupted. But the messenger told her on his own account that it was her mother who really needed her and that without her she would surely die.

Startled she looked at him.

'I have received no news that my mother is ill.'

'No, my lady.'

'Why not?'

'She did not want you to worry, my lady.'

'But,' cried Etheldreda, 'surely my father...'

The messenger looked uncomfortable. He had already exceeded his licence and was afraid to say more.

'What is it? What ails my mother?'

'She... she is with child my lady, but...'

Etheldreda's face darkened. Over the past few years the queen had had several miscarriages, each one leaving her paler and weaker. Why could her father not leave her alone, Etheldreda thought angrily. Surely he could control himself if he really loved her.

She told the messenger that she would return with him, and called for Heregyth. Together they started packing; Heregyth attending to her clothes, Etheldreda to the vellum pages of the half-finished psalter she was making for herself, and the pens, brushes and pigments her teachers were allowing her to take with her.

'"Make me understand the way of thy precepts, and I will meditate on thy wondrous works"[1],' she murmured as her eye fell on the words she had written that morning. How difficult to reconcile what actually happened in the world with how she expected it to be as the ever-present kingdom of God. Her father was a good man, yet he was destroying his wife.

'My lady,' Heregyth interrupted the train of her thought. 'Shall I keep the blue cloak out for travelling, or the brown?' Her eyes were bright and her heart was light. She had never been happy at Dunwich, though she had tried to make the best of it for Etheldreda's sake. She was delighted that they were going back to Rendilsham and all the bustle of the great hall.

'You decide,' Etheldreda said abstractedly, and looked sadly out of the window at the long low buildings that had been such a haven for her these last years.

* * * *

One night, a few weeks later, when Etheldreda and her father were watching together beside her mother's bed, she found it increasingly difficult to hold back her feelings of resentment.

'Why, father. Why?' she asked at last, fixing him with her accusing young eyes.

He did not answer for so long she wondered if he had heard her. He sat hunched with grief, a big man, his eyes clouded beneath bushy eyebrows, the downward droop of his lips hidden in his full beard.

'One day you'll understand,' he said at last in a low and broken voice.

'I want to understand now,' the girl said, an edge of hardness to her voice.

'I love your mother.'

'I know you do, but love is protective and caring, not destructive.'

'What do you know of it?' he said bitterly. 'You, a virgin! I love your mother. I care for her. I wish to protect her—but there are times when my longing for her is too strong. In other times a man in my position would have taken one of the women of the court or even a slave. But the Law of our Lord forbids adultery. My wife is the only one I may take to bed. I need her, Etheldreda. Is that so hard for you to understand?'

Etheldreda was silent, thinking of Eanfleda weeping at Eorconbert's wedding. She had never felt passion like that. No, she did not understand.

She rose and prepared to leave the room.

'Father I must talk to you tomorrow. There are things we must settle between us.'

'What things daughter?'

'Leave it until the morning. We'll speak then.'

A nerve twitched in his neck.

'Speak now,' he said gruffly. 'In the morning... who knows what the morning will bring...'

She hesitated. She felt as though something she did not yet quite understand was building up within her, pressing her to speak.

'I have decided,' she burst out at last, 'that I will stay with you only until my mother is well again, and then... and then I intend to take vows and become a nun.'

He looked up at her sharply, 'You are a princess. Your life is not your own to give away.'

'I know it. But it is the Lord Christ's and He has asked for it.'

'When? When did He ask for it?' demanded her father.

Etheldreda bit her lip. To tell the truth, until that moment, she had had no great resolution to become a nun, apart from the wish to continue learning from books. She had not been conscious of a dramatic 'call' from the Lord Christ. The words she had just spoken had come out of her mouth without her planning them, but as soon as they were out they seemed to carry with them a sense of conviction and relief, as though somewhere deep inside her she had been preparing for this moment all her life.

Her father turned away, knowing that if he spoke now he would speak in anger. As Christian he should welcome the news, but as king he knew that he could not. He had already lost two marriageable daughters to the church, one Etheldreda's elder sister, and the other his daughter Sathryd by his first wife. He indicated that she should leave and she obeyed quickly, needing time to think.

All night he knelt beside his wife's sleeping form, his face in his hands.

* * * *

Heregyth found Etheldreda one day looking through her mother's chest of clothes. The queen was feeling considerably better since Etheldreda's return and, although she could not rise from her bed and take her place beside her husband, she could sit up and speak quite cheerfully now. There was to be a particularly important feast at Rendilsham in honour of the exiled king of the West Saxons, Cenwahl, who had been living for three years as King Anna's guest. He had for a long time held out against the new religion, but at last had given in and agreed to be baptised. King Anna felt it a victory worthier to be celebrated than any he had won upon the battlefield. Cenwahl had been stubborn in his resistance and as he was a man whom Anna deeply respected it had been very disturbing to his own faith to be continually in argument with him. The baptism was to be made the occasion for general rejoicing, and Etheldreda had been asked by her mother to dress up in the queen's robes and to be hostess in her absence. Her friend and mentor Bishop Felix was to come from Dunwich to perform the ceremony and many sub-kings and earls were to come from the surrounding countries to witness the event.

King Oswin of Deira was to represent the north.

'What do you think of this?' asked Etheldreda, pulling out some fine silks from the chest and holding them against herself.

Heregyth looked at her. Her hair was golden and falling loosely over the cloth, her eyes shining.

'Beautiful my lady. Does it fit you?'

'Of course. My mother and I are of a height. Come help me slip it on.'

The two girls spent hours in the chamber taking turns to dress in the queen's clothes, laughing and joking like children. But the mood changed suddenly when Etheldreda lifted a fine circlet of gold and placed it on Heregyth's head. 'There you are! Queen Heregyth!' she said, but was so startled to see the expression on the girl's face, she reached up and took it off almost at once.

'It's only a game, Heregyth!' she said quickly.

'It is for me, my lady,' she said bitterly, 'but you'll be queen one day.'

'No, I shan't. I'll be a nun.'

'That would be a waste, my lady.'

'A waste, Heregyth? To serve the Lord every moment of the day and night!'

Heregyth flushed.

'Isn't it possible to serve the Lord in other ways than by shutting yourself up in a monastery and living on dry bread and gruel for the rest of your days?'

Etheldreda laughed, and placed the golden circlet she had taken from Heregyth's head on her own. It pinned down a fine veil over her golden hair, only a few curls escaping at her temples. Then she slipped on her favourite necklace of gold and pearl and held up a copper mirror to the light. Her face shone from the polished surface like a disembodied phantom, a stranger.

'How we mistake the image for the reality,' she thought. She touched her face wonderingly as though she were exploring a strange object she had never seen before. 'This is no more me than the sound I hear when I hold a shell to my ear is the sea.'

* * * *

Quietly and graciously the Princess Etheldreda greeted her father's guests, addressing each by their correct title, making them feel personally welcome.

Prince Tondbert of the South Gyrwes was there, a few years older and more gnarled since she had seen him. Elegant living was not to his taste and he stood awkwardly and clumsily in the background until the young princess took him by the hand and led him to his place at the table.

And then King Oswin of Deira entered.

There were stories Etheldreda had heard of him that made her take more than usual notice as she showed him to his place. He was a handsome young man, tall and fair, known for his generosity to high and low alike, his court a place where any man could come and speak his mind without fear of disfavour or sudden death. There was a story that he had once given Bishop Aidan a very fine horse, concerned that, as the bishop grew old, the long and arduous journeys he was wont to make on foot to preach to outlying districts would be too much for him. But the Bishop, who had walked everywhere since he had chosen the life he now led and had never allowed himself any luxury or comfort, gave the horse and all its expensive trappings to a poor and crippled beggar. It was said that when news of this came to King Oswin's ears he drew the Bishop aside as they were going to dine and asked why he had given the King's gift away.

'What are you saying, my King?' Aidan replied somewhat tartly. 'Is the foal of a mare more valuable to you than a child of God?' Bishop Aidan then took his place at the table, but the King stayed warming himself by the fire for some time.

Suddenly he unbuckled his sword and, handing it to a servant, impulsively knelt at the Bishop's feet and begged his forgiveness. The Bishop was deeply moved and rose at once, drawing the King to his feet, and placing him on his chair at the table.

As the night wore on Bishop Aidan became more and more reserved and eventually it was noticed that tears were flowing from his eyes. The earl who brought the story to King Anna's court said then that when he was questioned he said in a low voice that he knew that King Oswin would not live long, for such humility and Christian charity could not survive the violence of the times.[2]

As Etheldreda stood beside King Oswin and showed him where he was to sit, he looked into her eyes with a clear, pleasant gaze. It seemed to her that her heart turned over in her breast and her legs lost all their strength, and then, her hand resting on the back of his chair within inches of his arm, she could feel the flesh prickle as though he were touching her. She shut her eyes and in her imagination felt his arms about her.

'My lady!'

She heard his voice very close to her ear

so that his breath brushed her cheek. He had seen her shut her eyes and sway slightly as though she were about to faint. Solicitously he took her arm, but she drew it away from him at once, flushing deeply. And then with a quick, nervous bow she rushed away from him and left the room, aware that his eyes were following her.

Heregyth found her a few moments later trembling and weeping outside in the dark.

'My lady,' she cried. 'What's the matter? Princess, speak to me! What's happened?'

Etheldreda shook her head angrily, wanting to be left alone. So this was the desire she had seen so destructively at work in others!

'Lady...'

'Leave me, Heregyth. Leave me. You can do nothing for me.'

'But...'

'Please!' Her voice was sharp as she pulled herself away from her friend's reaching arms, and tried to control her sobs. 'I must be alone for a few moments. Go back and make sure that I am not missed. If you love me do this for me.'

Heregyth, seeing her determination and that she was already much calmer, returned to the hall.

Within a few minutes Princess Etheldreda

joined her and returned to her duties as hostess, her face composed.

At midnight a servant came to fetch King Anna and Princess Etheldreda from the hall. They left at once, their faces suddenly shadowed and anxious. The rumour that spread at once and brought a hush to all who heard it was that the queen was being delivered of her child and was herself near to death.

* * * *

Anna and Etheldreda found her writhing in agony, her face running with sweat and her eyes glazed with pain. Bishop Felix was on his way, but for the moment she was being attended only by her women.

Anna knelt at once by her side and took her hand. Etheldreda saw in his face such suffering, such love and tenderness, she felt ashamed of her recent anger.

At first the queen was in such pain she didn't notice their presence, but when Bishop Felix arrived and put his hand gently but firmly upon her heaving body, she seemed to become calmer and, although still very ill, could look at them with recognition. She turned her thin face, and her dark eyes sought her husband's. She could not speak but the relief in her expression at finding him at her side was beautiful to see.

Another contraction racked her frail form and she screamed. Etheldreda put her hands to her mouth and bit her knuckles until they bled.

'Pray for your mother,' whispered the bishop urgently. 'She is dying and we cannot hold her back, but we can ease her pain and ask for her acceptance into God's heavenly Kingdom.'

Etheldreda wept but could not pray for her mother's entry into the heavenly Kingdom. She could only think of how much she wanted her mother to stay alive.

'Take courage,' said Felix, 'angels are present.'

'I don't want her to go!' sobbed Etheldreda. 'I need her!'

The bishop pushed her gently away from her mother.

'Stay and help—or leave,' he said brusquely.

The queen gave one last desperate push and a squalling bundle of blood and flesh poured from her. Her eyes were suddenly clear and she looked directly into her daughter's face.

'Do not leave him. He needs you now,' she cried, and then fell back in death.

Etheldreda stared at her, but she was no longer there. There was a strange heap of something on the bed, but it was not her mother. Her mother had left.

Stunned, the girl suffered herself to be moved back as the women busied themselves with laying out the queen's deserted body, and washing the newborn infant.

Bishop Felix was praying and her father was weeping. Etheldreda put her arms around his shoulders.

'I'll not leave you,' she murmured. 'I'll look after you.'

* * * *

The baby was another daughter for Anna, christened Withberga.

* * * *

Over the next few months Etheldreda and Heregyth were busy. They found a wet nurse for the baby, but Etheldreda insisted on doing almost everything for her infant sister apart from the actual feeding. She was also concerned with keeping her father from total despair, and helping him to rule his kingdom. Since his wife's death he seemed to care about nothing and if it were not for Etheldreda's insistence and constant inspiration he would have abandoned most of his responsibilities. The sharp words of the man she admired so greatly, Bishop Felix, had roused her to action. 'Help—or leave.'

King Oswin had returned to his kingdom before she had a chance to see him again.

6

The hostage

'I will not let him go!' Eanfleda almost shrieked. Tears were streaming from her eyes and she was clasping her infant son to her breast with such fury and despair that she all but stopped his breathing.

Prince Egfrid added his voice to hers and howled disconsolately. He had no idea of the negotiations that had gone on between King Penda and his father King Oswy, the negotiations which had been at last settled and sealed with the agreement that he, Prince Egfrid, second son of Oswy and Eanfleda, would be given as hostage to King Penda as sign of Oswy's good faith, but he did know that he was extremely uncomfortable crushed so fiercely in his mother's arms.

Oswy looked at his pale thin wife, her eyes full of outrage, and his own face flushed with anger.

'Will not, lady? Will not?' he roared.

Eanfleda was afraid of him but she held her ground.

'I will kill him and myself rather than let him

go to that barbarous monster!' she screamed.

'You do that lady and you will kill us all. We live only at Penda's pleasure and Penda's pleasure is to have the child. He will have him! And you will give him up!'

'Never!'

King Oswy nodded at two of his men who were close behind the queen and before she realised what was happening she was roughly seized and the child ripped shrieking from her arms.

She tried to bite and kick and pull the child back, but the one man held him high above his head and stepped back out of reach as the other held her down. The men looked over her head for guidance from the king who nodded his approval and gestured for the man who held the child to hand it to Penda's two thegns waiting in the shadows.

As soon as they had the prince in their grasp they left the chamber, the queen's curses ringing in their ears.

The king let Eanfleda scream and cry and struggle for a while, but when he was sure that Penda's men had mounted and ridden off, he commanded that she be released. Sobbing hopelessly she fell to the floor and beat her fists against it. The king stood looking at her, the angry flush dying down, his eyes showing for the first time something of his own suffering, his own pity.

Suddenly a young boy who had been watching the whole scene from the corner of the room came forward and knelt beside her.

'My lady,' he whispered. 'Lady, do not weep. It'll only be for a little while. My lord the king will soon have Penda's head on a stake and your son will be restored to you.'

Tearfully she looked up at him, and allowed herself to be helped to her feet. Her face was ugly and red with weeping, but she knew that there was nothing she could now do to bring her son back. She was drained of all passion, numb with despair.

'Spoken like a man, Wilfrid,' said King Oswy with satisfaction. 'And you will help me put it there.'

'No,' said the queen with one last flicker of strength. 'I promised his dying mother that he would be a scholar and a priest, and I will not break that promise. He goes to Lindisfarne.'

The king shrugged. He felt it was a waste to send Wilfrid to a monastery and would have liked him for his shield bearer, but he did not want to cross his wife again so soon.

'He goes to Lindisfarne,' he said placatingly, and left the room.

Queen Eanfleda sat down on the chair Wilfrid

solicitously brought forward for her. Her legs felt weak.

'Wilfrid,' she said sadly. 'You are young and much that is sorrowful and hard has already happened to you. But it is nothing to what may still happen. If I let you be my lord's shield bearer you will have nothing in your life but killing and being killed. If you go to Lindisfarne, what you will learn there will be of more lasting value than putting Penda's head on a stake. You will learn ways of changing the hearts of men so that they can live together without this perpetual violence and hatred. You will learn how men can trust one another so that they will not have to take a woman's child from her to hold as hostage.' Her eyes were dry now, but there was still a touch of bitterness in her expression.

He was silent. He liked the idea of being a scholar and confounding them all with his knowledge, but he was not sure that he would take to the bare, uncomfortable life of the brothers at Lindisfarne. He came of noble family and was used to being rich and comfortable.

'Leave me now,' she said, 'but send Romanus my priest to me. I need to pray and have not the strength to do it alone.'

* * * *

Penda's queen, Cynewise, stared at the angry red-faced child and sighed. Another hostage. Her household was already complicated enough.

'It is obvious he needs feeding,' she said coldly to the thegn who held the child. 'Take him to the kitchens. When he is fed and cleaned, bring him back to me.'

7

Hilda AD 647

In the autumn the house of Anna had a visit from Hilda, a princess of the royal Deiran house, a kinswoman of King Oswin. She was on her way to France, to the monastery of Chelles near Paris, to lead the holy life like her sister Hereswith, widow of Anna's brother Egric. King Anna, sensing the restlessness in Etheldreda and fearing it, asked Hilda to winter with them.

She was a handsome woman of thirty-two who had had many suitors but found none to her taste, and had succeeded in keeping a fierce, proud independence, while running a well appointed household in Deira, the focus of travellers and scholars, priests and princes.

'What makes you head for France?' King Anna asked his guest after an evening of lively talk around the fire. 'Deira will be the poorer without you.'

She laughed.

'I will be the poorer if I stay in Deira,' she said. 'I seek my fortune in France, riches without price.'

'I heard you gave your land away, your house and all its contents,' King Anna said. 'Was that wise?'

'Very wise,' she replied cheerfully. 'The land was not mine, but God's, and what do I want with a house made of wood that can be burned by fire, and robes that the moth can gnaw. I am looking for more permanent possessions and I expect to find them.'

Etheldreda's eyes shone at the older woman's brave words, and Anna, seeing it, wondered if Hilda would exert quite the influence he wanted over his daughter.

'You are lucky you have no responsibilities,' he said pointedly. 'Some of us have people dependent upon us.'

'One must serve God in the best way one can,' Hilda said. 'Of course it is not right for everyone to leave for a monastery, but only those who are called.'

'How were you called?' Etheldreda asked curiously.

Hilda sighed and shook her head. 'It is almost impossible to explain,' she said.

'Did you have a vision?'

'Not exactly.'

'A dream?'

Hilda hesitated. 'No,' she answered at last. 'It was more like... more like "knowing" than anything else. I cannot explain it better than that.'

Etheldreda sighed. She had a 'knowing' too, but it was not consistent. Sometimes she had doubts. Sometimes she thought of King Oswin of Deira and prayed to God that her 'calling' would be to be his wife. At other times she 'knew' that her way was not the way of the flesh, but the hard, bright way of spirit, and that the only way to it was through self-denial.

Heregyth had found her crying in the night more than once, but the princess would never tell her what she was crying about.

The winter deepened.

The winds off the marshes were sweeping and bitter. Snow flurried through the grey air and lay on the hard icy ground.

Etheldreda told Hilda about an Irish monk called Fursey who had visited them when she was a child and how he had such control over his body that he no longer felt pain or cold.[3] Hilda was intrigued and at once suggested that they should start training their bodies in the same way. They started by leaving their fur capes off when they went for brisk walks across the crackling snow fields, and gradually reduced their garments and their comforts until they were sleeping on the hard floor of their bed chambers with barely a covering on the wildest nights. By Christmas they were both ill with the coughing fever and unable to take their place in chapel or hall.

When King Anna heard from Heregyth what they had been doing he was very angry. He stormed in to see Etheldreda and strode up and down her small room almost too angry to speak.

She felt terrible. Her eyes were streaming, her throat was so sore she could barely swallow, and her chest was burning and aching. She was sure she was about to die. She told herself that she ought to be glad that she would soon be in God's beautiful kingdom untrammelled by physical limitations, but she found herself longing to stay alive; there were so many things she still wanted to do, so many places she still wanted to see. Memory of the spring with its flowers and its bees haunted her.

Bishop Felix, himself not well, made the journey through blizzard and storm to spend Christmas with the king, and to see the two princesses.

'If you are going to follow Fursey,' he said as he sat beside Etheldreda's bed, 'it will take you much longer than one winter. It is not just a matter of leaving off robes and exposing yourself to the elements. Fursey trained himself day and night with rigorous disciplines for years—but even then it was the strength of his spirit that gave him control.'

Etheldreda sighed. Was there no easy way?

Bishop Felix laid his hand upon her aching head.

'Sleep my child. You always were one to try to go too fast.' He thought back on the years when she was at his school, and how she had insisted on learning everything as fast as she could. More than once he had given in to her wish to join a class that was beyond her, because of her eagerness. He had loved her for her enthusiasm and joy, and he blamed himself that he had allowed himself to be so charmed by it that he had neglected to teach her enough self-discipline.

He shut his own eyes, still resting his hand on her feverish head. Suddenly he had a strange sensation, as though he were touching a ball of light instead of a head of bone and flesh. He took his hand away quickly and opened his eyes.

There was no ball of light, but the impression had been so strong he crossed himself and, before he left, he knelt down on the dusty floor beside her in all his grand robes, and put his own head against her hand.

She looked at him with surprise, and then drifted peacefully off to sleep, the fever gone.

* * * *

In the spring when Hilda was making her final preparations to go to France she received a letter from Bishop Aidan of Lindisfarne.

He wrote most persuasively that Hilda should not go to France, but return to her own country to take her vows there and to found a little community of companions on the north bank of the River Wear. He spoke of the need for such communities in Britain and regretted that so many sons and daughters sought the holy life in other countries, neglecting their own.

'Sometimes it is more difficult to work amongst those we know, but sometimes it is necessary. If all who feel the call of Christ go abroad, how will we keep His word alive amongst ourselves? I feel you have a calling to establish places in this country which will become the jewels of our time, their light shining in a dark century, their spiritual riches sustaining an impoverished people.'

He reminded her that at the time of her birth her mother, in exile at the court of the British King Cerdic, had had a dream that must surely have been prophetic. She had dreamed that her husband Hereric, Edwin's nephew, was suddenly taken away from her, and, although she searched everywhere, she could find no trace of him. When all her efforts failed, she discovered a most valuable jewel under her garments, and as she looked closely, it emitted such a brilliant light that all Britain was lit by its splendour. Soon after this her husband was treacherously poisoned and her daughter Hilda was born.[4]

Bishop Aidan pointed out that the first part of the prophetic dream had come about, and it was now up to her to fulfil the second part.

'What shall I do?' Hilda asked Etheldreda. She longed to travel and to see her sister again. The monastery at Chelles was a centre of learning and culture. She would have the constant stimulation of people who had travelled widely and studied deeply, whereas at home she would have to provide the stimulation for the sluggish minds of those around her. But her admiration for Bishop Aidan was deep. Not to listen to his plea would be unthinkable. It had been his example that had inspired her to give away her riches and leave her home in the first place. He had come from Iona, his training in the tradition of Saint Columba and the Irish fathers to have no possessions, walking, even at his great age, over remote and windblown moors in every kind of weather, never doubting that he would find food and shelter when he needed it, never hesitating to give help and understanding to others.

She sighed.

Etheldreda took her hand and squeezed it. She knew that Hilda did not expect an answer from her.

* * * *

Hilda had not long returned to the north when Bishop Felix died. Sorrowfully, on hearing the news, Etheldreda left the crowded environs of the court and went for a long walk in the woods. Her mother was dead, and now her teacher and old friend. She felt very lonely. She wondered if she would ever see them again, and if she did, how changed they would be. She could not imagine people she had known without their bodies. She tried to visualise it, but failed.

She sat on the stump of a tree and closed her eyes. She whispered a line from the psalm she had so carefully and beautifully inscribed in the scriptorium at Dunwich.

'Open my eyes, that I may behold wondrous things out of Thy law.'[5]

The darkness behind her eyelids became blacker and blacker until she seemed to be falling into the most utter and complete darkness that had ever existed. She was afraid. If she was to have a vision she would have expected it to be of light. Was it the Lord of Shadow who had answered her prayer, and not the Lord of Light? And then she noticed that although she could see nothing, not even the little spots and imperfections that usually floated on the inside of her lids, she was intensely experiencing a vastness in which she was perfectly conscious, and that others were with her, whom she could not see, yet was aware of. Thoughts came to her, clear and powerful, as though she were thinking with the minds of others, better minds than her own. She knew suddenly and with great excitement that clarity of consciousness was not dependent on the presence of the physical body, but on its absence.

But even as she began to grasp what was happening and enjoy this new way of knowing... her body began to reassert itself and her eyelids itched to open. She fought to keep the experience, but it was already slipping from her. Her eyes opened and she stared astonished at the crowded visual complexity of the wood around her, the tangled green and vivid glimmer of sunlight that almost hurt her eyes.

She shivered.

By the position of the sun she knew that a great deal of time had passed since she shut her eyes. Yet it felt as though it had been no longer than a moment. She knew that she would never see her mother and Bishop Felix again as they had been, clothed in their curious sheaths of flesh, but it did not matter. She would be with them as they really were, and because she too would have sloughed her skin by then, it would seem natural.

'How stupid,' she thought, 'to think that things can never be anything but as they are at the moment.'

* * * *

Etheldreda took Heregyth and their two charges, Prince Aldwulf and Princess Withberga, to Kent to Easter with her sister. There she found a gloomy hush about the court, all the bright wall hangings of the great hall folded up and put away, and nothing but plain water served with the meals.

It was the children who explained it to the visitors.

'My father says for forty days before Easter we must fast and pray as our Lord did before he was crucified,' Princess Eorcongata said solemnly. 'Otherwise we will not be able to share in the resurrection.'

Etheldreda raised an eyebrow. They too kept the Lenten fast at home, but the whole court did not take on this air of dark desolation.

She looked at Eormengild, Saxberga's eldest

daughter, and saw that she had a bored, petulant look. It was clear the Lenten fast was an imposition on her from outside and was doing her no good at all. If anything it was driving her further from participation in the resurrection. The boy Egbert seemed indifferent to it and went his own way, pretending compliance when anyone was looking, breaking the rules when he was alone. Eorcongata seemed to be the only one in tune with her father's thinking.

'You see, it is very important,' she explained to Etheldreda, 'we have to empty ourselves of everything that is of the physical world in order to make way for the spiritual message God gives us at the crucifixion. If we look at it with the eyes of our body we do not understand it at all. We have to look at it with the eyes of the spirit, and then it all makes sense and is very beautiful.'

Etheldreda smiled. The girl was right. How wonderful to find such sensitivity in one so young. But—and here her face darkened as she looked at Eormengild—but the emptying must be from choice, not from imposition. What harm was Eorconbert doing to his eldest daughter? What harm to others of his people? She determined to speak to Saxberga about it, meanwhile suggesting that

Egbert and Eormengild should accompany Heregyth and the younger children to the woods.

Eormengild's eyes instantly lit up, and then darkened again.

'That would be enjoyment. We are not allowed to enjoy ourselves in Lent.'

'Nonsense!' said Etheldreda sharply. 'There is no quicker way to God's heart than to enjoy His works with love in your heart. The forest is full of His Presence. Go and be with Him.'

The children looked so uncertain and uneasy about what she had said, that she laughed. 'Don't worry. I'll speak to your father about it. I'm sure he will understand. Sometimes I find I am closer to God by enjoying a new leaf with the sunlight shining through it, than I ever am in my chamber on my knees.'

They needed no more encouragement.

They were away, Eorcongata as eagerly as the others.

* * * *

At Easter, on the day of resurrection, the release from the harsh discipline of the forty previous days was wonderful to see. Flowers and garlands of leaves were brought from everywhere to decorate the little stone church, the preaching cross on the green and all the houses. Children wore flowers in their hair and even Eorconbert wore his grandest, most colourful clothes.

After the singing of the praise and prayers at home Heregyth suggested that they ride into the country and see how the country folk celebrated. She had been finding the Kentish court oppressive and longed for the good times she and her friends had had at Easter when she was a child.

The royal party set off joyfully, even King Eorconbert relaxing and smiling at last. Etheldreda had been surprised at the change in him since she had seen him at her sister's wedding. It was as though the godless libertine days of his father Eadbald had so scarred him as a child that he was determined to devote the rest of his life to imposing their opposite.

The day was bright and light. Etheldreda rejoiced to hear the children chattering cheerfully again. Heregyth had suggested that they change into simple clothes so that they would not inhibit the locals with their royal presence, and they had been happy to do so. On more than one occasion they were pelted with petals.

The afternoon was nearly over and they had decided to turn back, when they saw a procession in the distance and agreed to witness this one more event before their return.

The children cried out with delight when they found that the procession was headed by a beautiful decorated cart, on top of which was a chair under a canopy, the curtains hiding what was presumably a very important person. Its progress along the lanes and over the fields was a noisy one, everyone singing and dancing and playing music. At each field it stopped and the canopied chair was taken from it and borne over the field on the shoulders of the slaves who had been pulling the cart.

'Who is in it?' cried Eormengild, her eyes shining.

'It is an old custom,' her mother said. 'The people used to believe that it was the Earth Goddess herself who rode in the cart, and she was going to give her blessing to the fields so that they would bear good crops. Now they know there is no Earth Goddess, but we still let them do it to keep them happy, otherwise they would blame us if the crops failed. The priests tell them it is the Virgin Mary and she is giving her blessing to the fields.'

'Is there a beautiful lady behind the curtains?'

'No.'

'Did there used to be when it was the Earth Goddess?'

'There never was an Earth Goddess. The

heathen priests used to say they "felt" the presence of the Goddess at certain times and the superstitious people believed she was there. No one ever saw behind the curtains.'

The procession was becoming noisier and noisier, and before they could stop them the children and Heregyth had climbed down from their horses and were dancing with the farmers and the villagers. The royal adults followed at a little distance, sometimes amused, sometimes embarrassed by the antics of the crowd. One hairy, bearded youngster had dressed himself up as a woman with a great deal of straw pushed into a bag over his belly so that he seemed very pregnant, and was swaggering and staggering about, pouring strong ale alternately down his own throat and over his neighbours' heads. Some youths and young girls were actually making love in the fields.

Etheldreda could see that Eorconbert did not really approve of what he was seeing, but remembering that Pope Gregory had told the English missionaries to tread carefully where old customs were deep-rooted, and rather transform than abolish them, he was keeping himself in check.

The sun was almost setting when they finally reached a lake and Eorconbert told Saxberga to call the children back because the festival was over and they had a long ride home before dark. It took a bit of time to locate the children and in that time the whole character of the light-hearted festival had changed.

Etheldreda sitting on a small knoll looking down at the scene, at first was surprised to see the cart and the slaves walk straight into the water, and was then horrified to see that when the slaves had sunk the cart in the water and were trying to walk out again, some of the men from the crowd, dressed in strange outlandish garments, which she later learned were the garments of their shamans, rushed in with whips and beat them back and forced them under the water.

Those who had not been expecting this began to scream. Only the older people did not seem surprised.

Eorconbert, when he grasped what was happening, suddenly gave a roar and kneed his horse to a gallop. Like an avenging angel he tore down to the lake swinging his sword, the water churning up around him as he beat back the shamans and freed the slaves. Unfortunately two were already dead, but the others struggled to the bank terrified and shaken.

'Lord in Heaven!' gasped Etheldreda. 'What is this?'

'The children!' shrieked Saxberga.

They could see Eorcongata standing by herself at the lake edge, drenched by the water that was flung up in the scurry, screaming with horror. Eormengild was running towards them. Young Egbert had rushed in beside his father and was beating at one of the shamans with a stick. The others, Aldwulf and Withberga, were safely with Etheldreda. She held them close, as Saxberga and Heregyth rushed to gather in the others.

As Eorconbert pulled one of the shamans out of the water by the scruff of his neck, the man turned on him a fierce and ugly face.

'A curse on you, profaner of the mysteries of the Goddess. No man may live who has touched her chariot. Plague strike you down and all who love you!'

Etheldreda, weeping, made the sign of the cross.

'Oh Lord,' she whispered. 'Oh Lord! Oh Lord!'

On the following day Eorconbert ordered the destruction of all heathen idols in his kingdom and the absolute abolition of the slightest heathen custom.

'We have been too lax,' he said. 'Always compromising, always trying to accommodate the old ways no matter how they conflict with the new. People have taken advantage and misused this freedom.'

'Sometimes things are difficult to understand,' Etheldreda said sadly, a little shocked by the ruthlessness with which Eorconbert's thegns were carrying out his orders. 'You forbid fortune telling by dreams and signs, yet in the Holy Book there are many examples of God speaking to man through dreams and signs.'

Eorconbert paced about impatiently.

'If my people could distinguish between the dreams and signs sent by God and those foisted on them by unscrupulous charlatan sorcerers, there would be no problem. For years we have given them the benefit of freedom and they have misused it. I have to take a firm stand now or we are lost.'

Etheldreda said no more, but she feared Eorconbert's over-zealous nature might destroy much more than he intended.

8

The vow

The summer of 651 was a turning point for Etheldreda.

It started quietly enough with the usual round of hospitality at court, the giving of gifts to new friends to buy their loyalty, and to old friends to keep their loyalty. There was much speculation as to whom the young princess would marry. At twenty-one years old she was already long past the usual age for marriage. She visited France, spending time with her eldest sister Ethelberga, her step-sister Sathryd, and her aunt, Hereswith. The people speculated that she would also visit the French court and perhaps make a marriage alliance with a Merovingian prince, but she returned to Rendilsham as beautiful and as unattached as ever.

Living at the monastery with her sisters had renewed her interest in the monastic life and she came home determined to make arrangements for her release from her court duties. But there always seemed to be something or someone preventing her taking the final step.

One of the distractions was Heregyth, who had become pregnant and was delivered of a still-born child. The young ceorl's son who had fathered it had heartlessly gone off and married someone else and Etheldreda felt impelled to nurse her wayward friend through the dark days of illness and sorrow, sitting at her bedside with her needlework, telling her stories of her time in France and how efficiently the monastery, which seemed more like a city than a house, was run. Heregyth turned her face to the wall and sighed as Etheldreda spoke of organisation and rules, but turned back to listen when she spoke of miraculous cures, premonitions and prophetic dreams.

* * * *

Then, in early September, messengers from Deira brought black news. Etheldreda arrived back one evening from an invigorating gallop through Rendilsham woods to find her father's house in deep gloom. People stood about in knots, either silently, or talking in undertones. Although the shadows were deepening rapidly, very few lamps and torches had been lit. The king himself was slumped in his chair, his chin in his hand, scowling into the darkness. At her entrance all eyes turned to her and one by one those around her father drew back so that she could be alone with him. She flung herself on her knees beside him and took his hands in hers.

'Father... my lord... What is it? What has happened?' She had not seen him look so old and so tired since the death of her mother.

'King Oswin is dead, my child,' he said gently, knowing no other way to deliver the blow.

She drew her breath in sharply, her heart missing a beat.

'It is God's Will,' he added.

She looked at him as though he were mad.

'God's Will,' she repeated dully, and then, with great bitterness: 'God's Will?'

'Yes, my child. We are all in the palm of God's hand and our going and our coming is as He wills.'

Her face had a terrible blankness. It seemed to her that everything in the world had suddenly come to a stop. The one man she could have...

'It is a bad business my daughter. The worst.'

'Tell me,' she said, forcing the words out.

'Oswy has had his eye on Deira for some time, wanting to unite the two countries under one king as his brother Oswald did. But Oswin wouldn't see it, though he was warned. Finally, too late, he was persuaded to raise an army.' King Anna paused with a heavy sigh and Etheldreda did not remove her gaze from his face for an instant. She sensed that he was going to tell her something that was worse than war and death in battle.

'They didn't meet in battle,' the King's voice broke. 'When Oswin realised his own force was inadequate to fight Oswy, he disbanded it rather than cause fruitless bloodshed, and he himself sought sanctuary with his greatest friend, a nobleman called Hanwald.' Here Anna's face twisted with bitterness. 'Hanwald! May his name be cursed from now to eternity! He betrayed his guest and friend, his king, his benefactor, to Oswy's murderer!'

A kind of keening came from the women in the court, angry murmuring and the sound of boots drumming on the floor, from the men.

'Why? Why did he do it?' Etheldreda cried out, leaving the shelter of silence at last, her heart breaking. 'King Oswin would not have hurt a living soul!'

King Anna bowed his head. He knew that Oswin's death and the manner of it was inexcusable.

Etheldreda stood up suddenly and walked from the hall. She could not bear to be with people any more. Everywhere she looked she saw the young king's eyes as he looked into her own.

Once in her chamber she sat for a long time

on the edge of her bed staring into darkness, not even lighting the lamp.

Through the dark square of her window a single brilliant star shone down on her, a bright needle of light, drilling into her head.

'God's Will!'

Her father's words repeated themselves again and again to her.

'God's Will!'

She tried to accept it. Tried to remember all the rich and beautiful arguments she had heard over the years from Bishop Felix and her teachers at school. Tried to remember her mother's teaching, her vows at baptism, all the years of acceptance.

The new religion was the only one she had known and so she did not turn, as the older generation sometimes did, to the old gods, in times of trouble, but to a terrible negative.

What if there was no God at all, but just blind events in a pointless, purposeless world? What was the point of trying to be as good and kind and just as Oswin was if God gave you no defence against your enemies? She could neither sleep nor weep. She sat all night and stared into the darkness. She had never felt so alone, so despairing. She tried to pray, but for the first time in her life she doubted that anyone was there to hear her prayer.

The dawn came and she was still sitting bolt upright on the edge of her bed. She heard a commotion at her door and Heregyth's voice demanding to be allowed in.

She drew the bolt aside and opened the door. Several women were outside and she looked into the faces of those she had known since early childhood, and saw that they were strangers.

A veil had come between them, and the veil was her passion and her despair.

* * * *

Her dark mood lasted several days and no one could talk her out of it. She avoided everyone, even Heregyth, going for long walks by herself in the woods, but finding even there that she was utterly alone.

One day Ovin, who had been watching her from a distance, ventured to join her as she walked alone in the wood. She looked up at him when he arrived, neither asking him to stay nor telling him to leave, and he paced beside her silently, his comforting bulk like her own shadow, causing no distress and no disturbance.

The next day he did the same.

On the third day she flung herself into his arms and wept. He held her like a father holds a child, though his heart was near to breaking.

At last she looked up at him.

'What is the meaning of it, Ovin?' she asked. 'What is the meaning?'

He did not know what to answer.

'I loved him, Ovin,' Etheldreda suddenly said. 'I loved him.'

Ovin stood before her, his shoulders hunched, his arms hanging by his side, her tears still wet upon his neck.

'Can you understand? I saw him only once but I felt I had known him all my life... longer than my life. Do you understand that?'

Ovin nodded dumbly.

'And now I wonder what was the point of our meeting. Is God cruel, Ovin? Or is there, perhaps, no God?'

'I think, my lady,' the young Celt struggled to express something that was so deep within him it almost hurt to drag it to the surface, 'I think God's love brought us into being, and it is only our love of God that keeps us in being.'

'God's love?' Etheldreda frowned. She felt she had been admonished. It was hard for her to think of God's love at this moment.

He flushed and turned away. He had accepted Christianity when he accepted his freedom. It 'felt' right to him, though he was not used to putting into words those secret and private insights that had been coming to him.

They said nothing more as they walked back together through the woods. The great trees rose around them, rooted in the earth, reaching to heaven.

That night when she went to her chamber she asked herself again and again what the words 'God's love' could possibly mean. And then a verse from Jeremiah often quoted by Bishop Felix came to her mind.

'You will seek me and find me, *when you seek me with all your heart*.'[6]

She knelt to pray and there was a quietness in her heart that had not been there before. Into this, words welled up from some deep source she had forgotten.

'Help me, O Lord. I believe. Help thou my unbelief.'[7]

* * * *

In the morning when she arose there were more messengers from the north. Bishop Aidan had died within a few days of his friend Oswin, some said from a broken heart, and there were stories that a young shepherd called Cuthbert, watching his sheep on the high moors, had seen a vision of his death.

'It's said that he suddenly saw a beam of dazzling light shining across the sky, coming from the direction of Bamburgh.'

Etheldreda joined the group that crowded

round the traveller, and the people drew respectfully back to let her approach closer.

'In the beam of light he could make out the transparent forms of shining beings rising upwards and bearing between them a sphere of flame. They carried it with great care as though it were very precious, and within it he could quite clearly see the soul of a man, untouched by the flame, protected by it.'[8]

Those who were listening gasped.

'How did he know that it was a soul?' someone asked.

'What did it look like?' another cried.

'I haven't heard what it looked like, but he knew it was a soul because the next day when he told his story, he learned that at the very moment he had seen the vision, Bishop Aidan had died in Bamburgh.'

Etheldreda moved away.

Coming as it did at the moment when her heart was seeking confirmation for her beliefs, the story moved her deeply. She herself had sensed things from the invisible realms, felt the presence of angels, had moments when she knew things that could not be explained to others. How could she have forgotten all this? Suddenly the dark doubts of the past days disappeared and she was filled with a tremendous certainty.

'For my thoughts are not your thoughts, neither are your ways My ways, says the Lord. For as the heavens are higher than the earth, so are My ways higher than your ways.'[9]

She had been expecting God to be like the people she knew.

She went at once, alone, to the little wooden chapel that served the court of Rendilsham, knelt before the cross on the altar and opened her heart in prayer.

'Lord who is the Source of All, Father, Son and Holy Ghost, mysterious Three in One, I offer myself now as a vessel to be filled by Thee. I swear to keep myself pure and empty of all the desires of the flesh, distractions of the flesh, corruptions of the flesh, so that all my energy shall be directed towards Thee. I pray that my life on earth, like a still pool, shall reflect Thy Will so that it may be seen on earth as it is in Heaven. Amen.'

9

Marriage to Tondbert AD 652

Etheldreda told her father that she was to take the veil, and that she would stay at court only long enough to see him married to a new wife who could take over her duties.

'I will not take a new wife,' said Anna. 'If you go, I will be alone.'

'Then that is your choice,' Etheldreda said firmly.

Anna sat for a long time after she had left the hall, chin sunk on his chest, his eyes dark and deep under his heavy brows.

The decision he had to make was not easy. As the only marriageable daughter of a much respected king, beautiful, cultured and charming, Etheldreda was a prize much sought after. Anna and his council had spent a great deal of time recently weighing up the relative merits of those who would be glad to seal an alliance with him by marrying the princess. King Oswin of Deira would have been perfect for her. But he was dead. Prince Tondbert, ruler of the South Gyrwes, had asked for her, but he was an old man, tough and uncouth. He held the key to the defence of East Anglia and he ruled the vast fenlands that separated the kingdom from the Mercians. On hearing the news that spies had brought of Mercian plans for a second and more formidable attack, the council that very day had persuaded King Anna that an alliance through marriage with Prince Tondbert would be a great advantage. Up to now the fen people had been fiercely independent, cut off from the world and its shifting politics. The only man who understood them and commanded their grudging respect was Tondbert. If anyone could make them take sides in a war between Mercia and East Anglia, he could. But he would not do it if he felt himself slighted. Mercia had its princesses and Penda would not hesitate to use one of them to obtain what he wanted. Anna called Etheldreda back; she had been a spirited child and he knew that as a woman there was a strength in her he would rather not challenge. But he had no choice. He told her about Prince Tondbert's request, and the council's decision.

'The council's decision?' she asked, her blue eyes looking straight into his. 'Does the king not have the final word?'

'My decision,' he corrected himself quietly, meeting her gaze steadily. There was silence for what seemed a long while, then Etheldreda turned away and paced about the deserted hall. He had dismissed all his companions, retainers, slaves and thegns and the place was uncannily quiet. Etheldreda could not remember a time when she had seen the hall so empty, nor when it looked so huge; the tall wooden columns at the sides seemed taller, the long tables and benches longer. She ran her hand along the beautifully worked tapestry that kept the draughts from blowing upon the king's back, and returned at last to stand before her father.

'I find it difficult to refuse you, my father,' she said quietly. 'I can see our safety depends on this marriage, but I have given my life as wife and mother away so that I may serve the Lord Christ. I have sworn an oath.'

The king looked old and tired. He knew the binding strength of such oaths. No man was more despised amongst his people than an oath breaker, the betrayer of the Lord's trust.

'Prince Tondbert is an old man, daughter,' he said thoughtfully at last. 'A Christian. He will understand that you can't break a vow to the Lord Jesus Christ and may be content to take you as wife only in name. Your presence at his court will hold the Mercians at bay for he has reason to fear them as much as we have. And your learning and your knowledge of diplomacy will help him bring his country out of barbarism. There are many favours you will be able to give him without the sharing of his bed.'

'Ask him, father,' the girl said in a low voice. 'For I will marry him on no other terms.'

She left him and went for a long ride in the forest. She longed to escape court life with its endless round of petty intrigues. She was bored with the monotonous bouts of drinking, the boasting of violent deeds, the greedy hands outstretched for favours or for presents from the king. Did no one do anything for love anymore? She missed the monastic life she sampled at Dunwich and in France, where every thought, every activity seemed charged with significance for eternal life. If she married Tondbert she would have to forgo the life she longed for, but it might not be for long. He was old and, although his muscles were still firm and hard like the roots of an ancient tree, his eyes had the grey rims to the iris that she had often seen in old people not long for this world.

* * * *

Tondbert did not like the arrangement Anna offered, but he agreed as long as the terms were not made public. The betrothal vows were taken at Christmas and the bride-price paid. He returned to his own country laden with gifts of armour and chests of silver and gold.

In early spring he returned for his bride.

Etheldreda was paler and thinner than when he had seen her last. The winter had been severe and she had spent much of the time on her knees in the cold little wooden chapel, trying to come to terms with the strange stirring of her heart for the religious life, while the court was joyfully preparing for her life as the wife of Prince Tondbert. Heregyth had been no help at all. The only flaw she could see in the prospect was that Tondbert was old and ugly. She was overjoyed that her mistress was to be married and that they were both to be rescued from the boring prospect of life in a monastery where all the talk was of God and art and books, and never of clothes and sex and food. She did not think ahead to the years of separation from her friends and relations, her isolation among people strange to her in custom and tradition. She enjoyed the immediate bustle of trying on clothes, ordering delicious foods, handling priceless gifts.

Etheldreda wanted to be married in a simple smock of white with no adornments, but a dress was prepared for her of eastern silk in blue and gold, with a cloak that shone like the sun. Her mother's coronet of garnet and pearl set in gold would hold the fine white veil to her head. King Anna was determined to make an impression with the wedding. Penda must be left in no doubt that Tondbert's support was now firmly committed to the royal house of the Wuffingas.

As the days went by and the wedding day approached, people began to wonder if the princess were ill. Heregyth reported hearing people saying that it was a shame she was to be married to such an old man, but that surely she would take a lover as soon as she was established in her new home.

Horrified to hear this she made an effort to appear more cheerful and instructed Heregyth to spread the word that she was well pleased with her father's choice for her.

A few days before the wedding feast was to begin, her sister Saxberga arrived from Kent with her husband and children, Bishop Honorius and two young men from Northumbria who had broken their journey to Rome in order to study a while with him.

On hearing her sister had arrived, Etheldreda rushed out of her bower, her hair undressed, her clothes ungirdled, and ran barefoot across the much trampled mud of the forecourt to fling herself upon her sister, covering her with kisses, tears of joy streaming down her cheeks. Here at last was someone she could talk to. Someone who would understand.

A tall, handsome youth on a well-accoutred horse, directly behind that of the Kentish queen, saw her beautiful, expressive face almost at his knee, her flying golden hair brushing his hand.

'Who is it?' he asked his Northumbrian companion, King Oswy's ex-thegn, Biscop Baducing, when the two women had walked off arms around each other.

King Eorconbert smilingly interrupted: 'It is the Princess Etheldreda whose wedding you have come to celebrate, my lord Wilfrid,' he said. The young monk's expression of admiration had not escaped his eyes.

Wilfrid acknowledged the king's words with a rueful bow. 'It is as well it is her wedding, my lord, as I have vows to keep!'

They all laughed, but Eorconbert wondered how well the young man was going to fit into the monastic life.

Etheldreda told her sister about her vow of chastity and her arrangement with Tondbert. Saxberga listened gravely.

'There are ways of serving God as wife and mother,' she said at last. 'You must not think it impossible.'

'For me it would be,' Etheldreda said firmly.

'Why?'

'I know my nature. If I give that powerful form of energy to a man I will forget God.'

'I know your nature too... It is full of warmth and love. A life of chastity will be hard and cruel for you.'

'It is the only way for me.'

Saxberga frowned, remembering something Heregyth had told her.

'Is it because of Oswin's death?' she asked bluntly.

Etheldreda flushed. 'No,' she said sharply. Then, hesitatingly, 'Not in the way you mean. At his death I turned away from God completely because I had longed for Oswin more than I longed for eternal life. But when I was in the depths of darkness, having forsaken all hope, all sense of meaning in my life, I suddenly had my faith restored a thousand times stronger than it had been before. I know now without any shadow of doubt that this physical life here is as insignificant to the life we are to lead in the spirit, as the little flittering mayfly in our fields is to the king who rules a kingdom.'

Saxberga was silent, thoughtful.

'It is a question of love, you see,' Etheldreda continued passionately. 'Whether you love with your eternal spirit or just with that part of you that is mortal. If I want to live in the spirit as the angels live, close to God, I must cast away the part of me that is of the flesh, that makes me female and not spirit.'

'But if God finds flesh so alien to His plans, why does He insist that we all pass through it on our way to Him? And I have heard you a dozen times saying that the beauty of this world is an expression of His love for us!'

Etheldreda stopped pacing for a moment, a frown between her eyes.

'Do you reject His gift?' Saxberga demanded triumphantly.

'I have not rejected his gift,' Etheldreda replied patiently, sad that her sister couldn't see what was so apparent to her. 'It is just that I have now seen that He has given me a special gift, and that there is more to this gift than I had at first dreamed of. There is fire that burns on the hearth and there is the invisible fire that burns in the love of God. Just as the ordinary fire needs fuel so that it may burn—the invisible fire needs the souls of dedicated people through which it can manifest. Knowing the weakness of my own nature and how easily it can be distracted from eternal matters, I have chosen to strengthen my resolution with a vow, and seal it with a sacrifice.'

Saxberga sighed. She acknowledged the strength in her younger sister with a bow of her head, and said no more.

* * * *

Prince Tondbert arrived a few days before the ceremony with his entourage of noisy, bearded companions. King Anna's thegn looked at them askance as they strode through the stockade gate, singing a ribald song. When Etheldreda walked out to meet them, greeting her betrothed with a curtsey, they crowded round her laughing loudly and shouting to each other in their barbarous guttural dialect.

Prince Tondbert let them say what they had to say and then took her hand and led her away from them. They fell back at once and turned their attention good-naturedly to finding food and drink.

* * * *

The fields around the palace enclosure were crowded with tents of many colours, some small and unpretentious, others grand and spacious. The travelling tent of Bishop Honorius was the grandest of all. He had learnt in Rome that bishops should impress with splendour if they wanted to convert, and his way of living was very different from the simple life of the Celtic missionaries from Ireland, Iona and Lindisfarne. The great Bishop Aidan of Lindisfarne would have scorned to sleep in anything but the lowliest peasant hut. Even at his death the canopy that was drawn over his ailing body was of the very roughest kind.

Wilfrid and Biscop attended the Kentish bishop wherever he went. They admired him greatly and were eager to learn all there was to learn from him while they were with him.

Biscop was twenty-five years of age and had recently left the service as thegn to King Oswy of Bernicia, to join the Church. He had been greatly shaken by Oswy's ruthless murder of Oswin and had begun to question the violence of secular life, and the immorality of earthly power, without wishing to go the whole way literally into the poverty and humility of the Celtic Church. Rome seemed much more to his taste, and so to Rome he decided to go.

Wilfrid too had lived under the protection of King Oswy, since his mother died and his father had taken to wife a woman who mistreated him. He had served at court as a child, and had been sent by Queen Eanfleda to Lindisfarne for education. He had learnt much and had been treated well, but he was impatient with the simple life of the monks. The monastery at Lindisfarne was cut off from the mainland at every high tide. It lay low in the sea, almost invisible from the Northumbrian shore. Sometimes Wilfrid felt they had been cut adrift from the world and were floating far beyond the reach of everything he longed for. He was intelligent and learned fast all the monks had to teach, the library of precious manuscripts his constant joy. But he had begun to hate the feel of homespun on his skin and long for a bright sword at his side and an embroidered cloak to fling over his shoulder. The chance to travel to countries beyond his own became his constant dream.

When it was known that Biscop Baducing was to go to Rome, Wilfrid had asked to share his journey. Biscop was by no means loath to take the youth, for although only seventeen, he was tall and strong, and the pilgrim route to Rome was a dangerous one, robbers being well aware that many pilgrims took treasures to buy their peace in St Peter's city.

In Kent they decided to break their journey with Bishop Honorius, and it was as his guests that they came to be at the princess Etheldreda's wedding.

* * * *

The wedding festivities lasted several days. In all that time the bride and groom, not yet united, walked amongst the guests, listened to heroic poems of other marriages and legendary love affairs, watched dancing, spoke politely to strangers. At night Etheldreda lay in her narrow bed, weary but unsleeping, wondering how it would be to live with the man she had seen so much of the past few days but with whom she had never once been alone.

At the wedding ceremony Bishop Honorius spoke a great deal about marriage being for the procreation of children.

Etheldreda shut her eyes. What if even now she were to say 'No!'? Would people die because of it?

She opened her eyes and found that she was looking directly into Tondbert's. He had been kind to her as a child and she had affection for him. But now she was afraid. Would he respect her vow? She could not read his thoughts. The Bishop's Latin words rolled over them, welding them together, making it impossible for her to change her mind.

* * * *

As they left her home and rode slowly through the cheering, smiling crowds that lined their route, she caught the eye of the younger of the two men who had come with the Bishop Honorius. It was dark and shrewd and looked boldly into hers. Troubled, she turned away, but she had the sense that she had not seen the last of him.

* * * *

At sunset Prince Tondbert's wedding tent was pitched for them and at nightfall they were ushered towards it, his men crowding and jostling, calling out to each other, and sometimes to their prince, their anticipation for the night in terms that made Etheldreda's cheeks burn.

It was only when the tent flap closed behind them at last that the men settled down with their jars of ale. But it was not long before the ribald songs began. Heregyth complained bitterly about the noise but was powerless to stop it. For the first time she wondered what kind of life she and her mistress were going to have among such uncouth people.

Ovin paced up and down throughout the night, sleep and peace of mind far from him.

* * * *

Inside the huge tent the lamps flickered and made monstrous shadows of the bride and groom, the only furniture a huge pallet of straw covered with furs. Etheldreda stood beside it, her heart beating painfully, hardly daring to meet her husband's eyes.

'My lord...' she said at last in a small dry voice, but then found that she could not continue. They stood in silence, trapped in the lamplight, aware of each other, aware of what was expected of them by the laughing men outside.

Tondbert moved at last and began to extinguish the lamps one by one. As each one went out a cheer went up from the men outside.

Etheldreda clasped and unclasped her hands.

As he came to the last one he paused and looked at her. The darkness was all around her; the flame of the last lamp dancing on her gold hair and the gold necklace at her throat. A muscle twitched in his cheek uncontrollably, but he said in a voice not much above a whisper: 'We must go to bed lady—but you needn't fear, I will honour the conditions of our betrothal though it destroys me.'

As the flame went out, she flung herself upon the bed and sobbed, trying to keep the sound of it from reaching the men outside. Her husband did not touch her, but lay flat on his back at the other side of the pallet staring all night at a small aperture in the tent that let the starlight in.

* * * *

By dawn most of the men had fallen drunkenly asleep around the dead and dying fires and when Tondbert drew the curtain flap aside and strode out into the pale morning air, beating his fists upon his chest and smiling broadly to show that he had had a good night, not as many of his companions as he would have wished were there to see the act.

But when the princess emerged later in her long silk robes, her hair dishevelled and her eyes showing that she had not slept, she was greeted with a cheer and Tondbert had to endure many an over-enthusiastic slap upon the shoulders and the back.

Heregyth was fetched at last and helped her mistress dress.

'These people are barbarians, lady,' she complained. 'You will never believe how they slobber over their food.'

Etheldreda smiled sadly. 'Their prince is no barbarian Heregyth. I've never met a nobler man.'

Heregyth looked at her in surprise.

'Truly, mistress?'

'Truly.'

Heregyth shrugged, but she was pleased. 'Ovin didn't sleep, my lady. I think he would have liked to beat some heads in to teach them some respect.'

Etheldreda laughed. 'Thank goodness he didn't.'

'Will you see him my lady, and assure him that you are all right. He is in a terrible gloomy mood.'

'Certainly. Send him to me.'

He came to her and helped her mount her horse. As his hands touched her she felt him tremble and looked at him, but with no understanding of what he was feeling.

'Heregyth tells me that you are worried about me?' she said gently, taking the reins in her small fine hands.

'Aye, my lady.'

'There is no need. All is well. As you can see—the sun is shining and everything is fine and new.'

He bowed his head, and stepped back away from her, her cheerfulness stinging like a cold wind. She rode off without a backward glance, the relief she felt at Tondbert honouring his promise making her light-headed. Her gaiety was instantly attributed to her husband's prowess as a lover.

* * * *

It was the custom for a groom to give his bride a present to celebrate the consummation. Tondbert gave Etheldreda the island of Ely which she had loved so much as a child, the best land in his princedom, wooded and standing free from the marshes, supporting six hundred souls. She received it humbly and gratefully, knowing that she had not earned it. At her request they rested there before they continued the last lap of their journey by boat. She wanted to talk to the people who were now her people and see how best to serve them. Near the end of her walk around the island they came across the charred remains of a wooden building that had once been a church. 'Consecrated by Bishop Augustine himself in my grandfather's time,' Tondbert told her.

'The Lord's house and it is lying in such ruins!' she cried.

'It was Penda's work,' he said gruffly, ashamed that he had not thought to rebuild it before he gave his gift to her.

A shadow crossed her face. 'Penda!' She picked up a piece of burnt wood and stood a long time turning it over and over in her hands, thinking, remembering Penda's invasion of her country.

Tondbert's men had gone to organise the shallow boats for the last stage of the journey and Ovin and Heregyth were bartering for food from the villagers. The prince and she were alone, and he, seeing that she was absorbed in contemplation withdrew, and stood awkwardly a little way from her, wishing that instead of the small island with its few huts and desecrated church, he could give her the world and all its riches.

He saw her stoop down and pick up a handful of grass and earth, and stand again, sifting it thoughtfully through her fingers. This was the first earth she had ever owned and she felt awed by the thought of it. This earth was her responsibility. She knew that she must rebuild the church... but not here. Penda's hate and violence had marked the place forever. She would find another place and she would know it at once when she saw it.

* * * *

Once they took to the punts, Tondbert's companions seemed less ungainly, less uncouth. They had been ill at ease on dry land and in the alien court, but in the marshes they were at home. The small, light punts glided swiftly, poled skilfully between the many hazards. Occasionally a man would draw a bow and arrow and shoot a bird from the sky. Etheldreda winced to see the lovely creatures fall, but when night came and tender marsh fowl was served for dinner she forgot her scruples and ate hungrily.

On the last day a sudden hubbub drew the attention of the Prince and Princess and they drew near to find a man floundering in the black, slimy water among the eels, the others gathered around shouting with laughter, Heregyth screaming and trying to reach him with the long punt pole, her boat rocking dangerously.

'What is it Ovin?' called Etheldreda.

'Nothing, my lady,' replied the big Celt with a grin. He, with Tondbert's men, was not sorry to see Edgils, a young thegn from Anna's court, get a wetting. He and Heregyth had been free with their insults since they had left Rendilsham and so one of the fen men, egged on by the others, had challenged him to a race and contrived to make him lose his footing.

'Help him out,' commanded Etheldreda, seeing that the young man was really struggling against the clinging water-weeds. So with great humour and not a few crude remarks they hauled him out and returned him, soaking and smelling, to Heregyth who instantly took him in her arms and covered his muddy head with kisses. Etheldreda and Tondbert joined in the general laughter and then turned back to the journey. 'So,' thought Etheldreda. 'Heregyth and Edgils, eh?'

* * * *

Tondbert's court had very few of the comforts to which Etheldreda had been accustomed throughout her life. The great hall was smaller than any she had known, dark, stuffy and overcrowded, and she was expected to sleep with him at one end of it, only a thin curtain between her and the noisy companions who occupied the rest of it.

At home, after the drinking and the feasting,

the talking and the singing, the royal family and most of the married couples of the court left the hall and found privacy in separate wooden chambers spread about the court enclosure. Only the unmarried thegns and bachelor visitors pulled out cushions and pallets and spent the night in the hall. Of course slave girls, peasants and servants thought nothing of copulating in public, but it was unthinkable that a princess should be subjected to the same indignity.

When Tondbert pulled the greasy furs from his pallet and indicated that this was where she was expected to sleep, tired as she was, her anger rose high and fierce.

'What of your promise now, sir?' she flushed at him with unusual haughtiness. 'Are we to be a nightly spectacle for your thegns?'

'There is a curtain, lady,' he said feebly, shocked at her sudden rage.

'A curtain!' she cried scornfully, and gave it a jerk with her white hand. It ripped at once and hung limply from its broken moorings. 'It would not obscure a midge!'

Tondbert looked embarrassed, aware that the noise of the hall had suddenly ceased and all eyes were upon them.

She turned from him and seized a torch, holding it high above her head.

'What kind of people are you?' she demanded, 'that you expect your prince's bride to sleep here among your snoring and your filth. I will not shut my eyes until you've built a separate house for me!'

An angry murmur started amongst some of the men, but she turned her fiery eyes upon them so fiercely that they were quiet at once. She was amazingly beautiful in the flickering light of the torch, and this, combined with the fact that they were a people who admired courage and outspokenness above all else, impressed them. Someone suggested that they rig up the travelling tent for her but she refused. She had said that she would not shut her eyes until she had a house, and she would not.

Tondbert tried to remonstrate with her, but she was adamant.

'In the morning my men will build you a house, lady, but tonight be content with the tent.'

'If I sleep in a tent tonight, a tent will be offered to me tomorrow night and the house will never be built. No, I have said I will not sleep until I sleep in my own house and I will not go back on that.'

'You might as well give up, my lord,' Heregyth said. 'My lady is very...' She hesitated, and then finished the sentence carefully, 'determined.'

Tondbert sighed. His men were looking at him and he knew what they were thinking. 'Very well,' he said. 'Stay awake if that is what you want. But the house will not be started until the morning.' And he strode back to his bed with dignity and, with a great show of being unconcerned, prepared to settle down for the night.

She remained upright in a chair all night staring into the shadows behind the torch flames, as, one by one, the men and women all around her fell asleep. Only Ovin stayed awake with her, standing behind her chair as though on guard. Heregyth tried to do the same, but in a very short time was slumped at her feet, fast asleep.

* * * *

At first light Ovin started to organise the building of her home. The marshlands had very little stone or wood, but reeds were plentiful. They wove her a house of reeds, cut sedge for the thatching, interlaced bulrushes for the matting to cover the ground, set rush candles at every corner to keep darkness at bay, the women preparing a huge mattress of soft marsh grasses and duck feathers, covering it with otter pelts.

At nightfall when the house was ready she and Tondbert were led to it proudly. Somewhere a lad was playing a reed pipe, its notes fine and clear; birds winged homeward over the water-lands and the sun sank, red and heavy, beyond the featureless horizon of a flat land. Etheldreda raised her arms to the green and gold of the sky.

'I want to give thanks to the Lord,' she said, 'for the people of this land, who were strangers, and are now my own people.'

10

Ethelhere at Penda's court

'What's happening?' shouted Egfrid, son of Oswy of Bernicia, as Wulfhere and some other Mercian youths galloped past him on the practice ground. Wulfhere called back over his shoulder, but the words were lost in the sound of hooves drumming on the turf. Egfrid stared after him, wishing that he could ride with him instead of spending endless hours sparring with old Enwulf and the boys of his own age.

Egfrid had served six long years as hostage at the Mercian court. Cynewise, the Mercian queen, had been kind to him, but Penda he feared, though he saw very little of him. Wulfhere, Penda's second son, now seventeen, was Egfrid's hero. He tried to remember that he was an enemy like the others and that one day he would have to kill him, but it was not easy when Wulfhere took him hunting and treated him like a friend and an equal.

Seeing that the younger boys would not settle back to their work after the disturbance, Enwulf called them together.

'You want to know what's going on? Well,

I'll tell you what's going on, but it'll do you no good to know it because I'm not going to let you stop work until you've finished what I've set you for the day.'

He looked round at the eager faces of the boys, all sons of thegns and noblemen, but in the sweat and dirt of the practice field indistinguishable from the rough slaves who served them. Egfrid's face stood out. It always did. He had a kind of sullen pride in his eyes, a lift to his head and a swagger to the way he walked, even at the age of nine, that told much about his future strengths and weaknesses. Ethelred, King Penda's youngest son, was in his group of pupils too, but it was Egfrid, the Bernician hostage, who was always at the centre of anything that was going on.

'Our lord the king entertains a special guest. There will be a display.'

A display!

The boys chattered excitedly amongst themselves. A display was the greatest excitement the court could offer apart from war, and was only put on for very special guests on very special occasions. It would mean that everyone would be in their finest clothes, the priests would be out in their feathers and their paint, the warriors would stage mock battles, the horsemen would compete with daring stunts.

Everything would be done to impress the visitor. Enwulf had been wise not to tell the boys earlier in the day. He could see they would take some stern handling now that the news was out.

'Who is the guest, sir?' Egfrid asked, his voice cutting sharply across the general hubbub.

Enwulf looked at him. What dark fires smouldered in that heart, what thoughts festered in that head? Did he resent his father for abandoning him to the enemy, and wait year after year in growing bitterness for his reprieve? Did he think now the honoured guest might be the Bernician king come to take him home?

'I think it is Prince Ethelhere of East Anglia,' Enwulf said mildly.

'Prince Ethelhere? Not even a king!' Ethelred said, surprised.

Egfrid said nothing, but Enwulf, seeing the disappointment on his face, knew that he had not guessed wrong about the boy's expectations.

'Princes may become kings,' Enwulf said. 'But not if they don't learn what kings must know,' he added pointedly. He clapped his hands.

'No more of this. You'll see the display, but first you must finish the morning's work.'

Unwillingly the boys returned to their practice—but soon Enwulf's problem became restraint. They were so excited that they were forgetting the disciplined moves he had been trying to teach them and they were fighting each other as they had seen men fight, to kill.

'Egfrid,' the teacher shouted sharply, and interposed his own sword as the young foreigner's blade drove towards Ethelred's ribs. Ethelred took advantage of the help to jump back, shaken and pale from his narrow brush with death.

Egfrid's face flushed darkly.

'Prince Egfrid!' he ground out between clenched teeth, his eyes blazing at Enwulf.

'*Prince* Egfrid,' Enwulf said as calmly and as firmly as he could for he too was shaken at the boy's sudden ferocity, 'you are losing control, the most important thing I am trying to teach you.'

Egfrid threw his sword down on the ground and turned on his heel.

All activity on the field stopped as the boys watched him stride off. Enwulf bit his lip.

'Come back here!' he roared. He had been challenged in front of all his pupils and he could not let Egfrid get away with it. But Egfrid did not turn round.

Enwulf seized a practice spear from the pile

and flung it with such skill that it landed just ahead of Egfrid, slightly to the right.

Egfrid stopped, but still did not turn round.

The boys watched breathlessly and crept nearer to get a better view of what was happening. Enwulf strode up to the boy.

'Do you question my authority, boy?' he snapped.

He confronted the lad, and only then did he realise why Egfrid would not turn round. There were tears making dusty runnels on his cheeks. For a second Enwulf hesitated and then he knew for both their sakes he had to finish what he had started.

He pulled the spear from the ground with one fierce movement, and shouted: 'Leave the field, whelp of a Christian dog! I'll deal with you later!'

Egfrid left, but to his friends, he still managed to leave with dignity, walking slowly and with his usual arrogant swagger.

* * * *

The display put on by the Mercian king for King Anna's brother Ethelhere was one of the most impressive they had seen for years. But for Egfrid the highlight was the display of horsemanship, his own special skill encouraged by his hero Wulfhere.

As the riders gathered for the start, the

boy's heart beat fast, knowing that Wulfhere would win, yet fearing that he might not. He clambered onto a small rocky knoll where he could view the scene better, pushing a couple of smaller boys off in order to do so. He could see Penda and his queen, the visiting prince, and all the most important eorldermen and thegns sitting and standing on the raised wooden platform beside the field where the race was about to take place. Someone blew a horn and the horses thundered past him, dust almost blinding and choking him.

'Wulfhere!' he shouted. 'Wulfhere! Wulfhere!'

Others shouted other names but he heard nothing but the drumming hooves of the horses, the wild sweet sound of the horn still echoing in his head and the name of Wulfhere beating like a pulse through his whole being.

Someone shook his arm. 'He has won,' a voice told him. 'You can stop shouting now!'

* * * *

Egfrid looked up at the sky with a shout of triumph. Wulfhere might be able to race the gods and beat them, but one day he, Egfrid, ill thought of, pushed around, forgotten son of a powerless king, would win, and the shouting would be for him. He would bow, laughing, before the throne of Penda, and he would receive the reward of gold and the giant aurochs' horn of mead! In his imagination he saw Wulfhere's eyes meet his and acknowledge that he was the better man. But that was the future. Now there were still the competitions of skill to watch and enjoy... the gallop past while stooping from the saddle to retrieve small objects from the ground... the jumping over water and over logs. How the dust flew, the crowds roared, the sweating riders yelled.

Egfrid jumped up and down, his disappointment that his father had not come for him forgotten. Who wanted to go back to Christian Bernicia after all! Was there not more adventure at the court of heathen Penda than at all the other kingdoms in the land!

Prince Ethelhere's eyes shone with excitement too. His ambitious nature had fretted under his brother's steady, peaceful reign, and, at last, tired of waiting for something to happen that would extend his power and give him personal satisfaction, he decided to take the kingdom for himself. But for that he needed help—and to take East Anglia Penda also needed help.

Prince Ethelhere sat now on the raised platform with the Mercian royal family, watching the display of power and skill with admiration and some alarm. Penda had sworn to put him on his brother's throne if he returned his kingdom to the heathen gods. This he would do without a qualm, but would Penda keep his side of the bargain and leave the ruling of East Anglia to him when the fighting was done?

He looked at the boy Egfrid, Oswy's son. Penda had a long arm and a ruthless heart. What hostage would he demand of him? He had no wife, no children. He had no one he loved enough to fear to lose. He was free and no one could touch him.

He smiled. Perhaps he would be the first to deal with Penda and come off best.

11

Ely

Etheldreda decided to start building a church on the island of Ely to take the place of the one that had been destroyed, and spoke to her husband about the possibility of founding a religious community there. He did not demur, and she set about at once looking for an appropriate place. She found a little hill, with a stream at its foot, and surrounded by a forest so green and bright it was almost luminous. She stood on its summit and looked out over her land, her heart knowing that she had found the place. It seemed to her that it had been a holy place before... there was a feeling of continuity... of abiding purpose...

'If God exists,' she thought, 'He has always existed and He has always been speaking to his people. He has spoken on this hill before in ancient times, before Saint Augustine, before the Romans, even before Ovin's people came to this land.'

She told her husband that she herself would undertake the consecration of the place and would stay there, praying and fasting for forty days as was the custom, before the church was built. Tondbert and Heregyth protested at once and Ovin offered himself as proxy for the fast, but she would have none of it. She forbad any of them to set foot upon the hill until the time she had chosen had elapsed.

Tondbert secretly saw to it that Edgils, fully armed and with a few good men, was stationed out of sight in the forest nearby. Ovin and Heregyth insisted on staying with them, Ovin to be as near as he could be to Etheldreda, Heregyth to be as near as she could be to Edgils.

Etheldreda constructed with her own hands a small bower of branches and leaves against the rain and chose carefully the amount of food she would allow herself, storing it in one simple wooden chest on which she set up the small crucifix of gold and garnet she had inherited from her mother, the precious Psalter she had made herself at Dunwich, and a battered volume of the gospel of Saint John that she had received as a wedding present from her father. She had a small earthenware beaker she could use for fetching water from the stream and a thick cloak of harsh, unrefined wool against the cold.

She kissed her husband and her friends gently but firmly, and told them to go away, to return only after forty days had passed.

* * * *

During the first few days, Heregyth, spying on her from the forest, saw that she moved about a great deal, pacing about on the hill top, walking round and round her small domain. Sometimes she rearranged the branches of her bower as though they did not satisfy her, and sometimes she stooped to clear pebbles away from where she intended to sit.

Heregyth reported back to Edgils and Ovin that their mistress was restless and she did not think it would be long before she would give in. But she was wrong.

* * * *

On the hill the passing of time gradually became meaningless to Etheldreda. Days and nights passed, clouds, sunshine, wind and rain... and she scarcely noticed them. Her body's presence on the hill was in a sense an irrelevance.

In the beginning it had been hard; weariness and hunger had bedevilled her and when she had tried to pray distractions had tormented her. During many of the early nights she had not been able to sleep at all, tossing and turning on the hard ground, trying to find a comfortable position and trying not to think about her comfortable mattress of duck feathers back in the house. Sometimes as the darkness of night grew heavier, and the sounds of birds and distant wood chopping that so often comforted her in the day ceased, she had felt very much alone and very much afraid.

One night after a fitful sleep full of doubts and bad dreams, she jerked awake, to find herself apparently surrounded by an almost tangible black cloud. She forced herself to keep her eyes open and to stare into the darkness, knowing that if only she could see the shape of her enemy, she would be less afraid. But there was no shape. There was only an overwhelming sense of the presence of evil.

Gasping for breath she pushed her way out of the bower and scrambled into the open air. She sensed the cloud was now behind her. She spun round to face it, but somehow it had moved and taken up its position at her back once again. Shuddering, she thought of returning to her husband and abandoning the hill to whatever or whoever haunted it. But then she stopped and her fighting spirit returned to her.

'This is the Lord's hill,' she said firmly, 'and no one shall take it from Him.'

She lifted her arms and called out in a loud, clear voice: 'Help and strengthen me, invisible Lord, Holy Spirit! Mighty angels protect me!'

Fiercely and angrily she demanded that the shade should leave the place and never return. She felt strong. She felt confident. She knew that when she turned round once more there would be no shadow at her back—and she was right. She was alone upon the hill. With a deep sigh of relief she looked up to the sky with a prayer of gratitude on her lips. Did she see a shower of stars arc across the dome of darkness and sparks of light fall around her?

* * * *

On another night it was as though she were above her own body, looking down upon herself. She saw ghostly shapes leaning over her as she slept. Terrified, she looked up and saw above the hill a tall figure of light. Now unafraid, she looked back at the place where she was sleeping and the shapes were no longer there. Her body looked peaceful, enclosed in a cocoon of light.

* * * *

Gradually she gained confidence. The hunger that had at first been such a distraction no longer bothered her. In fact she had to force herself to eat the ration of leaves and nuts and roots that she had sworn to Tondbert that she would eat. She slipped deeper and deeper into periods of meditation where whole days were swallowed up without being noticed. The shadow of evil she had been so conscious of in the early days was gone. She slept clear, untroubled sleep for a few hours each night, spending the rest in prayer.

The hill became a place of almost unbearable beauty. By the day she rejoiced in the soaring lark and the green and leafy wood below her: by night she rejoiced in the huge stars, and the moon, silver-rich, and magical. She knew the evil in the world was too huge for her to fight. She prayed only that this little hill, this centre, would be so charged with selfless love that those who came there would leave strengthened and refreshed. If evil spread, growing as it spread, from each cruel and selfish act, surely good could spread in the same way, each loving and unselfish act calling forth others, multiplying in every direction, from the centre.

* * * *

When the forty days had passed Tondbert came to the bottom of the hill and showed himself, and she, knowing this was the signal that they had arranged between them for the end of the purification period, ran to meet him, her face so full of light and joy that he was almost dazzled. She was thin beyond belief, her pale fine skin drawn tight about her bones, her eyes too large in her wasted face. But she was beautiful.

* * * *

When others came to walk upon the hill they found to their surprise that her pacing feet had worn a complicated pattern of paths through the grass. In following it they found that it was a maze, leading slowly and inexorably to a centre in which the pilgrim could reach stillness and meditate, before starting the long, slow twisting journey back to the outside world.

12

Anna's death and burial AD 654

Work was soon started on the new church at Ely, and Etheldreda returned to a normal diet and took her place at her husband's side. But one day dark news reached them from her father's kingdom. Penda had attacked again, skirting the southern reaches of the fenlands, storming the dykes across the Icknield Way and breaching the East Anglian defences that were under the control of Anna's brother Ethelhere.

Tondbert called all the men he could reach together immediately and set off for the south, sending word to the more distant villages for help and putting Edgils in charge of those who were to follow on. Etheldreda tried to stop the thought, but could not, that it was Ethelhere's treachery that had let the Mercians through. She had never trusted him.

Then messengers brought news that nearly broke her heart. King Anna was dead; the country lost to Penda. Dazed with sorrow she heard the voices of Edgils and the messenger as though they were speaking from a great distance.

'Is Penda himself upon the throne?' she heard Edgils ask.

'No. He has appointed Prince Ethelhere as sub-king, to rule under his overlordship.'

'Ethelhere?' King Anna's daughter heard her own voice shouting fiercely. 'I knew it! He has betrayed his people.'

Edgils was startled by the ferocity of her expression.

'My lady!'

'I must go to Rendilsham.'

'My lady, war is no place...'

'The war is over. I must see my uncle and decide what can be done for the country.'

'If he is as treacherous as you say, he'll be cunning.'

'I can be cunning too!'

Edgils looked upset. In the absence of Tondbert he did not know what to do for the best, but he was determined not to let Etheldreda ride into certain danger.

'If the war is over, Prince Tondbert will return. It must be his decision if you go to your uncle or not.'

'No, my lord Edgils, it must be my decision,' Etheldreda said sternly.

* * * *

On Heregyth's suggestion, Etheldreda and her party travelled in disguise. The news they gleaned from the villagers and peasants as they travelled was conflicting. Some said that Tondbert had passed that way with an army and was well on the way to reclaiming the country for his wife's family, but others said he had been defeated and was dead.

Etheldreda let nothing deter her.

At first she was puzzled that she saw so few signs of war's devastation. Many villages seemed untouched by the events of the past few days. Gradually she became more and more confirmed in her belief that the country had been won for Mercia by treachery and not by war. But nearer the heart of the country ugly sights became more commonplace. Apart from the usual places of execution where the shrivelled bodies of criminals hung from gibbets, there were heads on stakes, arms and legs strung from trees. The grizzly presence of a conqueror who sacrificed to Woden became more and more apparent. Her heart ached, her stomach sickened, but she would not turn back.

* * * *

At Rendilsham she found her husband and his men unharmed, Ethelhere installed as king and everything apparently peaceful. Penda's lightning attack had achieved its object and most of the Mercian troops had withdrawn with him in case Oswy should take advantage of his absence and attack the Mercian homeland. He had left sufficient of his men to help support his vassal's authority.

When Etheldreda entered the great hall and saw Ethelhere sprawling on her father's throne, it was all that she could do to hold her tongue.

A shadow crossed his face as he recognised her, and in that instant Etheldreda knew that her life hung in the balance. But Ethelhere was no fool. He well knew how popular his predecessor's beautiful daughter was, and to kill her now in front of everyone might well cost him the uneasy hold he had upon his brother's kingdom.

Etheldreda was no fool either and she could see that Ethelhere had too much power to challenge from her present position. She bowed to him with dignity and allowed herself to be led forward by one of his thegns to stand before him.

Tondbert's face was full of conflicting emotions. He was happy to see his wife, but he also feared for her. There was an underlying tension in the atmosphere that he could not understand. No one had accused Ethelhere of treachery and indeed there was no proof of it. But many were uneasy at the swiftness and easiness of Penda's advance through

Ethelhere's territory and the promptness with which Penda placed him on Anna's throne and left the country as though he trusted him.

'I'm glad to see you, niece,' Ethelhere said coldly to the princess. 'Had you not come I would have sent for you.'

She bent her head in acknowledgement.

He did not see her eyes.

'You are in time for your father's burial.'

She looked up at once, relieved that she was not too late.

'My lord, have you sent for Archbishop Honorius to come from Kent to speak at his grave? I know my father would have wished it.'

'No.'

'Bishop Thomas then, from Dunwich?'

'Neither, princess.'

'Who then, my lord?'

'Have you not heard that your father renounced the Christian god before he died? He will be buried as his ancestors were, under the protection of the real gods.'

Etheldreda was horrified. She looked from the sly face of her uncle as he said these words to her friends at court. It was only then she noticed that there was no Christian priest present, none of her father's closest companions, no one who could stand up to her uncle and give him the lie on this.

She swallowed.

'I had not heard this, sir. Was it witnessed?'

She stood very still and straight, looking him in the eye.

'Aye, it was witnessed.'

'Who witnessed it?'

'These men here.' He indicated a group of his closest friends.

'I would like to know exactly what he said,' she said, trembling, anger almost choking her, but knowing that she was dead if she showed it.

'He vowed when he went into battle that if his god gave him the victory he would build three churches to him, the finest in the world, but if he was defeated he would take it as a sign he had not been heard and he would never pray to him again.'

Etheldreda was silent. She knew for sure now that Ethelhere was lying. King Anna had discussed just this very type of bargaining with God with her on several occasions and she knew that he so disapproved of it he would never resort to it himself no matter how hard pressed he was. 'What! Threaten God that you will withdraw your favours from Him if He does not obey you! Offer Him presents if He helps you!' The thing was so ridiculous to him he had laughed aloud. No matter how many misunderstood God's nature and man's relationship to Him that they made such vows, Anna would not be one of them.

She looked around her carefully. She felt like flinging herself upon Ethelhere, seizing his own dagger and plunging it into his heart before he could do any more damage. She looked at her husband and his men. They were unarmed and placed separately amongst Ethelhere's armed men. Ethelhere was smiling, but being very, very careful.

Something of her old training at court stayed with her. She knew that she must smile and bow and show nothing of her true feelings lest they be used against her. She must bide her time, plan her action, making no aggressive move unless she were covered from every side by companions who could support her. In her father's days she had hated these lessons in hypocrisy and had spoken out against them, but now they saved her life.

Quietly and calmly she reminded herself of other lessons she had learned. Every act of violence brings with it more problems than it solves. To plunge a knife into another's heart wounds the soul of the aggressor more than the body of the victim.

'It surprises me, my lord,' she said at last, holding her voice steady. 'My father's works throughout his life are surely greater witness to his love of the true God, than a few words spoken in fear just before a battle.'

'If his god were "true" as you say,' Ethelhere said with an ill disguised sneer, 'why did he give a pagan victory over him?'

'The battles the Lord supports are not fought with swords and spears. Christ came to tell us that. Who are we to say he did not win a victory after all? The loom of the Lord is vast. No one can see the whole pattern of the weave.'

Ethelhere's face darkened and he rose from his chair impatiently.

'I have been gentle with you, niece, because of the sorrow you must be feeling for your father's death, but I have no time to sit and argue. Your father was a much respected man and I loved him as a brother. It is because I loved him I now rejoice that he has returned to the old and faithful gods, and I will see that he gets the burial he desired. If you wish to attend the ceremony you may, but I must demand that you speak no words blasphemous to the true gods. If you do not wish to attend, I will say nothing, but wish you well on your return to your own country.'

He stressed the words 'your own' as though reminding her that she was no longer of this country and consequently had no right to interfere.

She bowed.

'I will stay, my lord, and see my father buried.'

'And keep silence on pain of death?' He looked at her hard and menacingly.

'And keep silence,' she agreed.

'Good. We will waste no more time then.' He started to move briskly towards the door.

'My lord...'

'What is it now?' He paused impatiently to look at her. She knew that this was the last time he would listen to her.

'Is it to be a full pagan burial? My father to lie with all his war accoutrements and the treasures of his house.'

'Yes.'

'Have I your permission to bring a few of his personal things to lay beside him? Things I know he loved, though they were not of great value in the world's eyes.'

'You may do so, but you may say no words when you lay them down.'

'Thank you, my lord,' she said, and bent her knee to him as he strode past her and out through the door.

* * * *

Ethelhere had planned the whole thing well.

In order to return the country to the old gods to please Penda, and to ensure that he would be allowed to keep the limited power he had, he had to discredit the Christian God and show the people in one flamboyant, memorable act that even the man who had been so long a champion of Christianity had at last abandoned it.

The burial was to be spectacular, the site chosen among the burial mounds of their forefathers overlooking the estuary of the River Deben up which Anna's own pagan grandfather had sailed.[10] It was to be a ship burial harking back to the heroic days when men were under the protection of the old gods as they crossed the wild and stormy seas.

Ethelhere had had difficulty in finding priests capable of conducting the burial ceremony in the old grand way, for they had been long out of favour, living in secret, peddling only charms and curses to the superstitious peasants and villagers. But even when he had overcome this difficulty he was faced with others even more serious.

At the very last moment, when most of the crowds were already gathered, he was told that King Anna's body had disappeared.

'What?' he screamed. But rant or rage as he may he could not bring it back.

His first thought was that it was some mischief of his niece Etheldreda, but she was in his entourage and had been under observation ever since her arrival. He tried to think clearly. It was vitally important to his own grasp of power that Anna should be seen to have accepted the old gods.

It was too late to postpone the burial until the body was found, and unwise to let the people know that it was missing.

Indeed, if it were known the body were in the hands of the Christians to be given a Christian burial, it would be a mighty rallying point for all the dissidents in the country, and they were many.

He looked at Etheldreda, but her face showed nothing. 'She will pay for this,' he muttered to himself. 'I should have killed her when she first walked through my door!' He was certain that somehow she was responsible for the abduction. She had been a clever child, and as a woman she was accepted as equal by scholars and by kings. She had always made him feel uneasy, looking at him with those clear eyes, as though she could see into his very soul. But he was clever too, and this time he believed he would outsmart her. He mastered the outward signs of his discomfiture, took those aside who had brought the message and those who had heard it, swore them to secrecy, and sent them to organise a discreet search. His instructions were that if they were to find the king's body they were to kill all who had anything to do with its theft and hide it in a place only they would know, later to be revealed only to him.

He then took his most trusted thegns aside and some of the Mercian captains and ordered all that he could spare to disperse across the land, waiting for his signal to begin a purge of Christians and a punishment of dissidents if there were any sign of an uprising.

He then proceeded with the funeral procession as though nothing was wrong.

* * * *

There were huge crowds gathered for the burial in the sandy heathland beside the royal mounds.

For most people it did not seem strange that a Christian king should have a pagan burial. They were gullible and believed it when his brother, whom they had no reason to distrust, said that it had been his last wish. With some of them belief in the old gods had never really died, and bubbled easily to the surface again. With others Christianity was merely a convention, having no proper roots, easily abandoned. For such people a spectacle, a show of power and riches, was enough to influence allegiance, as the Roman Church had realised when it dressed its bishops in fine clothes and copes embroidered lavishly with gold thread. Ethelhere understood this too when he ordered the immense ship burial with full ceremony.

The new king was dressed magnificently as he climbed to the top of the huge mound of earth that had been excavated to take the hull of the ship. From the four directions of the wind mighty horns were blown to call the people's attention to him. When all was quiet Ethelhere raised his arms in greeting.

'My brother, King Anna, hero of our people...' He paused for the cheering to die down, and then resumed.

'King Anna prayed to his Christian god,' he said loudly and clearly, and there was scorn in the way he said the word Christian. '...prayed for deliverance from his enemies. He vowed to his Christian god that if he won the battle against Penda he would build three churches in stone that would last forever, the greatest in the world. But if he were defeated he would know his prayer had not been heard and he would pay homage to Penda's gods, the ancient gods of our people!' He suddenly raised his voice on these last words and the sound of his voice carried with tremendous power across the listening crowd. There was a murmur which he stilled with a gesture of his hand. 'He vowed before witnesses,' and here the men who claimed to be witnesses stepped forward and were pointed out triumphantly by Ethelhere, 'that he would have no Christian burial, but would be buried in the manner of his ancestors, under the protection of his father's gods. And this duty...' he shouted again, 'he charged me to carry out!' Again he paused for the murmuring to die down.

'He fought as a hero fights, but his god gave him no help. He died, chopped to pieces by his enemies, his members scattered across the fields... not even a body left for us to bury!'

The people swayed and keened. Anna had been greatly loved.

Ethelhere wept.

The people wept.

Etheldreda stood, dry eyed, angry.

Gradually the ceremony unfolded. Dirges were sung, and bards recited the heroic deeds of the hero king and one by one Anna's old companions brought treasures from his personal store and placed them where the priests dictated, within the burial chamber, amidships. Meanwhile the priests intoned invocations to

Woden and Thunor and Saxnet for protection for the dead hero, stressing his repentance that he had left their service for so long, and promising that his people would make amends for him now that he was dead.

Etheldreda did not move from where she had been told to stand.

At last Ethelhere gestured for her to move forward. His eyes gleamed dangerously into hers as she passed close to him, but, as before, her face was expressionless.

She had a few silver things of her father's wrapped in her shawl and she placed them carefully in the place where her father's heart would have been had his body been laid in the ship. There were ten silver bowls and two spoons her father had been given at the time of his baptism. She spoke no words aloud, but in her heart prayers to the Christian God for the protection of her father were deep and fervent.

No one noticed the words that were engraved on the silver spoons. Even if they had, no one present would have understood them. The writing was Greek and even Ethelhere was illiterate. One spoon had the name Saul engraved upon it, the other Paul. She placed them there as a secret token for anyone who might disturb the burial mound no matter how many millennia hence, that her father had been a pagan, but had been converted to the service of Christ, and died as Paul had done, still in that service.

The bowls she placed in two piles, upside-down, each fitting within the other, the Christian message of the flowering cross invisible, biding its time.

Gradually the burial chamber filled up. Her father's standard and his rod of office were laid to rest, his helmet and his shoes. His personal accoutrements were laid as though still upon his body.

She could not restrain the tears that came to her eyes when his belt was laid down and she saw the purse she had often seen him fondle containing a collection of Merovingian coins gathered by Sigbert during his long sojourn in the Frankish kingdom. It had been one of her pleasures as a child to be allowed to play with them, and he had promised her once that one day he would have a goldsmith make a necklace of them for her, and she had longed for it, spending much happy time visualising herself wearing the exotic foreign currency around her neck. But Ethelhere had decided to use the coins in the burial as symbolic payment for the forty spirit oarsmen who would row her father to the world his ancestors now inhabited, and had made the number up with three gold blanks, including two gold ingots for the steersman.

The huge drinking horns that Redwald, the great Bretwalder, had been so proud of and that had come from their homeland, won by a heroic ancestor from the rare and mighty aurochs, were carried in. Ethelhere was determined that no man would be able to fault him in the funeral arrangements or suspect him of collusion in his brother's death.

When it came time for Anna's sword to be placed in the chamber Ethelhere raised his arms theatrically and all chanting and music died down. He stood with his arms raised until there was complete silence in the huge crowd, those near enough to see and hear whispering to those behind them to be still.

'What now?' thought Etheldreda.

A man moved up beside Ethelhere and, bowing low to him, presented him with something wrapped in a blood-soaked cloth. Ethelhere whipped off the cloth and held the object high above his head for everyone to see.

There was a gasp. It was a man's right arm clutching a sword. Anna's sword.

Someone screamed, but on the whole the crowd remained silent, staring.

'This is my brother's right arm. His sword

arm. He died as you see, still clutching his sword in your defence. This is all we have found of him, but this is all we need for burial. His strong right arm will guard us in death as it did in life.'

The shaman took the grisly object from Ethelhere and laid it carefully with the other objects. The new king led the chanting as the slaves began to throw in the first sods of earth.

Etheldreda knew that that object was not her father's arm, but she said nothing. Some poor soldier must have been prevailed upon to grip the sword and then been killed, so that in death, his hand could be buried for the king's. She despised her uncle more than she could say, for not only had he turned against Christ, but he was mocking the old gods he purported to honour.

* * * *

Near the end of the ceremony, when Ethelhere, pleased by his success, had relaxed a little, she managed to slip away. The crowd began to surge forward, creating such a confusion that it was easy to elude the watchful eyes of Ethelhere's men. She found Tondbert and he took her in his arms. But still she did not weep. Heregyth joined them and together they sought out Ovin. He had horses ready for them, and news that King Anna's body had been taken by friends to Blythburgh where they would wait for Etheldreda's arrival to give it a Christian burial. It was decided that Tondbert and Edgils were to remain behind and organise the orderly retreat of Tondbert's men, for they could see that there was no hope of overthrowing Ethelhere with so many Mercian troops still in the land. Etheldreda, Heregyth and Ovin were to make their way as quickly and discreetly as possible to Blythburgh, going by sea for it would be quicker and less under the surveillance of Ethelhere's men. A fisherman agreed to take them and they cast off as the sun sank—the western sky blazing in gold and purple, while the east faded to a cool mother-of-pearl.

Etheldreda and Heregyth huddled close together, feeling the chill salt wind as the sky darkened, shivering with apprehension about the future.

When they disembarked at Dunwich the following day they found the town and the monastery crawling with Ethelhere's men.

The princess led them through the back streets as inconspicuously as possible, to the house of someone she had known when she was a student. They knocked and called a long time before the door was opened a crack and then it was only for the young boy inside to say with nervous hostility that he was letting no strangers in while his parents were away. He shut the door immediately after delivering the message, and they heard him bolting it.

Ruefully they looked at each other. The only comfort was that Etheldreda in her travel-dusty cloak and with her pale, tired face, had not been recognised. But weary as they were they knew their safest course was to leave the town as quickly as possible.

On the outskirts Ovin left the two young women sitting at the roadside in the dust, eating some dry bread the fisherman had given them, and went in search of horses.

He returned at last with a dilapidated cart pulled by one tired-looking mule, and helped the princess into it. The wooden wheels were by no means as round as they should have been. Their journey on the rough track to Blythburgh was extremely uncomfortable, but they were too tired to walk and Ovin had not been able to find any horses for them.

Half way between Dunwich and Blythburgh they were stopped while Ethelhere's men searched the hay and vegetables the cart contained.

They were just thinking that they would be free to return to the cart and continue on their journey, when one of the soldiers took

Etheldreda by the chin and turned her face to his. When she lowered her eyes he tipped her head back further, his hard fingers bruising her skin.

Ovin instantly sprang forward but was seized.

Cornered, Etheldreda looked up boldly into her tormentor's eyes, her own, cornflower-blue, unafraid.

The soldier laughed and with his other hand ripped at the front of her dress.

Ovin struggled desperately to free himself from the two men who held him but a third punched him in the face and kicked him in the groin. As he doubled up with pain the others set upon him. His last sight as he fell to the ground and darkness closed in around him was of his beautiful princess standing half naked surrounded by rough and leering men.

Heregyth screamed and tried to rush to her mistress's aid, but they held her back, laughing.

'Not so impatient,' they said, 'your turn will come!'

Etheldreda felt herself strangely detached from the whole scene. She felt the man's hands on her and she expected to feel sick and afraid. But instead she had a strange feeling, as though what was happening to her body had nothing to do with her. Her eyes rested a little above the man's head apparently on something he could not see. She looked quite calm.

He paused.

He had pulled off the cloth that held her hair in place and it had fallen down in golden splendour over her shoulders. Her body was pale and very beautiful, but cold as snow. Uneasily he turned his head to see what she was looking at, but could see nothing. He looked back at her, and then at his companions. They too looked uncomfortable, and were standing silent, embarrassed and awkward.

Calmly, regally, she drew her cloak around her.

'Come, Heregyth,' she said, 'help me put Ovin into the cart.'

The soldiers did not move, but stood and watched as the two young women struggled with Ovin's weight.

Suddenly one of the soldiers, no more than a boy, rushed forward and helped them lift him into the cart.

Unhurriedly, with great dignity, Etheldreda climbed up and took the reins.

Unhurriedly they moved off.

As though under a spell the men stood clustered together at the roadside staring after them.

* * * *

At the village of Blythburgh, on a hill overlooking the river's mouth, King Anna was given Christian burial, his daughter Princess Etheldreda leading the prayers, her maid Heregyth playing the music on a borrowed lyre, and her Celtic freedman Ovin, covered in cuts and bruises, standing watch.

At the end of the simple ceremony his grave was smoothed over and marked with the sign of the Fish. Bracken and brushwood was brought to cover the ground so that no one would disturb him.

* * * *

Etheldreda, Heregyth and Ovin were grateful to rest that night in a village house, but the following morning before first light they awoke and started on their long and hazardous journey back to the shelter of Tondbert's marshlands.

13

Death of Penda

'My lady, the dawn is not far off. Will you not sleep?'

The anxious voice of her maid cut across Queen Eanfleda's thoughts as she knelt at the altar of the shrine she had built on the site of King Oswin's murder. Normally monks prayed where she now was, day and night unceasingly, for the souls of Oswin and his murderer, her husband. Outside an icy wind rattled the bare branches of the trees and drove flurries of dead leaves against the door.

The floor was hard and cold and she was stiff in every limb from her long vigil. She suffered herself to be helped to her feet by two of her women. She was shivering in spite of her heavy fur cloak.

'My lady, you are pale! Come to bed!'

'Is someone ready to take my place?' she whispered. 'There must be no break in prayer.'

A young monk called Cuthbert, the same who had seen the vision of Bishop Aidan's soul being taken to heaven, emerged at once from the shadows and took Eanfleda's place before the altar. She looked at him with tears in her eyes. He had a rough peasant look, but his eyes had seen angels.

'Pray well, my friend, your sovereign's life and the safety of your countrymen depend on you.'

'I will pray for God's will to be done, my lady. There is no sense to a prayer that does not do that.'

She looked alarmed.

'But it is for forgiveness you must pray, forgiveness for the king. He goes into battle soon and with Oswin's murder on his soul the Lord will surely let his enemies triumph.'

Cuthbert bowed his head slightly, turning from her to the altar. Whether he had understood or not she could not tell.

Her women pulled her gently away.

'Come, my lady, the king's soul will be prayed for. Have no fear. But if you do not rest you will fall ill.'

The queen left the chapel, the wind swirling around her, the night shadows like so many wolves, circling her menacingly.

This was a terrible place where a terrible deed had been done. Fear and cold were in her heart. What chance had her husband against Penda without the help of God!

He had tried everything to avert war. He

had suffered the continual ravages of Mercian raiders without retaliation, knowing that Penda was too strong to challenge. He had offered Penda bribes to stop the raids. Treasure that would have bought a kingdom was taken by the Mercian king, yet still the raids continued. But now he had come to the point where he could afford to bear no more. East Anglia was now virtually a vassal of the Mercians and his own country would be next if he did not make a stand.

He called on his nephew, Oswald's son, who had taken murdered Oswin's place in Deira, to support him, but spies brought him news that the Deiran king had betrayed his plans to Penda and would fight against him in the battle.

He was alone.

Penda's heathen hordes were gathering like a vast wave to break upon his frontiers. The winter was coming on, the cattle that would not survive without winter feed already being slaughtered. The outlook was very sombre.

He rallied his men, making a public vow to God, that if he was granted victory he would give his infant daughter, Elffleda, to be consecrated as a virgin in His perpetual service, and he would arrange for twelve of his estates to be turned into monasteries.

* * * *

Penda, hearing of his challenge, laughed.

He called together all his vassal kings, including Ethelhere of the East Angles, and the temple of Thunor rang with the sound of metal against stone, as the thegns filed in in their thousands to dedicate their swords to Penda's favourite god. Sacrificial fires made the night almost as bright as the day and feasting and carousing was continuous as the men gathered from all over the kingdom.

Prince Wulfhere and Cynewise, who had grown fond of the Bernician hostage, Egfrid, advised him to lie low and keep out of Penda's sight. If Penda found him he would certainly be killed for his father's treachery. The queen even sent her most trusted slave to conduct him to a hiding place.

Egfrid, who trusted nobody, appeared to accept the help, and then when the queen's slave had left, he mounted up again and rode off into the night.

* * * *

Penda and Oswy met on the banks of the River Winwaed on a wild and blustery day.

Penda was confident the whole of Northumbria would soon be his. His troops outnumbered Oswy's by the thousand, his god rode with him in the fierce black storm clouds that were moving across the sky so swiftly and so ominously.

Ethelhere, leading the small East Anglian army that he had been able to spare from peace-keeping at home, was one of the first leaders Penda sent into the battle. Some said later Penda had deliberately sent him to his death because he despised a man who betrayed his people and betrayed his own god. The wind against him, his arrows and his spears went wide while Oswy's drove home.

Ethelhere was one of the first to die.

Penda sent another of his vassal kings.

Again Oswy prevailed.

Then Penda shook his battle axe at the sky and cried in a loud voice to his god.

Thunor answered.

The black clouds were riven by a jagged sword of light and Penda led his horsemen confidently into the river, while his archers shot over their heads to harry the Bernicians and prevent them attacking Penda's picked men while they were at a disadvantage. The Mercian horsemen were the terror of all the neighbouring kingdoms. No one could ride like them and many a villager had woken in the night to their dread hoofbeats, knowing that that would be the last sound he would ever hear.

Oswy's heart sank as he saw their number. He wiped his right hand as the sweat began to make it slippery, and then he gripped his sword hilt tight again.

The arrows were coming in thick and fast and many of his men were going down, but not as many as would have fallen had the wind not been against Penda.

'The Lord is on my side!' Oswy whispered, seeing this, and felt his courage rising.

'Charge to meet them!' he shouted. 'Do not let them set foot on our land!'

His men moved forward and the river ran red with the blood of those who were hacked to pieces in its turbulent waters.

Penda himself reached the far shore, his eyes blazing with the frenzy of battle, his formidable axe slashing left and right, his men close about him, wreaking havoc.

The far hills had disappeared under a deluge of rain. The thunder roared and rumbled.

Suddenly lightning struck a tall tree on the river bank. Instantly a column of yellow smoke rose from it, the crack of thunder that accompanied the awesome sight deafening many, causing others to drop their weapons and run screaming from the place, convinced that the supernatural was taking too personal an interest in the battle.

With all his force one of Oswy's thegns threw his spear a second before the lightning struck the tree, and—before the sound of the thunder had stopped reverberating—Penda toppled from his horse.

With a scream of triumph Oswy was upon him, his sword slicing through his neck while his left hand ripped off the helmet and held the grisly object aloft by its peppery white bush of hair.

'Penda's dead!' The roar went up. 'Penda's dead!'

Shocked, the Mercians hesitated. For as long as they could remember Penda had been the conqueror, the scourge and terror of the Seven Kingdoms. How could he be dead with Thunor roaring his support through the huge and echoing caverns of the sky?

Their hesitation was their undoing. Oswy's men took heart and swept forward. The Mercians were forced back to the river that they had with such difficulty just crossed, Oswy's men close upon them.

'Back!' shouted Oswy suddenly, noticing the fearful energy of the river... but only some managed to get back in time. The onslaught of rain the sky now unleashed and the flood waters pouring down the valley from the hills, washed many away.

It was said that when the storm passed, the dying and the dead were strewn for miles downstream of the battlefield, and there were more casualties on both sides from the storm's fury than from man's.

14

Death of Tondbert AD 655

The winter that followed the battle of Winwaed was severe.

Blizzards drove across the high moors and ice split rock from rock on the dark ridges. People huddled in their thatched houses, chopping and burning the very trees whose branches gave them shelter from the icy winds and whose roots held the earth firm beneath them. Rivers froze. Sheep were lost in snowdrifts. The old and very young died daily, coughing and shivering.

Oswy took steps to consolidate his dramatic victory over Penda. His eldest son Alfrid, who had fought with him at Winwaed, was installed as sub-king of Deira. Penda's daughter, Cyneberga, was given to him as wife and hostage. Peada, Penda's eldest son, was allowed to rule as sub-king of the Middle Angles, but Oswy wove such a web of spies around him and kept such tight control he was no more than a figurehead. He was forced to marry Oswy's daughter Alfleda and accept baptism.

The missionaries came to Mercia and Penda's old enemy, the Christian God, toppled the statue of Thunor in the temple and drove Frejya's cat women into hiding.

Wulfhere, bitterly resenting the change in his country's fortunes, took to the hills.

Egfrid returned home.

* * * *

In the marshlands of the South Gyrwe the winter was no less severe. An icy fog hung day and night upon them, not even the walls of the prince's hall strong enough to keep it out. Guttering torches and the sputtering fat of roasting animals added an acrid smell of smoke, and at times it was difficult to see across the great table.

Tondbert took ill and lay behind his curtain at the end of the hall coughing and wheezing. Etheldreda barely left his side, feeding him herb broth, mopping the sweat from his brow and holding him close against her as he alternately shivered and burned. She would have liked to have taken him from the crowded hall to the privacy of their own house, but his people would not let him go. Solicitously they hovered about him, offering him mysterious delicacies that were supposed to heal.

She could feel him slipping from her and held him closer, but the priest touched her arm and indicated that she should draw back allowing him to pray for the peaceful passage of her husband's soul.

She lifted her blotched and tear-stained face to him.

'Why?' she whispered. 'Oh why am I so weak in faith when I most need it? I should rejoice that he goes to the Lord, not weep that I am losing him!'

It seemed to her that she had not, in the three years they had been married, realised that she loved him until this moment.

* * * *

When Prince Tondbert's successor was chosen, Etheldreda withdrew to Ely. At last she could give all her attention to what had always been closest to her heart, the founding of her community. She and five of her closest women friends, Ovin and her priest Huna, built huts with their own hands from the trees of the Ely woods and thatched them with reeds from the marshlands nearby. They met for worship in the little church Ovin had built on the site Etheldreda had consecrated.

Heregyth was bitterly critical. If the princess was going to take to the religious life, she asked petulantly, why could she not have done so in one of the big monasteries as she originally intended instead of like a Celt in a hovel.

Only the Irish monks lived in gloomy isolated cells and had no comforts. The Roman priests Heregyth had met lived very well indeed. But Etheldreda herself was not aware of the discomfort.

It seemed to her a great luxury to have time to herself at last, with all the distractions of the world removed. She saw sustained meditation and prayer as essential if she wanted to adjust her inner hearing and her inner seeing to the eternal.

She did not ask Heregyth to join the community, for she could see that the life would bring nothing but misery to her. She gave her blessing to her marriage with Egdils and sent them both back to Rendilsham where Anna's younger brother, Ethelwald, was now king.

* * * *

In Mercia, after only a few years of rule, Peada was assassinated, some said with the treacherous help of his Bernician wife. Certainly her father Oswy benefited and moved in at once to take the leaderless country under his wing. But a year later a powerful group of Mercian noblemen brought the young Prince Wulfhere out of hiding and forced Oswy to accept him as the rightful king of their country.

Needing important allies, Wulfhere sent to Kent for Saxberga's eldest daughter, Eormengild.

Oswy, realizing that his position was weakening, sent his messengers to East Anglia and requested an alliance with Etheldreda's uncle, Ethelwald. The alliance was to be sealed by the marriage of Oswy's second son, Egfrid, to the widowed East Anglian princess, Etheldreda.

* * * *

King Ethelwald received the request with mixed feelings. To have Northumbria his ally was more than he could wish for, but, he knew his niece!

The last of the March snows were still lying when he set off for Ely, knowing that if he sent a messenger he would receive a polite but firm refusal to his proposition. His only hope was to appeal, as her father had done before, to her sense of duty towards her people.

* * * *

Etheldreda was chopping logs of wood for the fire when she received a message that the king was coming in person to speak to her. She paused a moment, straightening her aching back, and looked thoughtfully at the village lad who had excitedly brought her the news.

'How soon will he be here?' she asked at last.

'He is already on the island, my lady,' the boy cried. 'He had already landed before we realised who it was!'

She smiled.

'Well, then, you had better run back and guide him to us. You would not want a king to lose his way now, would you?'

Filled with a sense of importance the boy ran back down the hill.

Etheldreda put down her axe and without hurry tidied up her pile of wood. She would be pleased to see her Uncle Ethelwald, of whom she was fond, but she was a little anxious as to the reason for his unannounced visit.

By the time he arrived she had laid and lit a fire and found what simple furniture there was available in their community for him to sit upon. They had not seen each other for some time and Ethelwald was surprised to see how much she had changed. She was still thin, but she looked brown and healthy as though the vigorous Spartan life she led suited her.

If he had hoped that she would have found it too much for her, he was disappointed; her eyes were bright, her cheeks glowing with health.

His heart sank.

She sensed that something was wrong as soon as she kissed him.

'Why, uncle—there is a shadow on your greeting! What is the matter?'

He had not intended to tell her at once, but

had planned to introduce the subject tactfully much later. He tried to smile reassuringly.

'There is no shadow, niece, I bring good news.'

'What news, uncle?'

'Will you not let me rest a while and eat? I am hungry and cold.'

She bowed at once, and brought him warm bread and thin soup. She asked politely about court matters, trying to bring herself to be interested in them. She was sorry to hear that Heregyth had had another miscarriage and seemed not to be able to bring children full term to birth.

Taking advantage of her unguarded expressions of sympathy on this subject, King Ethelwald asked if she herself did not miss the joys of motherhood.

'So here we have it,' she thought. 'I knew there was something.'

She assured him that she did not and looked at him with such a penetrating gaze that he brought out Oswy's request sooner than he had intended and with no fine words to accompany it.

She laughed.

'Uncle, you've travelled through the snow for nothing! You must have known that I would not accept. Marriage is impossible for me.'

'Don't be so hasty,' he said. 'Think about it.'

'There is nothing to think about. I married once to save my father and it did not save him. There is nothing you can say now that will make me give up the way of life I have chosen.'

Ethelwald sighed deeply.

He was not a weak king and knew that if he commanded a thousand men they would do his bidding without question, but there was something in this woman that he could not bend.

'Come, uncle, I'll take you down to the village and make you as comfortable as it is possible to be on this simple island. Stay as long as you like with us and share our life. You'll see why it gives me so much joy that I dread to leave.'

He thought of all the persuasive things he had intended to say and wondered if he stayed longer whether he would be able to say them. He allowed himself to be led down to the village where all the islanders had gathered to do him honour.

* * * *

That night Ethelwald decided his mission was hopeless. He did not know how he was going to refuse Oswy, but he knew that there was no way to persuade Etheldreda. To force her at sword point was not only unthinkable, but would not work. He suspected that she would choose death rather than give in.

* * * *

Etheldreda settled to sleep regretting that she had had to cross her uncle, but with no doubt in her mind that she was doing the right thing. She began to dream that she was one of thousands of pilgrims walking towards a Christian shrine on the top of a hill. She knew that this shrine contained something unbelievably precious. There was a good, cheerful sense of purpose in her heart and seemingly in the people around her, but as she approached the shrine she sensed that something was wrong. The shrine seemed to have disappeared and people were walking over the place where it had been, looking anxiously for it. She noticed that some of them were crying. Others were walking away embittered, saying that there never had been anything there in the first place.

At first she stood helplessly by and watched, filled with sorrow, but not knowing what to do, when suddenly the gleam of something in the grass caught her eye and she stooped down to take a closer look. It was a simple gold ring. She picked it up, calling out to the others joyfully that she had found what they were looking for. But even as she did so she woke up with a start. The dream had been so vivid she found herself looking down at her hand expecting to find the gold ring upon it. But there was no ring.

She pondered the dream a long time.

Most dreams she ignored for they seemed inconsequential and were soon forgotten, but from time to time she had special dreams, dreams that seemed to be trying to tell her something. These she remembered in every vivid detail all her life. This, she knew, would be one of them, but what was it trying to tell her?

That Christ should not be taken for granted? That He should not be looked for only in the expected place, nor recognised only in the expected form? Was the dream trying to tell her that she might be wrong in thinking she could only serve Christ on the hill of Ely in the way she had decided? Was the ring she found telling her to take the marriage with Egfrid and seek there for new ways to serve her Lord?

Suddenly her life at Ely seemed not to have been a life at all, but a preparation.

* * * *

When Ethelwald came to say goodbye to his niece in the morning, he found her face pale and serious.

'Uncle,' she said, 'I see it is God's will that I should take my place in the world again. I will accept Prince Egfrid, but only on the same terms that I accepted Prince Tondbert.'

Astonished, King Ethelwald stared at her. It must be God's will indeed, for he had said nothing to persuade her!

15

Marriage to Egfrid AD 659

When Oswy heard the terms Ethelwald had laid down for the marriage contract he started to pace the hall, his face flushed red, his eyes sparking with anger. Eanfleda, not yet knowing what the gist of the reply from Ethelwald was, but knowing that sometimes the ungovernable rages of her husband could be very shaming and destructive, cleared the place at once of all other people.

When they were alone she watched him for some time, waiting her opportunity to find out what had happened. She knew that he had set his heart on the marriage alliance and from his reaction she assumed it had been refused. She was secretly glad. Egfrid was barely fifteen and Etheldreda was a widow of twenty-nine. Anna's youngest daughter, Withberga, was eleven. If there had to be a marriage between the two countries she had argued that it should be between Withberga and Egfrid, but Oswy would not hear of this. Etheldreda was an experienced and intelligent woman, her reputation for diplomacy at her father's court and for the way she had civilised the rough people of the Gyrwe was impressive. Though it had never been proved, the rumour was strong that she had outwitted the treacherous Ethelhere in the matter of her father's burial at Blythburgh. Such a woman Oswy wanted for Egfrid. Withberga was a pale and sickly child. She would be of no use to Egfrid. The boy had returned from the Mercians difficult and sullen. He seemed to fit in nowhere. He paid lip service to his father and mother, but there was no filial love in his eyes, and Oswy had caught a brooding look once or twice that had made him instinctively put his hand to his sword hilt.

Oswy had heard of Etheldreda's fervent religious bent and had decided that this could be an advantage. Egfrid had a smouldering strength that could lead to greatness if channelled the right way, but if left to itself could lead to a wanton destructiveness. Etheldreda was a strong and beautiful woman. She would be able to handle him, to mould him in a way his own mother no longer could. With her he might grow out of resentment and regret into a strong and practical man. This would still be dangerous for his father if it were not tempered with the Christian taboos and virtues. Etheldreda was definitely the one! But now that she said that she would marry him, but not bed with him, how would this affect the boy?

Eanfleda was pressing him to know what the terms of the marriage settlement were, and he looked at her from under lowering brows. She had not wanted the match in the first place and he knew this added complication would give her yet another argument against it. But would it be such a terrible thing after all? The boy could take other women to bed. The marriage was mainly important for the alliance it brought with it, and this alliance Oswy badly needed.

'The woman is to be wife only in name,' he said at last, harshly. 'Bring the boy to me and I will tell him.'

She knew him well enough to know that when he spoke like that no one argued. She left at once, considerably agitated.

Eanfleda herself had been Egfrid's age when she had been dragged from her home in Kent to marry a stranger, a much older man. She still shuddered when she thought of those early months, the revulsion she had felt against him, and the bitterness she had nursed against her mother for making her submit to him. She had hoped her own children would not have to suffer unwelcome marriages, but one after another they were being used as pieces in her husband's ruthless game of power. Alfrid to Princess Cyneberga of Mercia, Alfleda to Prince Peada of Mercia, Elffleda sworn to virginity by her father in exchange for help from God and sent to the monastery at Whitby to become a nun under the Abbess Hilda. Her daughter Osryth betrothed to Ethelred, the youngest of Penda's sons. And now Egfrid! All her children brought out of her body by her husband's lust, and doomed to serve his greed.

Sometimes she hated him!

He knew as well as she that Egfrid would commit adultery. Oswy was condemning Egfrid's soul to eternal damnation by forcing this marriage on him.

Tears of frustration came to her eyes, and part of it was envy that Etheldreda could make a marriage contract and dictate her own terms. How she would have liked to have done the same, but had not dared.

* * * *

Etheldreda travelled north with an entourage of her uncle's choosing, but amongst them he allowed her her old friends Ovin, Heregyth and Edgils.

Wherever they passed people flocked to greet them and to wish Etheldreda happiness—no doubt in anybody's mind that the alliance with Northumbria would be advantageous to them all.

Etheldreda smiled and talked with all who came. No one would have suspected how lonely she was as she left Ely and all it stood for further and further behind.

In the province of Lindsey they made good progress on the old Roman road, which, although overgrown in places, was still the easiest road to travel. It was usual for people to shun the ruins of the old Roman towns on the route, thinking that they had once been inhabited by giants, the huge columns and halls too big for ordinary men. But Etheldreda was intrigued and insisted that she would visit one by herself in spite of Heregyth's warning that she might well meet demons or the ghosts of the giants themselves. She fingered her mother's garnet cross now on a gold chain around her neck, and smiled.

'I've not met a demon yet that I could not quell with the Lord's help,' she said cheerfully.

'But won't you be afraid?' Heregyth asked, astonished.

'No. We hold the key to ourselves. We can open the door or not as we choose. I'll not open to anything that does not have the password of the Lord.'

Heregyth sighed, remembering how often

she had been deceived by men, let alone by demons! So there was some point to all Etheldreda's spiritual training after all. If only it were not so difficult!

Etheldreda would talk no more of demons or of giants. She went off to explore the ruined town, refusing any company.

As she wandered about the overgrown streets and sat on a broken wall in the sun, small flowers growing from the cracks, she wondered where they were now, the busy people, the men who drove the carts down these streets so often that their wheels wore out grooves, the stone-smiths, the millers, the merchants.

A snatch of an old poem came to her mind.

'Earthgrip holds them—gone, long gone,
fast in gravesgrasp while fifty fathers
and sons have passed.' [11]

Where were they now, her father, and her mother, and the years of innocence and joy? Where would Oswy's mighty kingdom be by the time one more of these stones had fallen from its place?

She was allowing herself to be caught up in the temporary again, and she feared its seductiveness. She must hold to her visions of eternity and never let them go, her visions of a beauty that was 'itself' and did not derive its quality by comparison with other things. If she could not avoid people and noise in her new life at the Northumbrian court, she must devise a 'place' within her, secret and invulnerable, where she could be alone. Without this, she would be lost.

A movement behind her made her turn her head.

Ovin stood a little way off.

She could not be sure that he had not been there a long time, sent by Heregyth to protect her.

She smiled. She was glad it was Ovin and no one else, for he was the one person who did not make her feel crowded.

* * * *

Egfrid sat in the great hall at York waiting for his betrothed, his knees drawn up under his chin, his brows knit in a scowl. His features were not unlike his father's and his brother's, but his expression was his own. He was disgusted that he was to marry a nun, an old one at that, and had pictured her pale and shrivelled, eyes cast down in humility, hands folded meekly. He did not bother to stand when she was ushered into the room, nor to look up. He heard voices giving formal greeting and then his brother angrily jogged his arm. Sulkily he raised his head and was startled at what he saw. She stood in a shaft of light in front of him, her head held proudly, her cheeks flushed with health. Her skin was bronzed by the sun, her blue eyes shrewd and lively. She wore a long cloak embroidered with gold, held with gold brooches at the shoulders. Above it her hair shone so much that the circlet of gold that held it in place looked almost dull. She did not bow her knee to his brother, but inclined her head very slightly in greeting, smiling pleasantly at Queen Cyneberga.

King Oswy and Queen Eanfleda were still at Bamburgh and had sent Romanus to deliver their welcome. While he droned on and everyone's attention was on him, Egfrid unfolded his legs and rose to his feet. He kept to the shadows, moving closer so that he could see her more clearly. If she was aware of him she gave no sign until his name was mentioned and then she turned her clear gaze upon him, looking at him steadily, appraisingly. She saw a gauche boy, standing awkwardly, his face slowly flushing angrily at her scrutiny. She saw his resentment of her, his restless, moody energy. She saw someone who had never known self-discipline, only the domination of others. She knew that their relationship was going to be a difficult one.

She moved towards him, her progress elegant, controlled, and he stepped forward to meet her with an expression of haughty condescension. But his foot caught a wooden stool which went crashing to the floor. He lost balance and stumbled clumsily. With an expression of disgust he kicked the fallen stool savagely away from him, and then turned his shoulder to her and stormed out of the hall.

Queen Cyneberga was the first to speak.

She rose from her husband's side and took Etheldreda's arm.

'You must forgive him, lady, he is still young and embarrassed by small things. Give him time and no slave would be more devoted to his mistress than the prince to you.'

'I hope not so, my lady,' Etheldreda said quickly. 'I have travelled all this way for a companion and a helpmate, not for a slave.'

'And that is what you shall have!' Alfrid rose now and joined them, speaking brusquely. 'Give him time. He is a good lad, but his manhood is insulted that you will not accept him as a man.' Alfrid did not like the chastity clause in the betrothal contract and was determined to do all in his power to break it down.

Etheldreda smiled at him unperturbed.

'Surely his manhood is founded on more

secure ground than whether I go to bed with him or not?' she asked blandly.

Alfrid looked irritated. The princess was not what he had expected either, and he could see his brother was not going to find it as easy as he had done, with Penda's daughter, to win her sexually. She would indeed be a formidable and valuable addition to the ruling family of Northumbria, but whether she would prove too strong a meat for his young brother remained to be seen.

'My lord, the princess Etheldreda is tired after her long journey,' Cyneberga intervened tactfully. 'May I take her to her chambers?'

He nodded at once, glad to be relieved of her disturbing presence. As she turned to go her cloak floated back and the curves of her figure showed briefly through the soft fabric of her dress. A twinge of desire stirred in Alfrid's heart and he conceived of a plan to help his brother.

'Such beauty wasted is an insult to God,' he told himself. 'No purpose is served by such denial. She could feed the poor, pray for souls, just as effectively if she were a normal married woman, better, for she would understand the human condition more intimately. When she is old and ugly, then let her join a monastery!'

He thought of his sister Elffleda. At the

age of one she had been vowed to perpetual virginity by their father in gratitude for his victory over Penda at Winwaed. When she grew to womanhood would she not curse him for this? And would she not be right to do so?

* * * *

The royal buildings at York were far grander than those Etheldreda had been accustomed to in her homeland. The central hall itself had colonnaded porches surrounding it where supplicants and visitors could wait out of the rain before they were admitted to the king's presence. Benches lined the walls, some of them elaborately carved. The spear-racks were enormous.

The sleeping quarters too were much more complex. There were many rooms joined one with another, as in Roman houses, except the rooms were smaller and the structure was of wood.

Cyneberga proudly showed Etheldreda the kitchens and the weaving rooms before she took her to her own bedchamber.

York had been a Roman town, one of the few the immigrant tribes had made use of when they sailed up the River Humber and its tributaries to make this land their own. Consequently part of the royal complex was in stone, the roads were well laid out and in workable condition, and there was a wall, well built and sturdy, though it had not always served to keep conquerors out. Knowing that Etheldreda was a friend of Queen Eanfleda, King Edwin's daughter, Cyneberga pointed out the place where Edwin's head had been left to rot upon the wall. There was a touch of pride in her voice that her father had helped to put it there.

Neither the Celts, nor the Germanic invaders, had skill in stone masonry, and the Roman town had been left to fall into disrepair. The elaborate system for central heating was no longer understood or used and in winter the winds blew cold over the moors and the frost worked on the crumbling stone buildings. York at the time of Alfrid was mainly wooden built, but the nearest thing to a city in the Roman sense the Northumbrians possessed.

Etheldreda's rooms were half Roman stone, half Saxon wood. Cyneberga drew aside a finely worked curtain to reveal a stone bath sunk into the floor. There were steps leading down to it. It was huge.

'Alfrid had this cleaned out when we were married,' Cyneberga said proudly. 'The roof had fallen in and so we built a new one of wood, but the bath itself is quite usable.'

'How do you put the water in?' Etheldreda

asked curiously, walking round the edge, marvelling at the size of it. It was by no means as clean as a Roman would have wished, but to a Saxon it was magnificent. Etheldreda had only ever washed in wooden buckets, the water boiled in iron cauldrons, carried by slaves or, recently, by herself.

'Slaves, of course. I have tried to use it once,' Cyneberga said. 'I had it filled, but it really was too cold. Would you like it filled for you?'

'No. No, of course not. But I would like a bucket of water if possible before I rest.'

Cyneberga sent one of her women at once for hot water, and then excused herself and left.

When the water came Etheldreda dismissed Cyneberga's slaves, but kept Heregyth with her.

Together they carried the bucket down the steps to the stone bath.

'Come, Heregyth, undress! I feel like a water fight!'

Heregyth had not seen the face of her mistress so alight with mischief for many years. She was quick to accept the challenge.

Naked, they began to splash each other with the water, laughing and shouting like two young children. Etheldreda knew she would have to be a royal princess again, a responsible and serious-minded diplomat on whom lives depended, married to a difficult and complicated man, but before she did, she would have one last joyous fling.

As the water flew and they darted and dodged, she remembered her childhood at Exning when life had seemed so simple. On summer days she and Saxberga had sometimes had such water fights in the little river that flowed through the valley.

Just as the last handful went into Heregyth's laughing face and they both stood dripping and exhausted, they heard a sound behind them and spun round to see that King Alfrid had entered above and was watching them.

* * * *

A few days before the wedding King Oswy and Queen Eanfleda arrived from Bamburgh. The occasion was to be used as a show of power and solidarity to impress King Wulfhere of Mercia and the other guests who were arriving for the wedding from every direction, at all hours of the day and night.

The quays on the River Ouse and the River Foss were constantly busy, and the children of the town were climbing on every available pile of timber or bale of wool at the quayside to get a better view of the distinguished guests.

The Roman road from the south was lined

with people too, watching for the baggage trains and the stewards, and guessing for whom the elaborate tents were being raised.

When the rumour got round that the Kentish royal family were due at the quay, the crush was so great Queen Eanfleda and Princess Etheldreda could scarcely get through. Many remembered the times of Edwin and were eager to greet his widow.

The boat came in sight at last, Edwin's widow, Ethelberga, standing at the prow, gazing out at the land and the people she had had to flee from in such distress so long ago. She had never met her grandson Egfrid, nor seen her daughter Eanfleda since she had forced her to accept marriage to Oswy.

Eanfleda herself took Etheldreda's hand and held it tight as she saw her mother, tall and elegant as ever, her hair as white as a swan's wing. Behind her stood Etheldreda's sister Saxberga and with her her two sons, Egbert, a tall and confident eighteen, and young Hlothere still very much a child though he was only a year younger than the bridegroom.

As soon as she saw her sister, Etheldreda ran down to the water's edge and flung her arms around her as she stepped off the small bridge onto dry land. She heard nothing of the calls and the cheers of the crowd, nor was aware of their good-natured pressure around her.

Queen Eanfleda stepped forward to greet her mother and the cheek she offered for her kiss was cold, her words of greeting formal. Many years had passed since they had last seen each other, and not all of them had been good for Eanfleda. Somewhere in the back of her heart she still carried resentment against her mother for insisting on her marriage with Oswy.

Ethelberga sensed Eanfleda's coolness at once, and tears came to her eyes. She turned from her only child to the crowd of strangers who sang her name, whose eyes were full of love and welcome.

Over her head Eanfleda sought Eorconbert, the image of whom she had carried in her heart all these years as she bore another man's children, wore another kingdom's crown.

Suddenly, a deep voice spoke beside her and she turned her head, her heart missing a beat. He was there, close enough to touch. She drew in her breath sharply. He had changed. He had grown heavier through the years, the fine lines of his face had gone. He was now bearded, almost gross of feature. His belly bulged above his sword belt. He was smiling at her, but all the magic was gone. He could have been anybody. He took her hands and she did not even feel the need to draw them back. She heard her voice greeting him, but it was a stranger's voice. By losing her long and secret dream she had lost a part of herself that had sustained her through the long and lonely years. Who would she think of now when Oswy made love to her?

She was kissed by Saxberga, by the young Kentish princes. She heard her mother's voice as though it was very far away. Politely she did all that was required of her as hostess and queen, nothing that was expected of her as daughter or as friend.

Had she changed much? She had borne six children and endured many years of danger and fear at the hands of Penda's raiders, and much sorrow from a husband who did not hesitate to kill her kinsmen if it suited him. She looked down at her own body. She had not grown fat, but the slimness of her youth had given way to a bony leanness. She knew her neck was wrinkled and her face was lined.

'How sad,' she thought. How quickly youth passed. Before one even knew one had it, it was gone. She looked at her mother with a sudden warmth, sorry that she had wasted precious time in resentment.

It was time to move. Horses were brought for the royal party, and in the bustle and confusion, difficult emotions were forgotten.

Eanfleda rode ahead with her mother, Etheldreda with her sister, and Eorconbert brought up the rear with his two sons.

* * * *

That night after the feasting and the songs and the speeches, Saxberga came to Etheldreda's room and they sat together as they had as children talking into the night. From time to time Heregyth looked in, bustled about and went out again, annoyed that someone else was taking her place as confidante.

* * * *

The following day the attention was turned to the road from the south. Wulfhere, the king of Mercia, was expected with his new wife Eormengild, the sixteen-year-old daughter of Saxberga and Eorconbert of Kent.

The mood of the crowd was very different to the one that had gathered the day before at the quayside to greet Edwin's queen and the Kentish royal family.

Mercia had always been their enemy and no matter how hard Oswy had tried to heal the breach after his victory over Penda by taking over the country himself and marrying his eldest son to one of Penda's daughters, and two of his own daughters to sons of Penda, the ill feeling between the two countries was still there. There was scarcely a village that had not suffered at the hands of the Mercians, scarcely a family that had not lost someone in the wars. If it had not been for the presence of Etheldreda and Queen Saxberga the crowd might well have turned ugly as the young king and his entourage came in sight.

The road through the hills was narrow and Etheldreda, Saxberga and others were nearly pushed off it as Egfrid suddenly galloped past, looking neither to the left nor the right. Etheldreda caught a glimpse of his face as he thundered by before the dust the hooves of his horse threw up temporarily blinded her. She was surprised to see how relaxed and happy he looked. On the few occasions they had met since she had come to York he had been so consistently morose and sullen she had feared that there would be no way to make him relax or smile.

She had heard good things of the young King Wulfhere and, although he was a Mercian, Saxberga had not been too averse to his marriage with her daughter. Unlike his father Penda, he had accepted that the tide had turned in favour of the new religion and had allowed bishops to set up their sees in Mercia.

'Your future husband needs to learn a few manners,' said Saxberga, coughing and trying to hold her own horse steady after Egfrid's passing.

Etheldreda laughed ruefully.

'I don't think he is going to take too kindly to my trying to teach him!' she said.

They could see him, already far ahead, reining up beside Wulfhere. Words could not be heard, but the two men were evidently very pleased to see each other, and there was a great deal of back-slapping as the two horses circled one another.

Saxberga saw her daughter behind Wulfhere and, forgetting what she had just said about Egfrid, she broke into a canter on the narrow path, inconveniencing the other riders.

Etheldreda thought to give them a few moments alone together and held back. King Alfrid drew up beside her. She felt the pressure of his knee on hers, and when she met his eyes there was a look in them that made her uneasy. Since the incident of the water fight she had avoided him as much as possible. When their paths had crossed he had not mentioned it, but his eyes always looked at her as though he were seeing her naked. She drew away from him now and cantered forward towards the Mercian party.

She knew that Oswy wanted her to greet the son of the man who had killed her father in a way that conveyed the desire for a peaceful future between them, while letting him know, very subtly, that the past was not yet forgotten.

She smiled bitterly. Had this not been the way she had greeted Oswy himself? She remembered how much it had cost her to bend her knee to him knowing that it was he who had murdered the man she loved.

'I am a stranger on the earth, O Lord,' she whispered from her favourite psalm. 'Hide not thy commandments from me.'[12]

'My lord Wulfhere,' she said quietly when she reached the Mercian king, and bowed her head to him. There was no memory of the long years of hate and violence between their two families, their two countries, in her eyes.

* * * *

That night her sleep was disturbed by Alfrid. His hand was on her breast before she realised what was happening.

She jerked awake as he lifted her into his arms.

Bewildered, she gasped and fought. Grimly he held on. His own desire was strong, but he told himself that it was for Egfrid's sake he wanted to break the iron barrier of her virginity. He could not get his hand between her legs because she struggled so violently, but he did get his mouth upon her mouth. But a kiss as brutally hard as that had no savour to it. He gradually withdrew his lips and with the lessening of the pressure she managed to bite his tongue.

He leapt back startled and enraged, releasing his grip on her and raising his fist to strike her. The candle he had lit when he came in to her chamber the better to see her, shone in her face, and he caught the look in her eyes. The enormity of what he was doing, or trying to do, suddenly struck him. His hand dropped and, after staring at her aghast for a few moments, he turned and left. She could hear his footsteps in the yard, the dogs barking at him as though he were a common thief.

Trembling, she drew her rugs about her. She had felt something in that moment of waking with his hands upon her breast that she did not wish to feel. She tried to forget it, and remember only the revulsion and dislike she had felt towards him when she was fully awake.

Shivering she fell on her knees and asked for help. Her breast tingled as though his touch was still upon it. And below, in the secret place of her body she scarcely knew existed, another feeling stirred that made her sob with chagrin and with shame.

* * * *

The next few days passed full and fast.

Etheldreda smiled and talked and did all that was expected of her, deliberately not seeking solitude. She had a strange feeling of unreality, as though she herself and all with whom she spoke were painted figures in a manuscript, and the real people were somewhere else. She forced herself to look at Alfrid, knowing that if she did not the memory of that night would grow out of all proportion.

When their eyes met for the first time the expression in his was wary, but when he realised she had accepted what had happened and put it firmly behind her, he bowed his head, and she understood he would not attempt to touch her again.

* * * *

One of the most honoured guests of the wedding was the princess Hilda, now the much-respected abbess of the double monastery at Whitby.

Etheldreda was impatient to be with her alone, believing that she was the only person who could help her resolve the conflict of her thoughts. As soon as she could she drew her aside and led her to her chamber, where she knew they could be undisturbed.

'What am I doing here?' she cried, throwing up her hands, her voice filled with bewilderment and distress. 'Jewelled clasps! Golden crowns! Fine silks! Hilda—this is not how I should be dressed! This is not how I should be living!'

The older woman in her plain woollen habit embraced her, kissed her eyelids behind which tears were gathering.

'Sssh... There must be a reason. You have been chosen for this as surely as I have been chosen as Abbess of Whitby. There are times I would give anything to be a simple nun alone in a cell with no worldly responsibilities, able to devote all my time to the visible kingdom of God.'

Etheldreda looked at her, surprised.

'Yes, I too feel I am wasting time with lists of provisions, with building projects, with letters and interviews and meetings. Sometimes at night I am so tired I fall asleep on my knees. The one moment of the day when I finally have time for private prayer—I fall asleep!'

Etheldreda laughed.

'You see, it is never what we envisage. You are a king's daughter and I am an abbess. We must make of our lives what we can. The realm of spirit is everywhere—in the great hall, in the abbey, in the village. Everywhere. You will not lose it by accepting the life you have been given if you remember always, in every decision, to consult the Holy Spirit within you.'

'Hilda...' Etheldreda paused. What she wanted to say she had not dared to think through, even to herself.

Hilda waited.

'Sometimes I wonder if I am doing the right thing by accepting marriage to a man and yet not giving him what a man has a right to expect from his wife.'

Hilda was silent for a long while.

'Egfrid knows what to expect from you? He has been told?'

'Yes, but...'

'You are offering him something far more valuable than physical love, which is demanding, temporary, limited. You are offering him spiritual love which will endure through eternity.'

Etheldreda sighed. Hilda was playing the stern abbess, the ruler of a great monastery. They were not walking in the forests of Rendilsham now with all the possibilities of youth open to them. They had chosen and were committed. There could be no compromise. No doubts.

The older woman saw more than she admitted. She reached out her arms to her troubled friend and held her close.

* * * *

In the great hall that night before the feast, King Oswy called upon Cuthbert, a monk from Melrose, to say the grace. The crowded guests shifted and muttered amongst themselves, surprised that with Bishop Finan from Lindisfarne there the king should ask this unlettered peasant to speak. He did not know himself why he did it. It was an impulse.

Cuthbert waited until there was silence and then lifted his head and spoke as simply and as sincerely as though he were speaking to someone visible in the hall.

'Thank you, O Lord,' he said, 'for the gift of life. Help us to use it wisely.'

And he sat down.

In the surprised silence that followed this brief plea, Etheldreda shivered, knowing that he had touched the realm of spirit and its secret sound was vibrating through the hearts of all who had heard it. Some would choose to ignore it. She would not. Everything that was good seemed suddenly easy and possible.

* * * *

But later that night when she passed Egfrid's quarters on the way to her own, his door opened and a woman, still straightening her clothes, came out, laughing at something he had said. Etheldreda drew back into the shadows and let her pass, watching the light that shone from beneath the now closed door. After a few moments it went out.

* * * *

The next morning she woke to find Heregyth fussing over her and her chamber full of slaves. Sleepily she allowed herself to be dressed, wondering why there were so many people in her room. It was not until Cyneberga entered that she began to remember it was her wedding-day.

Heregyth brought in the robes that she was to wear. They had come from Rome, of Byzantine silk.

Silently Etheldreda submitted to the attentions of the slaves, silently stared at her own image in a copper mirror as one by one the layers of fine cloth were put upon her, the jewels hung from shoulder to shoulder, the coronet of pearls placed upon her head.

'This is not me,' she thought. 'I am invisible. This... *this* will be married today. Not me. I am somewhere else where nothing can touch me, no one can reach me, somewhere where there is reality... not this charade of shadows!'

Saxberga burst in.

'Come! Come!' she cried. 'It is time. Why do you delay?'

Heregyth took her by the shoulders and turned her towards Saxberga as though she were a statue.

'Look at her! Is she not beautiful?'

Saxberga's anxious face broke into an admiring smile.

'Beautiful!' she cried with delight.

'You too, my sister,' Etheldreda thought. 'Even you cannot distinguish the real from the unreal.'

She thought of tearing the clothes off, of clothing herself in rags and blackening her face with dust and soot. 'This, *this* is the body!' she would cry. 'Tomorrow it will be gross and ugly. Why do you waste your time with it! Look for me somewhere else. Find me where I really am!' But she did not.

She was swept out of the room on a tide of excited women and washed towards the king's chapel where Egfrid had been placed, equally splendidly dressed, to wait for her.

As she took her place at his side she looked into his eyes.

His were dark and smouldering, those of an animal who could not leave his cage.

* * * *

When all the noise and clamour of the day

had died down Egfrid and Etheldreda faced each other for the first time alone, in a grand chamber full of tapestries and flowers.

Exhausted, she sank down upon a carved wooden chair and looked at him. He was so young. So old. So twisted and knotted in private bitterness. Was it the exile from his parents that had done this to him? Had he too seen the thinness of the skin of gold that covered the violence, the greed and the fear? But, being young, had he stopped there, and not looked further to find even deeper within the human heart the capacity for experiencing great and holy wonders, rich and lovely knowledge?

He sat on the edge of the bed, one knee drawn up to his chin, biting the knuckles of one hand, looking at her with deep resentment.

'My lord,' she said at last. 'Neither of us has asked for this marriage. Let us not be enemies.'

He did not reply, but continued to stare at her and bite his knuckles.

She waited for a while longer and then rose and started to loosen her outer garments and remove her jewels, ignoring him. Heregyth and the women who would normally have performed this office had been forbidden by her to enter the chamber.

He watched every move as she folded her clothes and put them neatly away. The lamps flickered on her long golden hair as she combed it out, on the fine white silk of her shift. When she was ready she brought out from among her possessions a small golden box, a reliquary containing a chip of stone from Golgotha, a wedding present from Bishop Honorious at her first wedding. On its lid was a fish, the cipher of Christ. She placed it on a low table and, still ignoring him, knelt down in front of it. She bent her head, and stayed absolutely still for a long time. The only sound in the room was the creak of the bed as he changed his weight from one leg to another.

When she was finished she arose and, still ignoring him, took some of the rugs from the bed and laid them on the floor. She then laid herself down upon them.

This time astonishment drew words from him.

'What are you doing?'

'I am going to sleep.'

'On the floor?'

'Yes.'

He stood up, staring down at her, frowning.

Within moments she was fast asleep as though on the most comfortable bed in town, on the most ordinary night of the year. He could hear her peaceful breathing.

He watched her for a while longer and then, realising that there was no one there to care what he thought or what he did, he pulled off his own clothes, dropped them in a crumpled heap on the floor beside her, and climbed into bed and fell asleep.

16

Wilfrid

Where had she seen the tall monk before? His appearance teased her memory, but she could not place him. He was smiling into her eyes as though he knew her, an amused lift to the corner of his mouth as though he knew that he was causing her confusion. He was handsome, dark-haired and dark-eyed, his skin tanned from the sun in Rome, his hair cut to the Roman style, the crown shaved and a circle of hair left around his head to suggest the Lord's crown of thorns. She did not like the Roman tonsure and hoped that it would not become customary in Northumbria, but she had to admit that it suited him.

'The Princess Etheldreda,' King Alfrid was saying, 'a jewel added to the family treasure since you left, Wilfrid.' Alfrid's voice had an edge of irony to it that Wilfrid picked up at once. He looked at Etheldreda closer. What had she done to deserve that hidden barb? She was even more attractive than he remembered her, the pretty girl mellowed into the beautiful woman. He had seen her at her first wedding when he was on his way to Rome and he remembered ruefully the way his blood had raced at the sight of her. But he was older now and more controlled. He would be careful not to let his emotions cause him such difficulties again.

'Wilfrid grew up with me, Etheldreda,' Alfrid was saying. 'He might have been my father's shield bearer had my mother not exiled him to Lindisfarne.'

'Exiled?'

'As good as.'

Wilfrid laughed.

'I know I was not too pleased at the time, my lord, but as it has worked out I have travelled further and seen more sights than I ever would have had I stayed at court.'

'That I envy you, my friend. Tell me of Rome!' Alfrid's eyes glowed at the thought of the great city, all the coming and going, the intrigues, the adventures, the power.

Etheldreda sat beside them quietly as they talked. The court at York had seemed busy enough to her during the year since her marriage. She found it difficult to find time to herself. But by Wilfrid's account of Rome, York was a quiet backwater, embarrassingly small and unimportant. The Church at Rome was more splendid than any royal court, ambassadors from all the kings of Christendom sought audience of its bishop. To have been there, to have won through the hundreds of miles of dangerous terrain and walked its ancient streets, lent a glamour to Wilfrid that was hard to resist. Etheldreda found herself looking at him more often and listening to him more closely than she had to anyone for a long time.

'The time is past when it is good enough for a priest to walk the countryside as the whim takes him, and preach the Word in fields and on hilltops to one or two hapless peasants,' Wilfrid said. 'We must have organisation now. We must use our resources to consolidate what we have won. Villages are growing into towns. We must have a settled, disciplined body of monks and priests. We must have order.'

Wilfrid argued that the discipline of the Benedictine rule would provide a framework, a backbone, for the ordinary monk and make him something more than he might otherwise have been. The ordinary monk, maybe, thought Etheldreda, but she wondered if it might not clip the wings of the great one. She thought of the Irish pilgrim Fursey who had so impressed her as a child. He would have chafed to be so cooped up behind walls, following a set routine.

'I think you forget the need for freedom of

inspiration,' she said suddenly. 'If you have so many rules that all the time is neatly parcelled out, this for prayer and that for manual work, are you not putting limits on the times when God will be "allowed" to speak? To me, one Cuthbert standing on a hill moved by the Holy Spirit, channelling the mighty energy of God so that it can sweep through him and out into the world, is worth far more than a thousand monks doing what they are told to do by an abbot.'

Wilfrid looked at her.

'Very few men can handle freedom,' he said. 'I'm sure Cuthbert would be the first to agree that reasonable, orderly discipline never hurt anyone, while too much freedom has.'

'I don't think he would.' Her eyes flashed. She almost disliked this arrogant monk who behaved and dressed like a nobleman and talked as though he had the sole right to the ordering of God's Kingdom.

'When have you known men not to abuse freedom?' he challenged.

'When have you known men not to abuse rules and laws?' she replied.

Alfrid was forgotten, the two faced each other with flushed cheeks and sparkling eyes.

'You seem to think that my way denies the possibility of inspiration,' he said.

'You seem to think that my way denies the possibility of discipline,' she said. 'I only say that it should be flexible enough to allow for the sudden inrush of inspiration.'

'If discipline is flexible it is not discipline,' he countered.

'What if someone is speaking with God and the bell goes for Vigils or for Lauds. Must he break off the conversation?' she asked sharply.

Wilfrid laughed.

'You are a woman of spirit I see, my lady. With a little more discipline you would be worth a great deal to the Church.'

Etheldreda went scarlet with annoyance. She bit her lip, too angry to speak.

* * * *

Alfrid displaced Cuthbert and Eata from the monastery at Ripon where they had been installed only recently by Oswy, and gave Wilfrid all the help he needed to extend the buildings and introduce the rules of the new Order.

* * * *

Etheldreda asked Egfrid to take her to Hexham, which had been his wedding gift to her. She felt restless and needed to get away from York. She was aware of Alfrid's desire for her and his resentment of her chastity vow, and tired of being always on her guard.

Egfrid had come to accept her role in his life with the kind of sullen resignation with which he accepted almost everything. In public he was as silent and morose as usual, but accompanied her without objection when his duties as second son of Oswy called upon him to do so. In private they hardly ever met. She chose to ask him to accompany her to Hexham because she hoped to make one more attempt to break through his resentment and reach some kind of friendly understanding. It was high summer and the sun was warm, the hills green, the forests ringing with bird-song. He too was restless, and quickly accepted the suggestion to leave the overcrowded town.

As soon as he was on horseback the awkwardness and clumsiness which characterised his movements about the court disappeared. He had learned something of the brilliant Mercian horsemanship during his childhood and was never so happy as he was in the saddle.

They started the journey with a race, Etheldreda's young mare giving his stallion a challenge that he found difficult to meet. But Egfrid won, and by the shine in his eyes as he did so Etheldreda knew that for that moment, at least, he was happy.

* * * *

They broke their journey north at Ripon, Wilfrid

entertaining them lavishly with pheasant and French wine.

Wilfrid was using stone in the church buildings, even importing French glaziers to work on the windows. Enthusiastically he walked Etheldreda round, taking her arm to lead her under scaffolding and over precarious planks of wood. She found it difficult to keep up the resentment she had felt at Cuthbert's displacement and began to see something of Wilfrid's vision of the future.

While Egfrid snored the day's exertions away, she rose in the small hours to the bell that called the monks to the chapel and for a few hours she followed the discipline of the monastery, finding that kneeling in a sacred place, praying in unison with others, charged the atmosphere with a certain powerful energy.

During the mass she trembled as the wheat touched her tongue, feeling that something of great power had entered her. The wine flowed in her veins transforming her.

* * * *

Egfrid brusquely refused Wilfrid's invitation to stay. There was something in the way the priest and his wife looked at each other when they spoke that gave him the feeling of being excluded. He didn't understand it, but he knew he didn't like it. For the first time since his marriage he saw Etheldreda as something other than a chain about his neck and was glad to be alone with her as they rode the high, bleak moors, the clean, fierce wind whipping her hair, and floating her cloak out behind her like wings.

On the last night before they reached Hexham, Etheldreda and he stood side by side looking at the stars. Neither felt the need to speak. Above them the immense dome of the sky seemed to wheel silently, the brilliant points of light imperceptibly changing position.

'Are we moving, or are they?' Etheldreda breathed.

He shivered, feeling the moments poised, precious, infinitely fragile. He wished he could say something that would please her, that would make her think of him as something other than a clumsy boy, but he could think of nothing.

'You are mad!' he said roughly, turning angrily away from her. 'How could the earth possibly move?'

17

Synod of Whitby AD 663

Etheldreda stood upon the very edge of the headland at Whitby and stared out at the sea, its silver folds, its deep mysterious depths, its vast impersonal reaches bringing a calm to her mind that had been sadly lacking lately.

Under King Oswy's patronage and with King Alfrid's help, Wilfrid had gone from strength to strength. He was at the Synod that was now in progress in the abbey great hall, an impassioned defender of the Roman computation of the Easter date, spokesman for Bishop Agilbert of the West Saxons, a Frenchman who feared his arguments would be impaired if they had to be filtered through a translator.

Etheldreda sighed. So many words. Such heated, angry faces. She could see Bishop Colman's Scottish monks from Lindisfarne now as they reacted to Wilfrid's withering scorn.

'Our Easter customs are those that we have seen universally observed in Rome, where the blessed Apostles Peter and Paul lived, taught, suffered, and are buried,' Wilfrid said. 'We have also seen the same customs generally observed throughout Italy and Gaul and through many different countries, in Asia, Africa, Egypt, Greece. In fact, throughout the world wherever the Church of Christ has spread. The only people who are stupid enough to disagree with the whole world are these Scots and their obstinate adherents the Picts and Britons, who inhabit only a portion of these two islands in the remote ocean.'[13]

Did it really matter so much on which date the festival of Easter was celebrated? It was surely the spirit of the Word that mattered, not the letter. But Oswy had called the Synod together, the greatest gathering of people powerful in church and state Britain had ever known, to settle once and for all this apparently trivial matter. For years it had been an irritation to him that he and his wife had different dates for Easter, he following the tradition of Columba on Iona, his wife, having grown up in Kent, following the Roman way. This meant that one of them was still suffering the privations of Lent while the other was celebrating with feasting the joyous Resurrection.

Etheldreda suspected that it was Wilfrid's agitation about spreading the neat orderliness of Rome that had made of this inconvenience a major issue, and that the Synod was by no means only about the date of Easter, but the wider question of whether the Roman way should prevail over the Celtic.

She found herself torn uncomfortably between the two.

Bishop Felix had been of Roman persuasion, Fursey of Celtic. Both men had influenced her as a girl. She did not see why the best of both ways could not be taken. Why must there always be confrontation and choice?

The men in the Synod were quoting authorities in support of their separate points of view and it looked as though Wilfrid's authorities would win. There was no arguing that the Lord *had* given the keys of the Kingdom of Heaven to Saint Peter and that Saint Peter was the founder of the Church in Rome.

The early missionaries who had come to Britain soon after the death of Christ (some said Joseph of Arimathea himself had founded a church at Glastonbury) had been strong men, inspired men, men who needed space to be alone with their God. In isolated communities they had preached the Word, no one to give them rules on how to do it. They told the Lord's story as they saw it.

When Gregory sent Augustine's mission to the heathen Anglo Saxons in 596 he found some of the conquered British population already Christian, holding to their independence jealously. Since then the two, the new wave and the old, had grown further and further apart. It was Alfrid's desire now to bring them together under the one authority. Wilfrid and he had spent many a long night in discussion on how it was to be done, both believing it was for the good of all that the Roman way should win.

Etheldreda could see that there was a certain sense in which it was important that Easter should be on exactly the same day throughout the Christian world. Many people concentrating their energies on a particular prayer at one and the same time would give that prayer greater effectiveness. If all the world were to appeal for renewal and for spiritual growth at the same moment, who knows what miracle of peace and transcendent love might not prevail?

But no one had mentioned this argument. This had not been made the issue.

She sighed. Was she wrong? Should she bend her way of thinking to authority in every instance? Sometimes she feared that she would be branded a heretic. There were so many things that she secretly thought that she suspected would not meet the Church's official approval.

She remembered the time when the angry

talk had been of Jerusalem and everyone was trying to think of violent ways to wrest it from the Arabs who had seized it when she was a child of eight, and were now, under the guise of their new aggressive religion, conquering half the world. She had caught herself thinking then that it did not matter who held Jerusalem in the worldly sense. The Lord was no longer there. He and his holy city were in the hearts of anyone who invited Him in.

A small boat sailed out from the harbour far below her. She could see the tiny figures of the fishermen going about their business unconcerned whether the heated and acrimonious arguments going on in the great abbey that overlooked their peaceful little town went one way or the other.

She took a deep breath of fine, clear air.

To the north as far as she could see were rocky cliffs and shadowy inlets. The green land came to the edge and stopped short.

Where she stood were the remains of a Roman lighthouse. The place was called 'the Bay of the Beacon'. Would this prove prophetic—or ironic?

Suddenly she heard a sound behind her. The decision must have been reached. The doors of the abbey hall had been opened and people were pouring out into the sunshine. The decision may have been reached, but there were obviously many who did not agree with it. Angry voices were still raised. By the ones who looked satisfied and the ones who looked dismayed Etheldreda could see that the eloquent priest Wilfrid had triumphed. He had been a favourite at court before; there would be no holding him now.

She caught sight of the Abbess Hilda who had been presiding over the Synod. She looked tired and discouraged.

Etheldreda pushed her way through the crowds to her side, lightly disengaging her friend from a group of argumentative monks, and drawing her away to a quiet spot.

'What do you think, my friend? Will you change to the Roman Easter?' she asked.

Hilda shrugged and sighed.

'I will change, but I do not like it.'

'There was a great deal said today that I didn't like,' Etheldreda said sadly. 'It became a general attack on the brothers of Iona and Lindisfarne in the guise of an attack on their Easter reckoning.'

'Wilfrid is a man to be watched. He's ambitious, I think, and not only for the Lord's Kingdom.'

'He has great skill with words. Saint Peter himself would find him difficult to outwit. Poor

Colman. He didn't stand a chance,' said Etheldreda. Hilda smiled ruefully.

'Wilfrid accused Columba of "primitive simplicity" as though it were something to be ashamed of,' Etheldreda complained. 'In fact it is this very simplicity that is his great strength.'

'It's Wilfrid's lack of it that will be his undoing,' agreed Hilda.

'What will be my undoing?' a cheerful voice said behind them, and they turned to find the handsome monk, glowing with his recent victory, smiling at them.

The women laughed, slightly embarrassed.

'I was saying your lack of simplicity would be your undoing in the end,' said Hilda.

Wilfrid laughed. 'That may well be, if simplicity is a virtue.'

'Our Lord...'

'I know our Lord spoke of it...' he interrupted, 'but times have changed. Our world is getting more and more complicated, populations are growing, enemies of our Church are thriving. We have to be strong and organised, presenting a unified front to the world. The old simplicity served its purpose. The new sophistication will serve its purpose too.'

A look passed between Etheldreda and Hilda.

'You are wrong, brother Wilfrid,' Etheldreda said, 'but I can't prove you so with words.

Nothing has essentially changed. The challenge of the world has always been as it is now.'

He opened his mouth to continue the argument, but Hilda raised her hand.

'I'm tired of talk. We have had too much of it this day. I'm going for a walk. You may both join me if you like, but if you do, you must keep silence.'

Hilda had such a natural talent for command even Wilfrid could not disobey her.

The three of them walked along the clifftop where Etheldreda had been before in silence, the fresh breeze tugging at their clothes.

The sea turned to gold and then to lead. When the first star appeared Etheldreda and Hilda turned back to the warm lights of the monastery, leaving Wilfrid alone on the headland. He knew the importance of the decision that had just been made in the council hall, and he knew that it had been made the way he wanted it because of his own personal power. He felt as though the world were at his feet and if he lifted his hand it would follow him anywhere he chose.

He took a deep breath. Success tasted good.

Above him the sky darkened and as it did so it seemed to grow vaster every moment. Depth opened upon depth, stars behind stars... His figure on the headland was very, very small.

18

Death of Oswy AD 670

One day in the spring of the year 664 Etheldreda was out riding with Heregyth. The day was bright and warm, the woods full of bluebells, when suddenly a sense of icy foreboding caused her skin to prickle. At the same time her sight seemed to be growing dim. Just as a thrill of fear touched her own heart, the gentle mare she rode upon reared up and whinnied. For the next few moments she was so occupied in calming it down that she was not fully aware of what was happening. Then she noticed that the landscape was rapidly growing darker.

She looked over her shoulder to Heregyth and saw that she too was having trouble with her frightened steed. Behind her an immense, cold, black shadow seemed to be advancing across the land. Strings of birds were winging purposefully towards the forests as they did at nightfall.

The two women drew close together as the darkness grew more and more palpable around them. The horses moved restlessly, breathing heavily, all senses alerted to danger, but held in check by their human companions' soothing words and caresses.

Heregyth crossed herself. Etheldreda did the same.

'Is it the devil coming?' Heregyth whispered. 'Is it the end of the world?'

A few moments before, this very thought had crossed Etheldreda's mind, but now she had another explanation and was no longer afraid.

'Be comforted,' she said gently. 'It's neither of those dread things. I've heard of this happening before.'

'Is the sun leaving us forever?' Heregyth's voice rose in horror.

'No. No. It's nothing. It will pass. A shadow crosses the sun. Who knows what it is... the wing of a dark angel... a moment of despair in God's heart as he looks at the world. It will pass. Learned men know of this. It happens from time to time.'

'How long will it last?' Heregyth was shivering with the sudden chill.

The darkness was almost complete. The air seemed thick and solid, the landscape insubstantial.

They looked up towards the sun and gasped. It was black, but around it a brilliant ring of light shone out, and suddenly at one side, in the split second their eyes could stand the strain, they thought they saw an immense jewel grow from the ring.

They clung together, their eyes burning and watering.

'God has given us a sign,' Etheldreda whispered.

'What does it mean?' sobbed Heregyth. 'My lady, what does it mean?'

'A warning... a reminder. He could snuff out this whole universe like we snuff out a candle if He wished. But the ring is His token, His gift of forgiveness and presage of glory.'

'See, the light returns!' cried Heregyth with relief. 'The light returns!'

But whatever their God might have been trying to teach them was not finished. Within a very short time of this eclipse news came from the southern kingdoms that plague was with them again. It was said that so many people had died in the country of the East Saxons that there were scarce enough left to work the fields. All the priests were dead and the people were turning back to their old gods. Amulets and charms were being sought, many bartering them for what little food was available. Temples were even being hastily rebuilt and Christian churches burnt down.

Following close on these dark rumours came news of the death of Eorconbert, King of Kent.

* * * *

Ovin, who was now apprenticed to the Herb Master of York, scarcely slept. He and his mentor, knowing that the plague would not be long in reaching their land, were preparing as best they could by laying in stocks of useful herbs. Sachets of garlic were prepared. Cauldrons of thyme and fennel, mugwort and plantain were boiled and set aside in buckets to administer when needed. They worked day and night, gathering and sorting, grinding some to powder, hanging others to dry, the old words of the Nine-Herbs Charm running through their heads...

'Thou has strength against three and against thirty,
Thou has strength against poison and against infection,
Thou has strength against the foe who fares through the land!'

Ovin secretly adding a fervent 'amen' every time.

Although it was time-consuming they both tried to keep to the old herb-gathering rules, the wort-cunning of the ancients, for the Herb Master was not that much of a new man that he did not believe that the natural properties of herbs were only part of their efficacy. Plants were alive and with encouragement and right treatment would yield their hidden energies to man, earth energies only they knew how to transform. If they were not handled properly these hidden energies would run back into the earth and the plant would be useless for healing. The Master taught Ovin to speak to the herb before he gathered it, telling it for what purpose it was being gathered and asking it for its co-operation. He was to be barefooted so that he himself was in direct contact with the earth. He was to use no iron, for iron destroys all ancient magic. If he had to dig he must use bone or bronze, wood, stone or even gold like the ancient Druids.[14]

Once gathered he must never let the herb touch the ground again or its power might leak back into the earth. He must remember to reward the earth with a little gratitude, an offering of wine or honey, bread, or even a small coin. The stars must be considered, the position of the sun and moon, even the direction of the wind should be taken into account. There was a great deal to remember and with the pressure of the approaching pestilence Ovin was fully occupied.

* * * *

By early summer the plague was in Northumbria and every day was a day of mourning. The king himself, Alfrid of Deira, was struck down, and died calling for Etheldreda. She came to him at once and strained to hear what his swollen lips were trying to say to her, but his throat was already closing and his eyes that gazed so desperately into hers one moment, the next were as sightless as stone. She thought of the night that he had come to her room, so strong, so confident. She thought of all that he had tried to do for the Church. 'O Lord, Thine is the only permanence, the only refuge from the howling storm,' she whispered. 'Keep this man's soul close to Thee.'

* * * *

News came from Melrose that Cuthbert, loved by all who knew him, was ill.

For the first time since the plague began Etheldreda retired to her room and wept. She had long passed the point where weariness demanded sleep. She was living in a kind of no man's land between sleep and waking, her heart raw and aching with pity for the victims of the disease that she and Ovin ministered to day and night, her soul still clinging fiercely to a belief that the Lord knew what He was doing and that in the long run it would prove to have been for the best.

She sensed that Cuthbert was one of the few truly holy people alive at that time. His great physical strength combined with his gentleness, his absolute unwavering faith, his visions, his capacity to heal both souls and bodies, all made him very dear to her. She fought to accept God's Will in this and found that she could not. She pleaded long into the night for his life, feeling somehow that, if he died, they would be lost and the dark tide of doubt that had swept over the East Saxons, and was already washing at their door, would overwhelm them.

Heregyth found her on the floor in the morning, slumped against the bed, and carefully covered her with rugs. Her face was pale and drawn, dark rings were under her eyes. She stationed a boy outside her door and warned him to let no one near the room to wake her mistress.

A full day and night passed and Etheldreda was not aware of it. When she woke she was greeted with some wonderful news. Cuthbert was on his feet again. It seemed that as he lay dying he became aware that his bed was surrounded night and day by his fellow monks praying for his recovery.

Suddenly he sat up and called for his stick. 'If I have such men as these praying for my health from such a God as we know exists—I must recover,' he said.

Still sweating with fever and covered with sores, he hobbled out of the room and down to the abbey church to pray. It was said he was already visiting other victims of the plague and giving them and their families courage and confidence. His fever was down and the sores healing.

* * * *

On Alfrid's death Egfrid became sub-king of Deira, Etheldreda his queen.

* * * *

In Kent her young nephew Egbert, Saxberga's eldest son, succeeded his father.

* * * *

In France, where he had been sent by Alfrid before his death to be consecrated as Bishop of York, Wilfrid tarried, enjoying the comfort and luxury of life among the French nobility. Months passed after his splendid consecration at Compiègne before he could bring himself to return to Northumbria.

Meanwhile King Oswy, thinking that he would not return at all, chose to make Chad, one of four holy brothers, the Bishop of York. He sent him south to be consecrated by the

Archbishop of Canterbury, but, on his arrival in Kent, he found that the archbishop had died on the same day as King Eorconbert, and no successor had as yet been appointed. He travelled on to the province of the West Saxons and was there consecrated by Bishop Wini and two British bishops from Cornwall. On his return to York he lived as simply as he had always done, being, like his brothers, Iona trained.

Wilfrid returned at last from France to find much had changed in his homeland. Chad was now Bishop of York, Alfrid, his particular friend, was dead, and Egfrid, whom he had never liked, was King of Deira in his place. Oswy was feeling old and tired, much depressed by the ravages of the plague.

Wilfrid rode up to Bamburgh to question his displacement from York, but came away persuaded for the sake of peace to return to Ripon and bide his time. He determined to make his church at Ripon an example to his countrymen of how a church should be. He had brought magnificent church vestments and furniture from France and these, with the new glass windows the French glaziers had installed, made it the wonder of the age. The stone walls rang to the sound of the newly introduced antiphonal chants.

As it turned out Wilfrid did not have to wait long for his return to York.

Since his arrival in Kent in May 669, the new Archbishop of Canterbury, Theodore of Tarsus, had been travelling throughout the Seven Kingdoms reorganising the Church the Roman way, giving the whole country a kind of unity it had never had before. At York he claimed that Chad had not been properly consecrated as bishop because the two bishops from Cornwall who had presided at the ceremony were not acceptable, celebrating as they did Easter according to the Celtic computation.

Wilfrid became Bishop of York and Chad, who had impressed Theodore immensely with his quiet acceptance of the change in his fortunes, was reconsecrated and sent to Lichfield to preside over the see of Mercia and Lindsey.

So powerful were Wilfrid's friends, so great his popularity, he was continually being showered with endowments for his minster and gifts for himself. His wealth and influence grew.[15]

* * * *

After the dark days of the plague York became a centre of light.

While Egfrid spent a great deal of his time hunting and sparring with his companions, Etheldreda ruled the kingdom, encouraging men of learning and talent from all over Europe to settle. Churches were built, monasteries were founded, the queen herself supervising much of the work, riding tirelessly between centres to check that all was well, hearing petitions, granting land and moneys where needed.

She assisted Wilfrid in every way to make the church at York as splendid as that at Ripon, finding herself more and more in his company, and more and more disposed to enjoy it.

* * * *

On a cold day in February of the year 670 King Oswy took ill and called Wilfrid, Etheldreda and Egfrid to Bamburgh.

They took the road to the north together, travelling over bleak and icy moors, the snowdrifts sometimes so deep that they were forced to spend several days and nights in whatever shelter they could find.

One night just as a blizzard looked as though it were setting in, they came upon a village huddled against the lee of a hill.

'We have to take shelter,' Wilfrid said, 'whether we like the conditions or not.'

Etheldreda at once dismounted, thankful to see the smoke drifting up through the thatch. Although she was clad in fur from top to toe her face was exposed, her cheeks were stinging and her nose seemed as though it would never feel like living flesh again.

Egfrid looked around with disgust.

'What a way to live!' he said. 'My pigs have better sties!'

'We must see what can be done about these people, my lord,' she said. 'It is not just that we live so fine and they so poor.'

'It is not just that we have to spend the night in such filth,' Egfrid snapped. He strode up to one of the huts and kicked in the frail door of woven twigs and straw. The men who travelled with them as protection strode in and hauled everyone out into the howling wind and driving snow.

'We will have this one,' said Egfrid, 'you take the others.'

Etheldreda's face went scarlet with anger.

'What are you doing, my lord?' she cried.

Men, women and children were unceremoniously pushed out of their house and stood bewildered and terrified in their rags in the freezing night. Some of the men seized sticks and tried to defend themselves against the rough treatment, their faces full of sullen bewilderment.

'Would you have us die in the snow?' said Egfrid impatiently to Etheldreda. Would this woman try to shame him before even the lowest in the kingdom!

'My lord,' said Wilfrid smoothly. 'We don't

need all these houses. Let some of the people stay with their neighbours this night and we'll take up as little of their space as possible. It would not be well, my lord,' he added softly in Egfrid's ear, 'if the King of Deira were seen not to care for the lives of his subjects.'

Egfrid shrugged. 'Arrange it,' he said. 'But be quick about it.'

Wilfrid took over and very diplomatically explained to the people what was happening. Within moments they were willingly vacating some of their huts for the royal party, the women looking out what food was available in the village and bringing it eagerly to the tall bishop and the beautiful lady, dropping frightened bows as they passed the surly king.

At last they were alone. The mutton broth had tasted vile and smelt worse, but at least it was hot. The fire was burning well and they were safe from the wind that was tugging at the roof, and the snow that was driving through the wild, dark air.

Etheldreda loosened her fur cape and Wilfrid helped her take it off. Her cheek touched his hand as she turned for him to reach for it. Shaken, they pulled apart, neither daring to meet the eyes of the other.

Egfrid was grumbling loudly that if they could have only kept going another few miles they would have been in the home of one of his father's noblemen and would have had a proper bed at least to sleep upon rather than this pile of bug-ridden straw.

'I think, my lord, it would be better if you slept on your cloak on the floor than on that straw,' Wilfrid suggested. 'My lady can have mine. I'll not sleep this night.'

'No indeed!' cried Etheldreda, trying to keep the tremor out of her voice, hoping that nothing of what she was feeling was showing on her face. 'I can't sleep either. Keep your cloak, you'll need it.'

'I insist, my lady.'

'I will have it,' Egfrid said sharply. 'My wife is used to sleeping on the floor, Wilfrid. I am not.'

Wilfrid looked from one to the other. Etheldreda had turned her face from him and he could only see the rich gold hair that the wind had tugged loose from its moorings, and the curve of her shoulder under the soft wool of her dress.

Egfrid was holding out his hand for the cloak impatiently. Wilfrid hesitated a moment and then handed it to him.

Egfrid took some time to get settled, swearing and grumbling as he tried various positions and found them all unsatisfactory. Wilfrid and

Etheldreda sat on either side of the fire on some low wooden stools that they had found. They said nothing. They looked nowhere but into the fire.

At last Egfrid fell asleep and there was no sound in the hut but his heavy breathing and the occasional crackle of the flames. Outside the sound of the blizzard seemed to be less than it had been. Etheldreda told herself that she should pray, confess her feelings to the Lord and repent of them, but she could not. Guilty as she felt about them, they were so intensely sweet she could not bear to part with them. She dare not look at Wilfrid, dare not wonder if he felt the same.

Although there were sounds, the breathing of Egfrid, the fire, the wind, a silence was between them that they could almost touch. It grew more and more uncomfortable until she could bear it no longer. She lifted her chin defiantly and looked him in the eye.

'My lord Wilfrid,' she said with determined brightness, 'it will be a long night. What shall we talk about?'

She could not see whether his dark eyes were as full as hers of feelings that he had difficulty in mastering, or whether he was amused at the earnestness of her proposition.

'Must we talk at all?' he said gently, and the

expression in his voice showed her that she was not alone in her confusion. She was determined that they should fight their feelings.

'What! The eloquent Bishop Wilfrid at a loss for words? I can't believe it!'

He laughed, and at last the spell was broken. They talked about their childhood and about Wilfrid's adventures on the way to Rome. They argued the finer points of theology, and the relative merits of various members of the clergy and the court.

Egfrid woke at midnight and heard an argument in full swing as to whether there co-existed two perfect natures, divine and human, in the Christ, or whether there was only one, and that divine.[16] He gave a groan and rolled over, pulling Wilfrid's fur cloak over his head so that he could not hear their voices. In the small hours Wilfrid stood up to put more wood on the fire and when he sat down again he sat on the floor close beside her. The conversation began to flag and sometimes there were long gaps, some even in the middle of sentences. Etheldreda wished he would not sit so close to her, but could not bring herself to ask him to move. At last she could bear it no longer and told him that she was now going to sleep. She rose from her seat and went as far away as she could from him. She lay down on the hard and dirty floor wrapped in her cloak and shut her eyes. But although there was now a whole room between them, the sleeping body of her husband and a fire, she could still feel his presence.

* * * *

At Bamburgh they found Oswy very pale and weak, but he rallied at the sight of them. He had been particularly eager to see Wilfrid and reached out his hands at once to him. The guilt of certain things he had done in his life had begun to weigh heavily on his heart and he longed to make a pilgrimage to Rome, to die in the city of Saint Peter and Saint Paul.

'My friend,' said the old king, taking the bishop's strong hand in his. 'I need your help for the journey. I need your guidance and protection. Will you come with me?'

Wilfrid put both hands over the king's.

'It will be an honour, my lord,' he said quietly, thinking that if this invitation had come at any other time how pleased he would have been, but now, to leave Etheldreda...

'I've sinned, Wilfrid, my friend! I've sinned,' the king repeated sadly, 'and all the deeds I've done to God's honour can't save me on the Day of judgement if I don't receive absolution.' He paused. 'In Rome they have holy relics of great efficacy. Their strength will flow into me, their goodness will fill my soul and wash away the stain. Come, sit by me, tell me of Rome. Tell me of the holy places there that we will visit.'

Etheldreda looked across the king's bed to Eanfleda. Oswy's queen shook her head almost imperceptibly and indicated the door. Etheldreda stooped and kissed the pale cheek of the old man.

'We'll leave you, my lord, to plan your journey. Come,' she said to Egfrid. He was sitting on a chair at the bedside of his father in almost the same position she remembered from their wedding night, one knee drawn up to his chin, biting the knuckles of one hand. He looked up at her with the same dark sullen eyes.

He did not move.

Oswy turned his eyes to him and there was a spark of the old impatience in them.

'Go, my son,' he said. 'I don't need you.'

Egfrid stood up suddenly, knocking over the chair. Without a backward look he strode out of the room, the door slamming noisily behind him.

A flash of anger crossed his father's face.

Etheldreda bowed quickly to him and hurried after her husband. She called his name but he wouldn't look back. He strode to the stables, took a horse and rode fiercely off, almost knocking her down as she ran after him.

She was worried. Lately the moodiness that had marred their early relationship had been less in evidence. There were times when he would seek her presence and be reasonably content to talk to her. But now... she had seen something in his face that made her afraid. She bitterly regretted Oswy's thoughtless words and knew that Egfrid would not forget them.

* * * *

Queen Eanfleda summoned Etheldreda back to Oswy's chamber in the later afternoon. The king was dying.

Wilfrid and Etheldreda, on either side of him, prayed for his soul throughout the night as his hold on the physical world gradually loosened. Eanfleda stood stiff and straight, dry eyed at the foot of the bed, thinking back over the years they had been together. There were many times when she had hated him, but they had been through much together and she could say now that she had grown to accept him and appreciate him for those qualities that made him a strong and positive man. He was impulsive and had done many things that he had later regretted, but the same quality had made him do good things, and she thought of these now, knowing that she would miss him, knowing that she loved him after a fashion and that perhaps he had loved her too. He had not been able to master the rigorous moral code of Christ, but there had been times when he had done good on such a grand scale in the Lord's name that she could not but hope it would help wipe away the guilt of the other deeds. He certainly would leave a rich and peaceful country, and his successor would have no cause to remember him with anything but gratitude.

Egfrid would now be king over the whole of Northumbria.

Egfrid? Eanfleda sighed. Where was he? It was typical of him that he was not to be found when he was needed. The night was almost through and he had not returned.

Wilfrid lent forward to answer a question the king had whispered. His gratitude for all those years when Oswy had treated him like a son showed in his face. A twinge of regret pulled at Eanfleda's heart. If only Wilfrid had in fact been one of their own sons and the country could have been left to him, with Etheldreda as his queen. What a partnership that would have been!

The train of her thought was interrupted

by a disturbance at the door. She turned to find Egfrid striding into the room, his hair and cloak covered with snow, cold and damp coming into the warm chamber with him. But he had arrived beside his father's bed too late. Oswy was already dead.

The lamps that flickered on either side of him illuminated a scene that Egfrid would never forget. The king's face pale and set but peaceful, his left hand clasping that of Etheldreda, his right hand Wilfrid's.

Egfrid gave a shriek of pain that split the silent air of the chamber like cold iron a skull. He flung himself upon his father and sobbed. For a moment the three others in the room stood back amazed.

Egfrid had never shown great affection for his father, and indeed his father had shown very little for him, but there was no mistaking the genuine suffering in those sobs. All those years of frustration when his feelings had to be held back because they found no answering emotion in his father's breast, found expression now. He was hysterical.

Etheldreda looked at the others and nodded to the door. Wilfrid understood at once and put his arm around Queen Eanfleda, leading her out of the chamber.

At the open door they found a woman about

to enter, also in a cloak with snow upon it, her eyes upon Egfrid. She was Eormenburh, the wife of one of Oswy's earls. Wilfrid took her arm at once and guided her out of the room beside Queen Eanfleda. She looked back as though she were contemplating breaking away from the bishop and rushing to Egfrid, but the sight she saw there made her change her mind. Etheldreda had gathered her weeping husband in her arms, and he had turned to her like a hurt child turns to its mother. His head was upon her breast and her kisses were falling upon his hair.

19

Queen of Northumbria

In the oak church at Bamburgh Egfrid knelt to receive the crown of Northumbria. Beside him his queen bent her heart to her God and prayed that she would have the strength to support him in this new and difficult role.

Bishop Eata of Lindisfarne, one of Saint Aidan's protégés, and Wilfrid, Bishop of York, were presiding, but Cuthbert, now Prior of Lindisfarne, knelt beside Etheldreda, his presence giving her a sense of comfort. She remembered that once when she had queried the arduous life he had led since his illness, noticing that he had to lean heavily on his stick and was frequently out of breath, he had said that nothing was ever required of him by God that he was not capable of giving. She must hold to this truth now, not only in the matter of the crown, but in the personal torment she was facing with regard to her feelings for Wilfrid. She was tempted, yes, but this did not mean that she would give in. She had strength to resist and she would do so. She forced herself to look at him now, the magnificent embroidered cope of Byzantine silk falling around him; his hand, long-fingered and fine, raised in the sign of the cross above her husband's head; his face in profile as though chiselled by a great sculptor.

Outside the wooden church the early March winds howled, the snow hurled itself through small cracks in the shutters like smoke, but inside there was the warm glow of flickering candlelight on the golden sacramental vessels on the altar and the crown that ringed the head of Egfrid.

The choir was good, but not as good as the one trained by Wilfrid at York. She must remember to ask him to spend some time at Bamburgh to train the choir. Even as she thought this tears came to her eyes. Was she so far gone in this secret sin that even on her knees she shamelessly thought of ways to see him?

Eanfleda saw the tears and misinterpreted them. She had been opposed to Etheldreda's marriage to her own son, but was now reconciled to it. She remembered her own feelings when she became Oswy's queen and how she had dreaded the long years of responsibility. She looked at her son wearing Edwin's crown. She remembered that day of horrors years before when, as a child, she had looked up to the walls of York and in the flickering light of torches seen the ghastly severed head of her father on a stake. Edwin had been a great man, now acclaimed a saint. Miracles occurred when people touched his bones or called upon his name. Oswy had worn his crown. He had been no saint, but he was a strong man and a courageous one. It did not seem right for Egfrid to be wearing it now. She could not imagine Egfrid a king of the same calibre as his predecessors. But there was no one else. Alfrid was dead. Alfwin was younger and had been made sub-king of Deira. Her other children were all daughters. Osryth would be Queen of Mercia when Wulfhere was dead, for she was married to his only remaining brother, Ethelred. Alfleda was a bitter widow, venting her guilt for her part in her husband's murder on all round her. Elffleda, her youngest daughter, now sixteen, was at Whitby, a novice under Hilda's protection. Thank God for Etheldreda, who had all the strength and the intelligence that was needed for the ruler of such a great kingdom.

Queen Eanfleda shut her eyes. She was tired. She would not live as her own mother lived at the Kentish court, a forgotten queen, a shadow doing homage to another generation. She would retire to Whitby and await her death and burial there, at least to spend her last years with the daughter who had been taken so early and so cruelly from her side.

* * * *

As Queen of Northumbria, Etheldreda found her days crowded with people to be entertained and decisions to be made. Her court was a sinecure for travellers from France and Italy and beyond, her counsel sought by churchmen and laymen alike, by rich and by poor. Egfrid left the burden of government almost entirely to her, spending his time exclusively on his new interest—confident that he had at last found a field in which he could outshine her. He began to build up the army Oswy had left. Edwin had had a fleet. He would have one too. His early training in Mercia, his admiration for the war-like Penda and his son Wulfhere, gave him the inspiration and the skill. His new occupation took the place of the long years of aimlessness that had been his as powerless prince and sub-king of Deira. Riding a stallion bred from Wulfhere's with his armed companions around him, he felt important and invincible.

He scarcely saw Etheldreda, for at night when he returned to the castle he took Eormenburh to bed.

Although her days were full, Etheldreda

found herself often lonely. Heregyth had chosen to stay at York. Since Edgil's death in the plague she had married one of Alfwin's thegns, a young man called Imma. Ovin stayed at Bamburgh for a while and then one day came to her and asked if he could be released to go to the monastery at Lastingham where Chad was now living.

'You may go, of course, my friend,' Etheldreda had said, 'but for what reason do you desert me?'

'I think you do not need me now, my lady,' Ovin said sadly, 'and besides...'

He looked so uncomfortable and unhappy Etheldreda was quite alarmed.

'Besides... what, my friend?'

'I find life at such a grand court not to my taste, my lady,' he said hesitatingly. 'I find it difficult to keep close to God here.' He didn't add that he had watched her gradually slip away from the standards that she had brought from Ely, and that it made him sad.

Her eyes shadowed.

'Go, my friend, pray for me. I too find that my life here is not always to my taste, but there are things I have to do.' She looked at him and he could see that she understood what he had been trying to say. His heart ached for her. He had watched her for so long caught between two worlds, trying to let neither down. How could he leave her? He stared at his feet, struggling to find words to express what he was feeling, what he was thinking. She waited patiently for him to speak, but he said nothing.

'Go, Ovin,' she said at last, 'with my blessing. Come back to me when I am worthy of you.'

He looked up at this, words rushing to his lips, words to tell her that it was he who would never be worthy of *her*, words to tell her that he would not go away but serve her, under whatever circumstances, for the rest of his life. But she had already turned away from him, and was greeting with a cool regality one of her husband's thegns who had arrived to ask a favour.

He decided to go to Chad and do what she had asked, pray for her.

* * * *

In need of a friend she turned to Wilfrid more and more. He rode between York and Bamburgh frequently, acting as confidant and advising her on many matters that should have been dealt with by Egfrid. They never spoke of their feelings for each other and they never touched, but there were some at court who did not believe this.

In late summer of her first year as queen

she gave Wilfrid all her lands at Hexham as a gift, all royal dues from it were to go to him. She wrote the document for this herself, enjoying the chance to use her skills as scribe again. It was witnessed and sealed with a curse on all those who might dispute the gift, as was customary.

When Egfrid heard of this he hit his fist against the wall and looked so angry Etheldreda was startled.

'My lord,' she enquired in alarm, 'what have I done wrong? The land was mine to give, I have no need of your permission.'

'The land was yours to give, my lady,' he said bitterly, 'because it was my wedding gift to you.'

'But surely... for the Lord's work...' Her voice trailed away as she realised how it would seem to Egfrid. She had thought of nothing but pleasing Wilfrid.

'I cannot speak as well as your fine bishop, lady, but that does not mean that I have not eyes to see!'

'What do you mean by that, sir?' she demanded haughtily, though her heart was beating very fast and painfully.

'You know what I mean, lady. I am no fool.'

She bit her lip. She would have liked to have argued, to prove him wrong. He was wrong in the substance of his suspicions, but not in the spirit. Although they had done nothing about their love, it was there and she could not deny it.

She turned away from him and strode out of the room.

Wilfrid must go away. She would insist that he accept the invitation of her nephew, King Egbert of Kent, that he had thought to turn down. Theodore himself had on several occasions tried to entice him away to help with Church organisation in the southern kingdoms. More often than not Wilfrid had refused, but now he must go. His work was suffering because of her, and she, because of him.

* * * *

After Wilfrid had left she tried to spend more time with Egfrid, arranging for him the nights of feasting and entertaining that he so enjoyed. A young poet called Ceric visited the court at this time with a version of the story of Beowulf, a heroic poem from the early days of the migrations that both Egfrid and Etheldreda had heard as children, but never so well sung or so beautifully worded. It was at Etheldreda's request that the poem was written down and given a twist that made of a heathen story of physical prowess, a Christian allegory of spiritual trial.

Whether Egfrid noticed the spiritual symbolism in it or not, it was his favourite poem, and he requested it almost every night, sitting in his chair with his foot drawn up under him and his chin resting on his knee, his eyes seeing nothing of the smoky hall but everything of 'the cold storm on the cauldron of waters... the lowering night...' and 'the northern wind' that fell on the intrepid band of adventurers 'in warspite'.

He longed for those days when the strength of a man's arm was all that was necessary to make him a hero.

'It was then that he saw the size of this water-hag,
damned thing of the deep. He dashed out his weapon,
Not stinting the stroke, and with such strength and violence
that the circled sword screamed on her head
a strident battle-song. But the stranger saw
his battle-flame refuse to bite
or hurt her at all; the edge failed
its lord in his need. It had lived through many
hand-to-hand conflicts, and carved

through the helmets
of fated men. This was the first time
that this rare treasure had betrayed its name.
Determined still, intent on fame,
the nephew of Hyelac renewed his courage.
Furious, the warrior flung it to the ground,
spiral-patterned, precious in its clasps,
stiff and steel-edged; his own strength would suffice him,
the might of his hands. A man must act so
when he means in a fight to frame himself
a long-lasting glory; it is not life he thinks of.' [17]

To Etheldreda the fact that the man's sword failed him and he had to rely on his own inner courage and strength to reach the 'long-lasting glory' of the Kingdom of Heaven was explicit in this passage. The 'mere-wolf' he had to kill to do this was the evil lurking in his own heart. To Egfrid it was confirmation that he was the heir of Beowulf, *he* had a sword handed down through the generations, 'precious in its clasps'. *He* had immense strength in his arms. He gave gifts of gold and precious stones, of weapons and horses and land to his companions just as these ancient heroes did. He would ride out with his twelve companions and seek adventure!

* * * *

Unfortunately, the first adventure that came to his mind was to attack the province of Lindsey and wrest it from the hold of the Mercians.

Wulfhere at this time, with the conquests that he had made and the alliance with the Kentish royal family through his wife, was overlord of all the southern English. His power and influence was growing stronger every day, and since Oswy's death rumours were being brought to Bamburgh that he was plotting to extend his influence north of the Humber, thinking that Egfrid was no match for him.

This rumour was too much for Egfrid. He wanted to show his childhood hero his newfound strength, and test his skills against him. He also wanted to make sure that no one thought he was a weakling under the thumb of his wife.

Against Etheldreda's advice he took his men south, and Lindsey once more became a pawn in the game of power between Mercia and Northumbria.

Wulfhere was not expecting an attack, all his advisers and spies having told him that

Egfrid was useless at everything except drinking, womanising and playing at soldiering. He was occupied on his western borders when the attack on Lindsey came, and Egfrid won an instant victory.

Beside himself with excitement at his achievement he rode back to Bamburgh. On his arrival he did not go straight to Eormenburh as he normally would have done, but strode, still clad in his dirty fighting clothes, into the bedchamber of his wife.

He held a torch above his head and looked down at her triumphantly.

Startled, she woke and sat up, staring at him in amazement, her long hair flowing around her like silk.

'Lindsey is mine. I have taken, it,' he announced, and waited breathlessly for her commendation.

It did not come.

She drew her wraps about her and stared at him.

'All those people killed—for what?' she said coolly.

The flames danced on her gold hair, her pale, cold skin.

His face went black with rage.

'For me!' he shouted. 'For my kingdom and my throne!'

'Egfrid...' she started to say, horrified at the passion in his voice.

He pushed the torch into the iron wall socket and then strode back to her bed.

'I have taken Lindsey and I will take you,' he said bitterly, seizing her shoulder and tearing her wraps from her.

She slipped from his grasp and fled to the other side of the room, pulling her clothes on with shaking hands. He lurched after her but lost his footing, the small mat beside her bed caught in his foot, and, cursing, he grabbed a chair to save his balance. By the time he was in control again she was gone. Furious, he seized the torch again and flung it on the bed.

When the agitated servants came running they found him standing in the room staring at the flames that had consumed the furs and were now roaring towards the tapestries. Tears were streaming down his cheeks.

'My lord!' they cried, some taking his arms and hauling him out of danger, others beating at the fire.

* * * *

Etheldreda had run straight from him to the stables, saddled her horse, and with only a young groom to accompany her, ridden down to the harbour. The groom woke the startled master of a boat that lay to at the quayside and demanded that it be made ready to sail the queen south to Whitby as soon as the tide was right.

The groom was then sent back to the king with a message to be delivered as soon as the boat was under way.

* * * *

No news had come to Hilda of what had occurred at Bamburgh. She greeted her friend warmly and insisted on her having food and drink as soon as she arrived.

Etheldreda sat quietly listening to the gossip of the great abbey, her head throbbing, but saying nothing about the reasons for her sudden visit. Eanfleda and her daughter, the young Elffleda, were present and she didn't want to talk about Egfrid in front of them.

After the meal Hilda insisted that she listened to a song although she protested that she was not in the mood for singing.

'Listen to this one song, my friend,' Hilda said. 'It is no ordinary song, I promise you.'

A rough looking peasant was brought in. Etheldreda was told his name was Caedman, and that he had received the gift of song in a dream, from an angel. She was so tired she could hardly concentrate. Everything seemed to be swimming around her, the firelight, the faces of her friends, the flickering shadows.

She longed to sleep. Then Caedman began to sing, and his voice was unbelievably fine and pure, his words falling into her mind like crystals dropped into a clear pool, the ripples of their meaning travelling outwards from the centre far beyond the words of any song she had ever heard. He sang of the Lord of Creation. He sang of the earth. Etheldreda's agitated thoughts were stilled, her weariness forgotten. She began to see her relationship with Egfrid and what had just happened with such clarity she knew that the fault was by no means all on his side.

The song ended and Hilda was eager to tell her about the singer. 'There is no doubt that something really extraordinary took place here,' she said as soon as the man left the room. 'Up to a few weeks ago he could scarcely put two words together. He has been looking after horses all his life and hardly had occasion to talk with men. In fact, when he was with others and the harp was being passed around after a meal he would slip out and go back to the stables to avoid the embarrassment of having to take his turn at singing.'

'The song he sang was beautiful,' Etheldreda said, still half dazed by the power of it.

'His word-hoard is as rich as a poet who has been storing and using words for a long time,' Eanfleda said with tears of pleasure in her eyes.

'One night,' Hilda said, 'he was sleeping in the stable when he saw a man standing beside him. "Caedman" the man said, "sing me a song." Caedman shrank back and told him that he couldn't sing, but the man reached out his hands towards him and looked into his eyes. "You will sing for me," he said. Caedman felt suddenly wonderfully confident. He even laughed to think how all those years he had refused to sing. "What shall I sing about?" he asked cheerfully. "Sing about the creation of all things," the man said, and immediately Caedman found that words and melody were flowing from him as easily as water from a spring. When he woke he could remember the song vividly and the next morning he sang it to the reeve, who brought him to me. He sings for us every day now,' Hilda said happily. 'We tell him a story from the Bible and he puts it into a verse straight away.'[18] She paused and looked hard at Etheldreda. Something was wrong. 'What is it my friend?' she asked. 'Surely this story should make you happy. It's a sign of God's continual grace to us.'

Etheldreda shook her head and the tears began to flow. 'I know,' she sobbed. 'It's a lesson to me. I've been so busy with worldly matters lately I've scarcely stopped for a moment to notice if miracles were happening or not!'

Eanfleda and Elffleda quietly and tactfully withdrew, leaving the two close friends together. It was some time before Etheldreda stopped weeping but when she did she lifted her blotched and desperate face to Hilda and told her everything that had occurred and everything that she feared.

'What must I do? Oh, Hilda, what must I do? I can't go back to him and yet I can't leave him. The people need me. I know he is not capable of ruling them.'

Hilda shook her head. 'I can't tell you what to do. There is only one who can—and that is the Lord.'

Etheldreda was ashamed. This was advice she herself had given to many people in her life, and yet she had to receive it now from someone else. Hilda, seeing the expression on her face, kissed her wet cheeks.

'Spend the night in the chapel,' she said gently. 'I'll see that you're not disturbed. But I'll give you one piece of advice. Think of Egfrid—not only of yourself. I think you have thought too little of him over these years, my sister.'

Etheldreda bit her lip, the tears welling

up again. Caedman and Hilda together had opened a door she had been trying to keep shut. 'I tried, after Oswy died,' she said sadly. 'I truly tried. But there was so much to do. There never seemed to be any time.' Her voice trailed away. How often had she pointed out to others that the moments were there and it was our choice what use we made of them?

That night in the chapel she tried to pray as she used to pray, and realised with a shock that even in prayer her mind had become too busy and too worldly. She found herself asking for things, pleading and wheedling.

'Egfrid is a burden to me,' she caught herself thinking. 'Please take the burden off my shoulders.'

At Ely she had learned to pray a different way, a way that she had known was right by the feeling of joy it gave her. It had been a gradual going into Silence, a listening, and a waiting. She had learnt that when you asked the Christ-God for help for yourself or for others you did not list and specify and bargain. You offered the problem to Him for His help confident that He knew better than you did what was needed.

'These things I have spoken to you, while I am still with you. But the Counsellor, the Holy Spirit, whom the Father will send in my name, he will teach you all things, and bring to your remembrance all that I have said to you.'[19] Of all the gospels, Saint John's was the one that spoke most directly to her.

She bowed her head, knowing that she had lost the art of listening to His counsel. Her days were governed by what she wanted to do and how she thought it should be done. First one thing and then the other had led her further and further into the noise of the world, further and further away from the quiet inner voice of the Counsellor.

Just before dawn she went for a long walk, down the steep hill from the headland where the monastery was built, through the little village that nestled in the bay. The tide was out, and so instead of the sea beating against the cliffs there was a long stretch of beach for her to tread. First light was touching the wave tops, making the cliffs look darker in contrast. The first gull winged above her seeking the return of the first fishing boat.

She shivered at the beautiful, cold clarity of it all, the feeling of renewal and excitement that dawn always brought with it. She thought of something she had heard about Cuthbert when he was at Coldingham. A brother monk had noticed that after the others had performed the last office of the day, instead of going to sleep for the few hours that were allotted to them for this purpose, he crept out of the building and disappeared into the night. Thinking that he would catch him at some sinful work, he followed him. Cuthbert took the path down the cliffs to the beach, the monk close behind him. To his amazement Cuthbert walked straight into the sea and stood there for the rest of the night, only his head showing above the water in the moon-light. Stiff and cold and ashamed the brother monk returned to the monastery knowing that the bell for the early vigil would soon be rung. Cuthbert was not late for the vigil. His clothes were dry, his face fresh and peaceful.[20]

The brother told his fellows and several accompanied him on another night. The same thing happened. But this time two young seals followed him as he came out of the sea and for a while the brothers watched the three of them playing on the beach as though they were children. The exercise and the frequent rubbing of their fur against him made him dry.

Etheldreda removed her shoe and touched the water with her toe. It was freezing. The air was prickling with invisible ice.

She remembered the Irish monk Fursey from her childhood and how Hilda and she had tried to emulate him by walking in the snow with bare feet.

She took off her other shoe and threw them both back up the beach out of reach of the sea. Then she stepped into the water and gasped as her legs almost buckled under her with cramp. The sky blazed with sudden fiery brilliance as the sun came up over the horizon and a shaft of dazzling light shot across the watery leagues and drove like an arrow into her heart. She cried out and the cry was of a lonely child seeking its Comforter, its Counsellor, its Protector and Mentor.

Suddenly she felt no cramp, no cold. She found herself walking along the golden path that led from the beach to the sun, the air filled with singing and with a million sparks of light. Beings swirled around her, bodiless yet recognisable to her in bodily form. It was as though all the barriers between the realms were down.

* * * *

A fisherman returning from the sea found her lying on the beach unconscious, the waves washing over her.

20

Eormenburh

Etheldreda lay ill at Whitby for some time, but when she recovered she returned to Bamburgh. She was much paler and thinner than when she had left, but she was calmer. She had resolved to ask Egfrid to allow her to leave the castle and become a nun, realising that for his peace of mind as well as for her own, the arrangement they had had for more than ten years could not go on. She was also sure that she could not do justice to either world by straddling both as she had before.

The king was away when she arrived, and, hearing that Wilfrid was at Lindisfarne, she decided to go there at once to ask his advice.

The holy island was only an island at high tide. At low tide miles of pale sand stretched out towards it and it was possible to walk to it. On the mainland shore, where the sea did not normally reach, the sand was held against the wind by tall grasses that shivered and stirred in the sea breeze, and caught the gold of the sun.

Etheldreda insisted on going alone, walking

over the dry sea bed at low tide, listening to the sound of sea birds and the distant hush of the water. From time to time she stooped and picked up shells until the little leather pouch she carried at her belt was full. She looked at the heavy rings on her fingers and they seemed gross and crude compared with the exquisite delicacy of the sea treasure she was gathering. Her heart ached to return to the natural life, the holy life, close to God's infinite wisdom.

As she drew nearer to the island there were times it disappeared from view behind a sand dune, as though it didn't exist and she was following a dream. But it was there and where the land rose enough for grass to grow, boats were drawn up like stranded fish and some of the brothers were working on the nets.

She was shown at once to the guest hut and was given cold, hard boiled gulls eggs and fresh rye bread to eat while a novice went in search of Bishop Wilfrid.

'He is probably in the library,' she was told.

When she had rested and eaten she wandered out and looked around her at the church, built of sturdy oak beams and thatched with reeds. The monks' quarters were huts, part drystone, part thatch and turf. She smiled to think of the elegant Wilfrid living for so many years under these primitive conditions.

Wilfrid came to her at last, his eyes alight with the pleasure of seeing her. He took both her hands in his, looking down into her eyes with such an expression in his that she lowered hers, the blood rising to her cheeks. She had hoped after the long separation they could meet without her heart pounding and her mind floundering in confusion. But it was not to be. She pulled her hands away quickly and drew back, turning slightly from him so that when she spoke he could not see her face.

'I have come to ask your advice,' she said in a low voice he could scarcely catch, 'not so much as a friend this time, but as bishop.'

He pulled himself together and tried to mask his feelings. 'Shall we walk in the sun, my lady, or shall we sit indoors?' he asked formally.

'Oh, let's walk in the sun!' she cried, and for a moment she lifted her face to his and he caught the joy she felt in being with him. This time he turned away from her.

They walked on the little path that wound around the island, flowers and soft grasses nodding at their feet, the sky immensely domed above them. They did not talk again until they could trust themselves, then Etheldreda told him what had happened and what she had decided. He listened, although he already knew of the incident with Egfrid. If she had not returned when she did, he would have gone to Whitby at Egfrid's request to fetch her back.

'Egfrid's request?' she cried in astonishment when he at last told her this.

'Yes. He called me back from Lichfield as soon as you fled. He seemed to think I would have some influence over you.' He looked at her sideways when he said this, a slight, light smile lifting the corners of his mouth.

Her eyes shadowed and she did not respond to his amusement. It troubled her to think that Egfrid wanted her back so badly he was even prepared to call on Wilfrid's help.

Wilfrid and she talked and walked a long time. It was decided that Wilfrid would visit the monastery of Coldingham and request the abbess there, Egfrid's aunt Ebba, to take Etheldreda in as novice, preparatory to her taking the full and formal vows of a nun. Being his aunt, Egfrid might well be persuaded to accede to this arrangement where he would have opposed another. Wilfrid himself, who seemed now to have gained something of the king's trust and friendship, would use all his persuasive powers.

Much comforted, Etheldreda returned to Bamburgh castle to await the return of Egfrid.

Since she had been away the lady Eormenburh's influence had increased at court. Her husband had been despatched to Lindsey to keep order, and she had moved quite openly into the king's private chambers.

She greeted Etheldreda with cold disdain as though she were the queen and Etheldreda the wife of a minor earl. She had even been entertaining foreign guests as though she were the mistress of the castle.

Etheldreda found herself trembling with the effort to control her anger after their encounter and went to the chapel to pray for patience and good sense.

When she emerged she was met by a delegation of women who begged her to dismiss Eormenburh from the court. They told tales of the wantonness and corruption of those around her, and of her own arrogance and foolishness. 'The king listens to every word she says, and she harms everything she touches.'

'I can't send her away,' she said. 'She is the king's friend. Besides, I myself will be leaving soon.' At this such a wail of protest went up she was quite startled. She tried to explain to the women why she had to go but they wept and pleaded with her, describing in vivid detail what they feared would happen to the kingdom if it were left in the hands of the king and Eormenburh.

At last they left her alone, confused and anxious again. What they had said was probably true. If she left, Eormenburh would take her place in the state as she had in her husband's bed. The country would then be defenceless against the king's vagaries of mood, and ill-considered judgements. She wrestled with her conscience and finally knew that she had to stay, at least a while longer, to work out if she could how to unseat Eormenburh from the king's affections, and to arrange the affairs of the country in such a way that her presence would no longer be essential.

When Egfrid returned she said nothing of leaving for Coldingham, but knelt at his feet and asked forgiveness for all the pain she had caused him.

Eormenburh, instantly suspicious of this new approach, made a point of telling Egfrid that the first thing the queen had done on her return from Whitby was to go to Lindisfarne to see Bishop Wilfrid. She herself desired the handsome bishop's attentions and, having been coldly rejected by him, she was determined to destroy both him and Etheldreda if she found the opportunity. It was clear to her that, in spite of everything Etheldreda had done to him, Egfrid still desired his wife. If she could only catch her with Wilfrid in a compromising situation she would have revenge on both of them at the same time, and ensure Egfrid's dependence on herself.

Over the next few months Egfrid was torn between the two women. He had never been good at judging character and seeing through rogues. The friends he chose to spend his time with were worldly wise, having no love for him, but only desire for what he could give them. Eormenburh manipulated the king and his companions brilliantly, and he never suspected it.

Etheldreda thought now of nothing but how she could help him to take proper control of his kingdom and his own destiny, trying desperately to undo the harm her indifference to him over the years appeared to have done. She spoke against Eormenburh, but only with careful tact, knowing that the woman's hold was strong and could easily become stronger if she herself lost her tenuous hold on him.

The court at this time found the king's moods almost intolerable. He swung from mildness of temper and reliance on Etheldreda, to sudden rages when he suspected every word she spoke, and every gesture she made. At times he hated Wilfrid, and at others he would call him and give him lavish presents of land and treasure.

Wilfrid now ruled the Church from Lindsey to the land of the Picts, and his position seemed invulnerable.

Eormenburh bided her time like a spider in its web.

* * * *

One day, suddenly, Ovin returned.

When Etheldreda heard the news she dropped everything she was doing and ran down to the stables to greet him.

'Ovin! My friend!' she cried, tears in her eyes, taking both his work-roughened hands in hers. 'I can't tell you how thankful I am that you've come back!' Just the sight of him reminded her of happier days when it had seemed so simple to live as she desired, and when good had followed easily from good intentions.

His face shone at her words with embarrassed pleasure, and she could see by his eyes that his affection for her was still as strong as it had always been.

'I heard of Bishop Chad's death. I am sorry for your loss, my friend, but I am sure he will be happy to be close to our Lord at last.'

Ovin nodded. 'I heard angels, my lady. There is no doubt that he is happy.'

'Ovin! Angels? Tell me about it!'

'It must have been angels, my lady.'

'Tell me!' she cried eagerly. Oh how she needed to hear something of the real world again. She had grown so weary of the shadow-play those around her mistook for life.

'I was digging in the garden. Bishop Chad was alone in his oratory, his brothers in the church, when I heard the most beautiful music I've ever heard coming down from the sky. It seemed to come from the south-west, hover over the oratory for a while and then enter it... filling it... so that the whole building seemed to be shaking with it.'[21]

Etheldreda's eyes were wide with interest.

'Did you see anything?' she breathed.

He shook his head.

'It was music. I saw nothing.'

'How long did it last?'

'I don't know. I seemed to stand there for ages listening to it, afraid to move, thinking it would go away if I moved.'

'What happened then?'

'It rose to a peak, and I tell you my lady tears just poured from my eyes it was so beautiful!' Ovin's face shone.

'And then?'

'And then it gradually withdrew, rising to the sky and finally fading away.'

Etheldreda shivered with the pleasure of knowing that such things were possible.

It seemed that, when it was gone, Chad opened the window and clapped his hands as he often did to call Ovin to him. His face was joyful and excited. He instructed Ovin to fetch seven of the monks and bring them to him. When they were before him he announced that he had received a message from angelic spirits that he was soon to die. He wanted to instruct them in all they needed to know to carry on his work, and to strengthen them in their faith.

He died as had been foretold, but Ovin, having heard the music, felt no pain at his passing, only gladness that what he believed had been proven true. He told Etheldreda he had then felt a strong urge to come to her and tell her of his experience, feeling that in some way it would be particularly important to her at this time.

'My friend, you don't know how important your story is to me!' she said with feeling. 'I truly needed it.'

21

Coldingham AD 672

One day in April, not long after Ovin's return to her and the story he brought of Bishop Chad's death, Etheldreda took advantage of the fact that Egfrid had for several days been calm and pleasant to everyone, and apparently cool to Eormenburh, to seek private audience with him and tell him that she wanted, more than anything on earth, to go to his aunt at Coldingham and take the veil as a nun.

'I find, my lord, this life at court drives me further and further from what I know to be my true life. I spend my days on sand-castles washed down by every passing wave, while the Kingdom of Heaven which stands forever is ignored by me. When I married you, you were no more than a child. Your parents arranged the marriage for political reasons and for political reasons I have stayed. But now that you are a man you no longer need what I can give.'

Egfrid drew his right leg up onto his chair and put his chin upon his knee, looking at her with brooding eyes. He said nothing. She could almost hear her heart beating in the silence.

'Have I your permission, my lord?' she said at last, in a low and pleading voice.

He still did not reply.

'Because we have never consummated this marriage, you will be able to marry again, my lord.' She talked rapidly, nervously. 'You could take a princess of a royal house to wife who will bring with her at once a dowry and an alliance that would be beneficial to your kingdom.'

'And who...' he said with a dangerous edge to his voice as though he were holding himself in check very carefully, 'would you suggest?'

She hesitated, sensing the danger, but knowing that she couldn't leave the subject yet.

'It would be your choice, of course, my lord, but Northumbria needs to strengthen links with the southern kingdoms to balance Wulfhere's hold. I hear that my friend Cenwahl of the West Saxons has a beautiful and intelligent daughter who would be an asset to the throne and to your bed.'

'Eormenburh my cousin is a cousin of the King of Kent. Would she not make an admirable wife?' The bitterness was only very thinly disguised now.

Etheldreda flushed.

'She is already married, my lord,' she said quietly.

His face darkened, and he stood up suddenly, towering over her.

'And so am I, my lady! So am I.'

'But only in name, sir.'

'That is not of my choosing.'

'Nor of mine, my lord. It was God's choice.'

'Did God come down and speak to you? Did he say "Etheldreda, you may not lie with a man, not even your husband"?'

'How it happened is of no moment now, my lord. It is enough that I vowed my life to His service in chastity. I have so far kept only part of my vow. I had thought I could serve Him and still be queen, but lately I have found more evil comes from my presence here than good... and the time has come for me to serve Him every moment of the day and night in the way I feel is right for me.'

'I will not let you go,' he suddenly snapped. His eyes bored into her fiercely.

'I can't help you any more. My presence here disturbs your peace of mind. Cenwahl's daughter–' She broke off, seeing his expression.

He pushed a heavy chair out of his way and strode about the room, clenching and unclenching his hands, cracking his knuckles.

'Why do you hate me?' he muttered. 'Other women fight to share my bed. Only you reject me!'

'I don't hate you, sir,' she cried quickly. 'If I could make you happy, I would have no greater pleasure. But I can't give you what you want. And what I can give, you scorn.'

'Have you no love for me after all these years?' he turned to her and she was moved by the suffering in his eyes.

'Yes, my lord, as sister to brother.'

His face clouded over and he kicked the leg of the table.

'Go then!' he shouted furiously, his face darkening again. 'I want no sister's love from you!'

She slipped out of the room at once, trembling, her heart pounding, as unhappy as he, but determined to make the break now while something like permission was still ringing in her ears. She would speak to Wilfrid and perhaps he would be able to persuade the king to marry Cenwahl's daughter.

Without waiting to gather her belongings she rushed to the stables and started to prepare her horse, telling the stable lad to run at once and bring Ovin to her. 'If I am not here when you get back,' she called, 'tell him to ride fast and meet me on the road going north. I will wait at the first crossroads. Give no one but Ovin this message.'

The boy, amazed at the queen's agitation, for he had always seen her as a calm and gracious lady, ran as though the hounds of hell were after him and breathlessly delivered her message to the Celt.

Ovin was with her before she reached the crossroads.

'My lady, what is the matter? What has happened?'

'Ovin, my friend,' she said, her face full of relief to see him. 'I'm sorry if I alarmed you but I need your help. The king has given me permission to do what I have always longed to do, to become a nun in God's holy service. Because my lord's moods are sometimes changeable, I decided to leave while he was in the mood to let me go. Bishop Wilfrid has already asked permission of the Abbess Ebba to allow me to join her at Coldingham. Would you be kind to me, my friend, and take a message to the bishop advising him of what has happened and asking him to come to Coldingham.'

'Of course, my lady, and I'll ask your women to follow you with your clothes and belongings.'

'I've no belongings, Ovin. I leave the world as I entered it, with nothing but the spirit I had from God, and the body that temporarily clothes it.'

He bowed.

'I'll tell my lord bishop where you are, my lady, and then, if you'll allow it, I'd like to join you at Coldingham. Would you speak to Abbess Ebba for me?'

'Of course, my friend. But please—hurry now.' She watched him go and then took one last lingering look at Bamburgh castle perched as high as an eagle's eyrie. Her time there had not always been happy, but it had been interesting, and although one part of her rejoiced that she at last would be able to live in a monastery, another part of her warned her that she might well miss the challenge, the bustle and the adventure of the worldly life.

* * * *

Because Ovin went straight to York thinking to find the bishop there and then had to retrace his steps to Ripon where Wilfrid was supervising some new buildings, it was some time before he could deliver his message. As soon as Wilfrid received it he began preparing to leave for Coldingham, sending Ovin on ahead to reassure the queen. Before Wilfrid himself could set off, however, Egfrid arrived unexpectedly at Ripon with a huge entourage, bearing gifts and insisting on setting up a feast at his own expense with delicacies he had brought with him. Wilfrid could not help but look for the hidden claw in the proffered hand, knowing as he did that the queen had left and that in the past Egfrid had been suspicious of their relationship. But he played out the game Egfrid set before him.

Wilfrid's larder was by no means bare, and his plate and furnishings were as grand as that of any king's. With Egfrid's gifts of food and foreign wine the feast was magnificent and prolonged. Throughout they made no mention of the queen.

At last Egfrid stood up and, swaying slightly, took Wilfrid's arm as though they were the best of friends. 'Show me your library, prelate,' he said, his voice slurring. 'My wife tells me that you have some of the best books in the country.'

Wilfrid conducted him to the library. He had taken care not to drink too much, knowing that he would need his wits about him for whatever Egfrid had in mind. He managed to hold himself in check while Egfrid, his hands still greasy from the feast, handled the priceless, rare manuscripts.

At last Egfrid decided to come to the point of his visit.

'You're a man of the world, Bishop, though you talk a lot about God. I need your help.'

Wilfrid raised an eyebrow and waited.

'Have you nothing to drink in here, man?' Egfrid said suddenly, looking round impatiently. He saw the shelves of books, the benches and long low tables for the monks to use when studying, light falling only dimly from the narrow windows. 'This is a gloomy place, Bishop, and my glass is empty.'

Wilfrid went to the door and called a servant to bring wine.

'You were saying, my lord, that you need my help?'

'Aye... it is my wife, sir. My wife.'

Wilfrid said nothing.

The king lurched about the room and came to rest at last by one window, gazing out unseeingly at the huge tree that grew outside.

The wine was brought, Wilfrid poured it carefully and slowly. He presented Egfrid with a glass, but took none himself.

'She has left me,' Egfrid said as he took the glass.

Wilfrid gave no indication that he knew of this, but kept his face expressionless.

'You're a cold fish, Bishop. I tell you that my heart is breaking and you say nothing.'

'I'm sorry, my king. I don't know what to say. If it is the Lord's will...'

'Of course it's not the Lord's Will!' shouted Egfrid. 'It was the Lord's Will that she should marry me. It is her own will that she will not lie with me!'

'I think...'

'I don't want to know what you think, sir. I want you to help me.'

'How can I do that, my lord?'

'You can persuade her to come back to me. You can persuade her that what she is doing is not God's will. God's will is for her to be a wife to me in every sense. Otherwise why should He give me these feelings for her?'

There was a painful silence between them for what seemed a long time, broken at last by Egfrid.

'You know what she said to me before she left? She said that she loved me!' he raised his glass triumphantly a few inches from Wilfrid's face. 'What do you think of that? You thought she loved you!'

For a moment Wilfrid's control broke.

'Aha!' cried Egfrid. 'The man of stone is flesh and blood after all!'

'I am not of stone, sir. I feel very deeply for the queen, but not as you imply.'

'I'm no fool, sir,' Egfrid's voice was bitter now.

'I can see through masks as well as any man and I can see what you are thinking when you look at my wife.'

'I pity you, my lord, if you think the only love there is is of the flesh.'

'Pity me, do you!' screamed Egfrid. 'Well, I pity you too, sir, for you'll not have her either. She has gone to Coldingham to be a nun.'

Wilfrid stood very still, forcing himself to take control again.

'It was on my advice that she went there, sir. I think you'll find, when you have taken time to think, it will be the best for everyone.'

Egfrid's anger and bitterness suddenly seemed to dissolve in self-pity.

'I must have her, Bishop. I can't live without her. Help me to get her back.'

'I can't, sir, if she has decided.'

Egfrid took his arm, his eyes full of tears. 'You can persuade her, Bishop. She'll listen to you. At Whitby you persuaded the most stubborn-minded people in the world to change their ways. One woman should be easy.'

'No, my lord.'

'She loves you Wilfrid. That I know. She'll listen to you. If you tell her to do anything in the world she will do it.'

'No.'

'If you just tell her to come back to me.'

'No.'

'I have brought treasure with me. If it is not enough you will have more. Ask for anything you want in my kingdom. You want land and revenues? I'll give them to you. All you have to do is persuade her that I need her. Is that so much to ask?'

'It is too much to ask, my lord. I think you should ask yourself how you will face the judgement seat of God when you have made a woman break her oath to Christ for nothing but the lust of flesh for flesh. She is a remarkable woman and has much to give the world in example of holy living. She has given more than ten years of her life to you. Be grateful, and let her go now.'

'She has given me nothing! Nothing! My country may have benefited. But I have had nothing!'

'That's not true.'

'What do you know of it! Have you stood day after day beside the most beautiful woman in the world, given you by God in holy matrimony, and known that you can never touch her? Never!'

Wilfrid was silent. He too had felt the power of Etheldreda's beauty.

'I cannot help you, my lord,' he said sadly. 'Cannot. Not will not.'

Egfrid caught the finality in his voice and sat down on a bench, slumped in despair, all fire gone out of him. He laid his head upon his arms on the long table and sobbed.

Wilfrid stood helplessly beside him. He knew this was the time, as bishop, he should have drawn Egfrid's mind to higher matters, but, as man, he could not. He shared too many feelings with him.

* * * *

After this Egfrid seemed to give up the attempt to bring Etheldreda back. He hardly left the castle all summer. His skin became pale and sallow, his eyes dull. He did not go hunting and refused even to go down to the harbour to see how the building of his fleet was progressing. Wilfrid visited him several times at Etheldreda's request, trying to persuade him to consider Cenwahl's beautiful and intelligent daughter as his queen, but he would not listen. Even Eormenburh found herself rejected and bitterly turned to others for consolation, playing one thegn off against another until the court was in worse ferment than before.

* * * *

Meanwhile, Etheldreda was living the life of a novice at Coldingham, finding the daily routine congenial where some of the other noble ladies, who had joined on a wave of enthusiasm to be with her, found the discipline rigorous and uncomfortable.

In any monastery periods of time are allotted for adjustments to be made before the full vows are taken, but Etheldreda was impatient to take hers at once and pleaded with the Abbess Ebba to allow her to do so.

'Should I treat you differently because you are a queen?' Ebba asked, her eyes gazing with uncomfortable penetration into Etheldreda's. There was a slight mocking smile on her lips. 'Is that what you are asking?'

Etheldreda flushed and shook her head.

'It's just that...' Her voice trailed away.

'It's just that when you are irrevocably committed.' Ebba finished for her, her voice still having that slight edge of mockery, 'you think you will be safe from the desires of your own flesh and the importuning of others.'

Etheldreda was silent, but her face showed that there had been something of this in her impatience.

Ebba shook her head sadly.

'Oh my child, you of all people should know that "motive" is the key that opens the door, and if you have the wrong motive you cannot enter the room no matter how much you long to do so. Stay with us a while longer. When you're purged of all that drove you to us in such haste, we'll think about your vows.'

Etheldreda sighed. She knew the abbess was right.

* * * *

In the autumn Abbess Ebba relented and summoned Bishop Wilfrid to hear Etheldreda's final vows of commitment.

Many years later when misfortunes came thick upon him, and he lay manacled in Egfrid's prison, Wilfrid thought about that day, the pale October light shafting through the chapel windows on to the head of Etheldreda, the fine gold of her hair hidden under her veil, his own heart tugging two ways, for joy at her dedication to a life he knew with part of himself to be the only way for either of them to reach their God, and pain that so much had to be given up to do it. The words he was speaking came through him as though spoken by another. The choir singing seemed bodiless and remote, like the choir Ovin had described at Chad's death.

'O Lord,' he had whispered in his heart, as his mouth gave out other words, 'may I no longer desire this woman. May our hearts be as chaste as our bodies and Thy Will be all that we desire.'

'Amen,' Etheldreda said softly, as though she

had heard his secret plea, and, for a second, she looked up and met his eyes.

* * * *

In November the abbess burst into the dormitory where the nuns were sleeping and called Etheldreda out.

The two women stood in the cold passage, Etheldreda in nothing but her coarse woollen shift, the winter winds whipping under the door at the end and whistling round her bare feet.

'I've just received news that Egfrid has decided to come and take you back, by force if necessary.'

Etheldreda gasped.

'But...'

'It seems, from what I hear, that it is not so much his idea as his friends. My information is that since you left he has hardly left his chambers. He sits and sighs and groans half the time, and does nothing. I didn't tell you of this before because I thought my nephew would soon pull himself together. In fact I'm guilty of the very thing I warned you against, wrong motive. I agreed to your taking your final vows as soon as I did because I thought that once that was done, he would accept the fact, and return to living his own life. But it seems it hasn't been the case.'

'My poor Egfrid! Why did God ever make me come into his life? I have done him nothing but harm!'

'What? Questioning God's good sense?'

Etheldreda winced at the older woman's sharp taunt.

'What am I to do? I can't go back.'

'No, of course not. We must make a plan. Come, we'll go to my room.'

The two women were about to leave when the door of the dormitory creaked. Ebba pushed it sharply and revealed a whole group of women crowded round it trying to hear what they were saying. Ebba couldn't help laughing at their expressions.

'Well, seeing that you are awake we might as well have our discussion here.'

Among the women in this particular dormitory were some who had been at Ely with Etheldreda. Their love of God was sincere, but often became confused with their love of Etheldreda. They would follow her anywhere and suffer anything for her. It was decided that she and those who would not be parted from her should leave just before dawn, making for the south as fast as they could, hoping eventually to reach Ely where, among her own people and protected by the fens, she would be safe.

It was already time for vigils and Etheldreda insisted on staying for this service before she left. She put her head down before the altar in the great cold chapel and gave herself into the protection of the Lord.

She was still praying when Ebba hurried in and pulled at her arm.

'You must go, my child. Egfrid and his men have been sighted not far from here.'

She allowed herself to be bundled into her cloak and onto a horse, her women friends chattering excitedly around her. She saw the great bulk of Ovin beside her and felt a wave of relief that he was coming with her. He took her bridle and led her out, warning her to duck her head beneath the old black beam of the stable door. The air was crackling with cold around them, the grass white with frost. As the horses breathed, great puff-balls of mist rose from their nostrils.

Ovin gave her horse a slap and started running beside her with great loping strides. There were not enough horses for all of them and some had to ride two to a horse, plunging through the fields and the woods, seeking the coast road to the south, but skirting the part of it that Egfrid and his men would be using. The horses stumbled over the rough ground and sometimes trees loomed out of the gloom causing them to shy and whinny. The women were shivering with fear and cold, some sobbing openly.

'It will be better when we are through the woods,' called Ovin, his breath coming in short bursts, his chest beginning to ache from the cold and the exertion. But the woods seemed to go on forever. There was a track, but it was almost overgrown and brambles caught at their skirts as though to hold them back. Ovin pushed branches away, wishing the light would come and the icy fog that lay so heavily over the low-lying ground, creeping and sliding around the tree trunks, would lift.

Eventually he called a halt, finding a sheltered place under an overhang of rock. He scraped dry leaves out of the crevices under the overhang and tried to make a fire, but there were not enough dry twigs to give it body.

'We must press on,' said Etheldreda. 'See, it is much lighter now and the fog is lifting.'

The fog lifted because a wind arose and blew it in ghostly filaments and threads across the fields towards Coldingham and, as the light grew, the wind grew, cold and fierce, whipping at their faces. The sky that had been clear when they set off soon filled with swirling cloud, keeping the temperature low and the aspect gloomy. They had to pause from time to time for Ovin to rest, and to take their bearings. None of them had been this way before.

At last they saw the sea, but even as they did so they sighted Egfrid and his men at the crest of a hill moving towards them. He was a hunter, with a hunter's instincts and had found his quarry.

The women wailed.

'Sssh,' hushed Etheldreda somewhat impatiently. 'You are in no danger. The king will not harm us.'

'I wouldn't be sure of that, my lady,' whispered Ovin to her. 'The messenger who brought the news to Coldingham said that most are Eormenburh's men, and they lead Egfrid by the nose.'

'You think that they'd harm us?'

'It's possible.'

'But why? My husband wants me back. He doesn't want me dead.'

'*He* doesn't want you dead my lady,' one of the women said. 'But Eormenburh does!'

'Come, my lady,' Ovin said. 'I think we must move on and find somewhere to hide.'

They continued in haste, slipping and slithering down the steep slope to the sea. Before them was a jagged rock promontory reaching out into the water. Ovin suggested they sent the horses on as decoys towards the south while they themselves hid on the rocky sliver of land.

The women at once started clambering over the rocks, the wind howling around them and the waves reaching for their feet. Ovin himself led the horses away, Egfrid's men out of sight behind the brow of a hill. He took them as far as he dared, giving them a beating to start them careering on their way.

He managed to get back to the women before their pursuers came in sight. They had found shelter from the wind under an overhang that the sea had excavated but which was now well above water-level, lifted out of reach by the ancient restlessness of the earth. The women were clustered together shivering and frightened, trying to get as much comfort from each other as possible. Etheldreda was slightly apart, sitting on a rock, a deep quiet around her as though she were not part of the wild and stormy scene. Ovin stood looking down at her for a moment, his heart filled with anxiety for her, and yet, even as he studied her, her calm began to affect him and he felt confident that no harm would come to them.

He began to look for driftwood and found enough to make a fire if necessary. Perhaps when Egfrid's men were gone they could rest a while and warm themselves before continuing on their journey.

But Egfrid had not been fooled by the tracks of the horses. He was at this very moment scrambling down the slope towards them. They were trapped.

Ovin gripped a piece of driftwood ready to use it as a club.

'There'll be no need for bloodshed,' Etheldreda said, seeing the expression on his face. 'If it is God's Will for Egfrid to take me back I will be taken. If it is not, all the men in the kingdom will not prevail against me.'

Ovin was ashamed that he had doubted. The Etheldreda he had admired so much at Ely had returned. Her face was flushed with the buffeting of the wind, her eyes bright with determination.

The women could hear the men shouting from the rocky beach and thought that they were surely finished, but the wind howled louder and a great wave broke fiercely over the entrance to the promontory. Sleet began to fall, driving its sharp ice needles into the faces of the men who were trying to reach them. The sea rose higher with every gust of wind and roared across the narrow entrance, throwing up columns of spray as high as Bamburgh Castle.

'God in Heaven!' exclaimed Ovin, awed.

The women crossed themselves and clung closer to the rock.

There was no chance of anyone getting across the channel between the shore and the promontory. The men could see it and looked for shelter nearby. But there was very little.

They waited all day for the storm to abate, but it did not. It persisted even through the night and at the following dawn it was as fierce as it ever had been. Luckily the women had taken provisions for several days from Coldingham and now, protected by the overhang, they began to laugh at the discomfiture of Egfrid's men who had neither shelter nor food.

On the third day Egfrid called off his men.

'This storm is not natural,' he said, 'Etheldreda has asked for the Lord's protection and she has been given it. I can't fight Him. I'm beaten. He can have her!'

The men who had set off so full of arrogance and high spirits a few days before were soaked and miserable, hungry and exhausted. They were also frightened. What if the Lord God Himself really *did* exist, and really was on Etheldreda's side! They made their bedraggled way back to Bamburgh and, within a few hours of their leaving, the wind and rain stopped, the sea returned to normal, and the women could cross the neck of the entrance on to the mainland shore.

* * * *

Etheldreda had now no doubts that what she was doing was God's Will.

* * * *

Cautiously, slowly, they made their way through the country, keeping off the main roads, splitting up into groups of two or three, seeking shelter from cottages and churches all the way south to Ely.

It was the mildest winter they had ever known so far north, and although they were cold and hungry and tired more often than not, they suffered no hardship that they could not endure.

When they needed rest or when the weather took a turn for the worse, they settled in a village and became part of its community, sometimes for several weeks at a time. In later years wherever Etheldreda had stayed became a place of pilgrimage. Churches were built, sometimes no more than tiny chapels of wood and reeds, sometimes more substantially of stone.

In all this long journey Etheldreda was coming more and more to terms with her eternal self. It was as though that strange storm had blown her mind clean of all confusions. She knew now with unshakeable conviction that all that struggle for worldly power and glory that she had been part of was as pointless as two straws fighting over which one of them is to be king while a fire is sweeping towards them over a field.

She thought back to the court where jealousies and rivalries occupied the days, where the clothes and jewels worn by a person were what people judged him by. She thought of Wilfrid whom she loved and yet who played the power game with kings. He had left the true Path as surely as she had when she was queen.

Now, walking the road, her shoes worn through, a rough and prickly wool against her skin, no one knowing her as queen but only as a nun walking, she knew that she was nearer to the Path than she had ever been.

She thought of Ely and what she would do there when they reached it.

Something in her longed to be an anchorite, to live alone on her beautiful island with no one but God. But over the years as queen she had learned that she had a natural talent for inspiring, teaching and guiding. She believed that talents must be used, for they were gifts from God and always given for a purpose. Her apprenticeship had been in the world. She would now practise what she had learned exclusively to the glory of God. She would found a community and a school that would bring light to a dark and savage world.

22

Death at Ely AD 679

Etheldreda arrived at Ely in the spring of 673. The island had never looked lovelier. The leaves in the wood were the colour of pale green silk. The homesteads were nestling in clouds of apple blossom.

She set about at once to organise her community. Ovin was to be her steward, and the faithful women she had brought from Coldingham were the first to be provided for. Her nephew Aldwulf, King of East Anglia, joyfully visited her, offering to help in any way he could to establish the buildings of her community. Wilfrid, on his way to an important meeting of the Church called by Theodore at Hertford, stopped off and stayed, sending a proxy in his place to a synod that proved to be of a great deal of importance in the future of England's Church history. He performed the ceremonies that made her Abbess of the new house, and lent her some of his own stonemasons to ensure that the new church she was building would be beautiful and strong.

The year passed busily and pleasantly. She

had never been so happy. She was at home at last and at peace with what she was doing.

She managed to run a community that was rapidly growing in an orderly way, treading a careful path between the individualism and the simplicity of the Celtic way which she admired so much, and the more organised and disciplined way of the Roman Church. There were certain rules and regular services, but there were no compromises made to the values of the worldly kingdom.

The poor and needy were tended and whatever was elegant and rich about Ely at that time was produced by the skills of those who lived and worked there. A school was started that became greatly respected, also a scriptorium whose manuscripts were distributed throughout the world like seeds of some rare plant to grow and flower amongst people of many different nationalities and many different times. Ovin started an infirmary and installed famous herb masters and healers. Embroidery done by the nuns became sought after in Rome and Byzantium.

All the skills that Etheldreda had amassed over the years, from the formal scholarship of the school at Dunwich under Bishop Felix, to the tactful guidance of people and the diplomacy learnt at her father's court and at York and Bamburgh, were put to good use. She lived a life of extreme abstemiousness, regretting the damage she had done to her soul during the years of rich living at court. She demanded no great sacrifices of others but for herself she wore nothing but the simplest, roughest clothes and ate no more than was barely necessary to keep her alive. In order to have time for personal prayer and meditation after a full day with her community, she took to staying up most of the night when the others were asleep. She was determined not to lose that lifeline of communication between herself and the Counsellor that she felt she had lost at Bamburgh.

* * * *

Meanwhile, in the outside world, the flux and flow of events were continuing.

Her nephew Egbert, King of Kent since his father's death of the plague in 664, died suddenly, and her younger nephew Hlothere took his place. Their mother, her sister Saxberga, retired from court to found a monastery at Sheppey.

Cuthbert withdrew from active life as a prelate to a wild and lonely island off the coast near Lindisfarne. His brethren tried to dissuade him, as the place was well known as the haunt of demons, with no fresh water and no vegetation. Etheldreda was amused to hear how he, with his customary unshakeable faith in God, took himself to the highest point on the island and there, in a voice of thunder, commanded the demons to be gone.

'And did they go?' she asked her informant.

'None have been seen since,' he replied, 'and within days the holy father found water by digging for it. It's said he has planted some barley seed and some onions, and has built himself a hut with a high wall surrounding it, so that he can see nothing but the sky.'

She sighed.

'What joy to live so close to the earth, so close to the sky, and above all so close to the God he loves. He must be very happy.'

'Are you not happy too, my lady?' one of the nuns asked, seeing the slight shadow that crossed her face.

'I too am happy, my friend,' she said, the shadow lifting, the light returning. 'The happiest I have ever been.'

* * * *

At Whitby the Abbess Hilda had fallen ill with a fever not long after Etheldreda had last seen her, a fever which was not to leave her for seven years and which eventually would destroy her. In spite of the pain and discomfort she refused to accept that she was ill and continued to rule her house and act as hostess and adviser to any who called upon her.

Etheldreda and she did not see each other again but kept in touch through letters and mutual friends.

* * * *

The news of Egfrid was that he was building up his force of fighting men and his fleet, an activity watched closely by Wulfhere.

The year after Etheldreda came to Ely, Wulfhere launched the attack on Northumbria that everyone had expected he must make in reply to Egfrid's growing aggressiveness. The two forces were well matched, but the Mercians were driven back and Wulfhere killed.

The news saddened Etheldreda—the image of the two straws fighting for supremacy in a burning field rose once again to her mind. She prayed for peace and for Egfrid's restless energy to be channelled towards something more creative, but she accepted that the ruthless rivalry of kings was not her concern now, while the running of her community was. She saw her work as providing a rich and fertile seed-bed from which a burnt and desolate world could regenerate itself. But Wulfhere's death was a blow. She had admired him and knew that her niece loved him. Egfrid had said on several occasions that Wulfhere was the only true friend he had ever had. What demon drove him to provoke a situation from which there was no way out but through the death of one of them?

The Mercian defeat was not such that Northumbria could boast of conquest. Wulfhere's brother, Ethelred, married to Egfrid's sister, Osryth, became king of a Mercia still powerful enough to overlord most of the seven kingdoms.

* * * *

Over the next few years while Ely grew as a centre of light and Theodore of Canterbury was busily preparing a unified Church of Britain, the countries that had been held in a state of political equilibrium during the time Etheldreda was queen began to shift and move.

Ethelred of Mercia ravaged Kent, burning churches, destroying villages.

Egfrid harried the British and the Picts to the west and the north, while keeping his southern borders with Mercia heavily guarded.

* * * *

After three years as her steward and much longer as her close friend, Ovin died. Etheldreda sat beside his body through the night, her heart closer to breaking than it had been for a long time. He had always been so strong, a certain comfort to her in everything that alarmed or frightened her. Now he had left her, and no matter how much she told herself that she should rejoice for he was with their Lord, her sense of loss was deep and painful.

Now she was alone. The child who had cried in the wake of Penda and turned to the Celtic slave for comfort was dead too. The future might be vast and rich, but the past, crouching in the heart, would always cry in the night for things no longer possible, for a loved one no longer to be touched.

The cross she erected for him said simply, in Latin:

'Thy light to Ovin grant, O God, and rest. Amen.'[22]

* * * *

Eormenburh's husband had been killed in the battle against Wulfhere and she at last achieved what she had long wanted, the position of Egfrid's queen. One of her first deeds was to poison Archbishop Theodore's mind against Wilfrid. Egfrid had never forgiven him for refusing to help him with Etheldreda, nor for having her friendship and affection still. Eormenburh had no trouble in enlisting his help to destroy the man who had rejected her.

Theodore was in the process of reorganising the Church and of dividing the huge bishoprics.

He did not hesitate, on Egfrid and Eormenburh's advice, to unseat Wilfrid and divide his see between Bosa, Bishop of Deira, and Eata, Bishop of Bernicia.

Indignant at the injustice of this, Wilfrid chose to go to Rome like Saint Paul, whom he admired above all men, to present his case. He did not see Etheldreda before he left, though she heard of the events and was greatly distressed to think that it was his friendship with her that had caused Egfrid to hate him so. That it may have been Egfrid's fear of his growing power and influence and jealousy of his great wealth that made him seek his downfall, did not occur to her.

* * * *

In early August of the year 678 a comet spanned the sky, bringing with it to everyone who saw it feelings either of fear or of elation.

Etheldreda rejoiced in its beauty and went out in the fields long before dawn to watch its progress, her feet wet with the dew, her eyes shining with the promise of glories to come in God's Kingdom, if the sky, which after all was only His antechamber, could contain such splendours.

Wilfrid, resentful and restless on the boat bearing him to France on the first lap of his journey of protest to Rome, saw it as the

Sword of justice raised threateningly by God above Egfrid's head.

Egfrid himself, locked in battle with Ethelred of Mercia, saw it as a sign of God's favour and a promise that he would win, while Ethelred claimed it as a sign from God to him that he would have the victory.[23] As it happened, neither won, but many of their loyal subjects were slaughtered on the banks of the River Trent, and the popular young King of Deira, Alfwin, Egfrid's brother, met his death.

Heregyth was faced with the loss of her husband Imma and, heartbroken, made her way south to Ely, returning at last to Etheldreda, ready to take the vows of a nun. Age and sorrow were beginning to wear her down, and Etheldreda found her friend much subdued.

In the spring of the following year she took the veil and settled to a calm routine of work and prayer, never reaching the heights that Etheldreda reached, and yet finding a kind of peace of mind at last.

In June this peace of mind was shattered.

Etheldreda received news from her nephew, King Hlothere of Kent, that a young man called Imma, claiming to have been once a thegn of hers at York, was requesting ransom money in her name to free him from slavery.

Trembling with excitement she rushed to find Heregyth.

The two women could not imagine what had happened, but Heregyth was given at once an escort to take her to Kent, and a letter for King Hlothere asking him to pay anything that the slave-master asked, to free Imma, who was indeed known to her and much loved.

The story Heregyth heard when she at last was reunited with the husband she had thought dead was an extraordinary one.

It seemed he had been knocked unconscious in the battle of Trent and had lain insensible for hours. When he recovered consciousness the battlefield was deserted. He managed to get away before the burial parties came, but, still dazed from the blow on his head, he was not clear in which direction his homeland lay.

He was found by some Mercian soldiers and taken before Ethelred. Fearing to say that he was one of Alfwin's thegns, he said he was a peasant who had followed the army with food.

Ethelred ordered him to be put in chains and kept as a slave. But the manacles that were put upon him slipped off. New ones were brought but they too slipped off. It was found that no manacles would stay upon him no matter what was done to make them fit.

He was brought back before Ethelred.

The king looked at him long and hard.

'I think you have lied to us,' he said. 'You are no peasant.'

Imma confessed that he was not, and gave his real identity.

'How do you account for the fact that my blacksmith can't make manacles to stay on you?'

'I don't know, my lord, but I have a brother who is a priest, and who surely will be praying for my soul. Perhaps his prayers are keeping me from being chained.'

Ethelred was uneasy at this thought and decided he would take no more responsibility for the man. He sold him to a Frisian in London, who on finding that he had the same problem as Ethelred in keeping him chained, and hearing Imma's explanation, gave him the opportunity to buy his freedom.

It was at this point that Imma went to King Hlothere for the ransom price.

Hlothere gave it to him gladly in Etheldreda's name, and when Heregyth and he were reunited gave them a great feast of celebration.

At the end, when it was time for bed, Heregyth began to weep.

'What is it, my love?' Imma asked, concerned.

'I've taken vows of chastity!' wailed Heregyth. 'Oh why wasn't I given a sign that you were still alive!'

They talked all night, trying to find a solution, but neither, after Imma's experience, would consider breaking a vow to God.

Wearily, sad-eyed at the dawn, they agreed that there was no way for them but for Imma too to take such vows, and join Etheldreda's community. At least they would be together, though they would never again share a bed.

* * * *

On their return to Ely they found that the dreaded shadow of pestilence hovered over the community. Guests had brought it from where it ravaged the East Saxons. Heregyth was told that Etheldreda was already ill, but that she refused to let them be distressed by it.

'Just after you left a family came asking for shelter,' one of the sisters told Heregyth. 'The widowed mother pleaded to be allowed to test out the holy life to see if it were suitable for her and her family. She and her children looked perfectly healthy to us but within a few days they were ill of the plague. Our holy mother did not look at all surprised when we told her of it. She said she had seen a dark shadow behind the woman that was not cast by the sun. We asked her why she had allowed her to enter, having had this premonition.

'"Should I have turned her away because she carried suffering with her?" she said. "Is it not suffering that we are here to alleviate or endure in God's name?"'

'We felt shamed. She then told us how many of us would die and how many of us would live through it, but she wouldn't tell us the names.

'"Only one name I will give you," she said, "and that is my own."'

'Will you be among the living or the dead?' we asked.

'"The living," she replied calmly, "but no more on this earth."'

'We then understood that she was to die, but she wouldn't let us weep or mourn. Since that time she has been arranging everything about the place to run smoothly without her.

'Huna has been instructed that her burial must be as simple as that of an unknown peasant, her coffin wood, her grave unmarked.'

'I must see her!' cried Heregyth.

'She is very ill.'

'No matter. She and I have been like sisters since childhood. I must see her.'

She found her in her little cell with no more comforts than she usually had, her face flushed and wet with fever and a horrible swelling on her neck, under her chin.

On seeing Heregyth, a lovely smile came to her face.

'I was hoping you would come.'

Heregyth knelt down beside her.

'No, don't weep, my sister. You must know by now, death is not what it seems. Besides—I've been told Imma's story. So pray for me when I'm gone—it seems to be very effective.' She gave a mischievous smile at this, which brought further tears to Heregyth's eyes.

The surgeon Cynefrid lanced the swelling on her neck a few days later, and for a while it looked as though she would recover. She had her bed moved out during the daytime into the garden, where she could hear the birds sing and see the flowers growing. One by one the whole community came to her side and spoke with her, receiving courage and inspiration from her.

One day Heregyth could keep up the brave face no longer and burst into tears in front of her. 'I hate to see you suffering,' she sobbed.

Etheldreda looked concerned. 'My friend,' she said gently. 'It is you who are suffering, and for that I'm truly sorry. For myself I find the pain in my neck a relief. I see it as a penance for all the times I have put worldly matters before the eternal. Remember the necklace I used to wear with such delight? Well, this jewel of pain reminds me that beneath the surface of everything that shines with earth-light alone, is darkness.'

* * * *

The temporary improvement gave way to a higher fever and during her short periods of consciousness it became increasingly difficult for her to speak the words of comfort and encouragement those around her had grown to expect.

Heregyth never left her side. One night when she was alone with her she murmured something and Heregyth leant down to hear what it was.

'The candle... the candle flame is dark...' she thought she heard.

'Dark, my lady?'

'Dark against the light I see... blow it out Heregyth... we want no darkness here!'

Heregyth blew the candle flame out, but she could not see the light Etheldreda was talking about.

* * * *

Etheldreda died on the 23rd of June 679 with her friends around her, and was buried as she had wished, simply.

Exactly the number of monks and nuns

died at Ely that she had foretold. When the number was reached, the pestilence abated and the community returned to its normal working round.

Epilogue

Exhumation 17 October AD 693

The pavilion flapped in the stiff breeze, tugging at the wooden pegs that held it to the earth. Saxberga, Abbess of Ely, had herself made sure that it was firmly tied before the ceremony began, testing the ropes with her own hands, knowing that autumn could be changeable and that although they might start the work in calm sunshine they might have to finish it in storm.

She stood now before the entrance, an old woman but still holding herself as regally as when she was Queen of Kent. It was to be her command that would set the two monks digging at the grave of her sister.

When Etheldreda had died fourteen years before she had been insistent that she was to lie in a plain wooden coffin amongst her brothers and sisters of the monastery, and that there was to be nothing that would mark her grave out from theirs. They had respected her wishes at first and there had been nothing on the grave to show a passing stranger that in it lay a woman who was the daughter of a king, once herself Queen of Northumbria, and the founder of Ely. But pilgrims had still come and found her grave. The grass was worn thin around it, the earth-level sinking as the dust was carried away in thousands of little flasks and leather pouches to be used for healing or for protection against demons.

It was decided that her bones should be moved from their present exposed position and transferred to a stone coffin more fitting for such a great lady, within the protective body of the church.

It was for this purpose that they were now gathered together at her graveside.

Wilfrid, now the Bishop of Lichfield under the protection of King Ethelred of Mercia, stood beside the abbess, his face lined, his hair grey from all the misfortunes that had befallen him in the last years, but still handsome, and still lordly in his bearing.

On his return from Rome with letters from Bishop Agatho declaring that he had been unlawfully dismissed from York and that he must be reinstated, he had been flung into prison by Egfrid, who declared that the letters were forgeries. Eormenburh had taken the valuable relics he had purchased in the holy city with his own money, and had had them set in a gold chain which she wore around her own neck. The proud bishop rotted in Egfrid's dungeons for almost a year before Abbess Ebba of Coldingham secured his release by pointing out to Egfrid that the fits Eormenburh had begun to have were probably a form of punishment for the way they had treated Wilfrid, and the way she had profaned the holy relics.

He stood now beside the grave of the woman he had loved, deep in thought. The years when she had been queen were golden in memory. Everything had come easily then, comfort and riches seemed his by right. Stripped of everything in prison he had thought of her until he feared he would go mad. She was dead before he returned to Northumbria and he would never see her again, but something she had once said to him finally pulled him through the dark days and gave him strength. The last talk they had together had been of the foolishness of trusting to worldly riches and worldly power for security. Had she known what the future held for him? She had said, and he could see her now saying it, 'When we are flying through a storm it is the strength of our wings and our courage that keeps us going, not the colour of our feathers.'

Saxberga raised her hand and the two choirs, monks to the right and nuns to the left, began to sing. Sweetly the music rose above the tent where Etheldreda was lying in her old, plain wooden coffin. The abbess raised her other hand and two monks moved forward and entered the tent. The implements for them to use were already beside the grave.

Saxberga lowered her hands and her head, and shut her eyes.

It had not been an easy decision to make to go against her sister's wishes, but once made something happened that appeared to show them that the decision had the Lord's blessing. Because the flat marshlands that surrounded the island of Ely yielded very little rock, they were hard put to find a slab suitable for the coffin. They were debating what to do when a young nun told them of a dream she had had in which they had been searching on water and had found a coffin washed up like a boat on a shore, lying against a wall. Impressed by this they took to the river and went south, coming at last to the crumbling walls of Roman Grantchester. There, as the young nun had described, they found a fine stone coffin lying waiting for them, the exact size they needed for Etheldreda.

* * * *

Heregyth's eyes filled with tears as she listened to the words that were being sung.

'Teach me, O Lord, the way of Thy statutes;
And I will keep it to the end.
Give me understanding, that I may keep Thy law
and observe it with my whole heart.
Lead me in the path of Thy commandments,
for I delight in it.
Incline my heart to Thy testimonies,
and not to gain!
Turn my eyes from looking at vanities;
and give me life in Thy ways.
Confirm to Thy servant Thy promise,
which is for those who fear Thee.
Turn away Thy reproach which I dread;
for Thy ordinances are good.
Behold, I long for Thy precepts;
in Thy righteousness give me life!
Let Thy steadfast love come to me, O Lord,
Thy salvation according to Thy promise...' [24]

It had been her suggestion that Etheldreda's favourite psalm should be used, the psalm that had seen her through so many bad times.

'I am a stranger in the world, O Lord, hide not Thy instructions from me.'

Now even more a stranger without Etheldreda to guide her, Heregyth felt lost and lonely.

She tried to talk to God, but God seemed so difficult to understand, so formidable and harsh. She found more and more that she prayed to Etheldreda, asking for her help, pleading with her to intercede with God for her. Oh that she could rise up from the grave now and be amongst them again, smiling, laughing, turning everything to joy around them.

During the years since her death it had been difficult to keep faith. There was so much evil in the world, so much hardship. Etheldreda had always found a way of accepting it, of understanding it, and finding how it led to good. Heregyth found this almost impossible to do. There was civil war in Kent, Saxberga's grandson contending for the throne with her son, both dying in the struggle. Egfrid following one bloody massacre with another, invading Ireland, invading Scotland, at last himself being tricked into death by the Picts, his people slaughtered in revenge for his greed for power. Plague followed plague. Disaster followed disaster.

Heregyth shivered. How could she stand beside the grave of Etheldreda and think such black, despairing thoughts? Etheldreda had once said that through all the shadows there were always fine lines of light to follow, each one an individual spirit finding its way to God.

No matter how the storm raged these lines would never break. All that was needed was trust, and courage to hold to them.

'Etheldreda, lady,' Heregyth whispered, 'give us a sign that we can hold to in the dark!'

The singing stopped, the two monks came out of the tent and bowed to Saxberga. The coffin was ready to be opened.

Stooping, the abbess entered the tent.

Silently the community waited. The stone coffin was ready to receive Etheldreda's skeleton. Even the wind had dropped, the last leaves hanging poised from the trees as though time had stopped.

Wilfrid clenched and unclenched his hands. He dreaded to see the woman who had been so full of life reduced to dusty bones. He wondered if he could effect the transfer and conduct the whole service without looking at her.

Suddenly there was a commotion in the tent and Saxberga came rushing out, her face blazing with excitement.

'It is a miracle!' she cried. 'Praise be to the Lord.'

'What... what is it?' he gasped and rushed forward.

There was pandemonium, everyone was rushing about asking everyone else what had happened.

Weeping with joy the abbess told them that Etheldreda's body was as fresh as the day that she had been buried. The corruption of the grave had not touched her.

Wilfrid knelt beside her looking at her calm and beautiful face. He could think of nothing but that he was seeing her again and that he loved her.

Behind him Cynefrid the surgeon crowded into the tent and gazed down at her, prepared to disbelieve Saxberga's words.

'Even the tumour that I lanced has gone,' he murmured, crossing himself.

Heregyth fell down on her knees.

'Mistress, I will never doubt again,' she sobbed. 'Never! Never again!'

Some of the community were singing, others had joined hands and were dancing around in circles; the whole scene was more like that of a fair than an exhumation.

Gradually they quietened down, realising that night was falling and they must transfer her to her new resting-place before the cold dews of evening fell on her.

The coffin was sealed and carried lovingly to the chapel.

No one slept. No one left her side.

She was with them still and would never leave!

Map

PICTLAND
Iona
Coldingham
BERNICIA
Lindisfarne
Bamburgh
NORTHUMBRIA
Hadrian's Wall
Hexham
Whitby
Lastingham
DEIRA
Ripon
York
MERCIA
LINDSEY
EAST
ANGLIA
Lichfield
Ely
Dunwich
Exning
Rendilsham
Sutton Hoo
ESSEX
London
KENT
Canterbury
WESSEX
SUSSEX

Chronology

Certain relevant events with the dates usually associated with them.

461—Patrick died in Ireland.

563-565—Columba established himself and his twelve companions on Iona.

570—Mahomet born.

597—Augustine landed in Thanet, sent as missionary to the heathen Anglo-Saxons by Gregory the Great. Columba died on Iona.

605—Augustine died.

616—Ethelbert, Christian King of Kent and Bretwalder of Southern England, dies. Succeeded as king by his heathen son Eadbald. Redwald of East Anglia becomes Bretwalder.

622—The 'flight' of Moslems to Yathrib—the starting point of the Moslem era.

625—Redwald, King of the East Angles, dies.

627—Edwin, King of Northumbria, baptised at York. Edwin converts Eorpwald, Redwald's successor in East Anglia.

630—Etheldreda born at Exning.

632—Penda of Mercia and Cadwalla the native British king attack and defeat Edwin of Northumbria. His head is put on a stake and his queen, Ethelberga, their children and her priest Paulinus, flee back to her home country, Kent.

633—Oswald and Oswy return from exile on Iona. Oswald becomes King of Northumbria.

634—Wilfrid born. Monastery founded on Lindisfarne by Aidan (from Iona).

635—Cynegils, King of the West Saxons, converted to Christianity.

636—Bishop Felix in East Anglia. Also the Irish monk Fursey (whose visions centuries later influenced Dante).

640—Fursey leaves for France. Eadbald of Kent dies. His son, Eorconbert, succeeds him. Penda attacks East Anglia. Egric, the king, and Sigbert, the ex-king (who gave up the throne to become a monk), are both killed. Anna becomes King of East Anglia. Saxberga marries Eorconbert.

641—5th August—Oswald is killed by Penda at the battle of Maserfield. Oswy becomes King of Northumbria—sends for Eanfleda of Kent.

643—Cynegils of Wessex dies. Succeeded by Cenwahl (pagan).

644—Paulinus dies. Egfrid born.

645—Cenwahl of Wessex expelled by Penda, flees to East Anglia. Lives three years at Anna's court and is converted to Christianity.

646—Wilfrid at court of Oswy and Eanfleda.
647—Hilda in East Anglia.
648—Bishop Felix dies.
651—Oswy murders King Oswin of Deira. Bishop Aidan dies. Cuthbert sees vision of his soul being taken to heaven.
652—Etheldreda marries Prince Tondbert of the South Gyrwe. Wilfrid in Kent on his way to Rome; stays to study with Bishop Honorius.
654—Penda attacks East Anglia and kills King Anna. (Sutton Hoo burial? See British Museum.) Ethelhere King of East Anglia. Penda is killed in Battle of Winwaed against Oswy. Ethelhere of East Anglia is killed fighting with Penda. Oswy vows his infant daughter Elffleda to perpetual virginity in gratitude for his victory. Ethelwald now King of East Anglia.
655—Tondbert dies. Etheldreda widowed.
656—Peada, son of Penda, baptised on marriage to daughter of Oswy. Later murdered. Wilfrid in Rome.
657—Wulfhere of Mercia rises to power.
658—Cenwahl of Wessex drives British back as far as Cornwall and Devon.
659—Etheldreda and Egfrid married.
660—Wilfrid returns from Rome and is given the Abbey of Ripon to Romanise, by King Alfrid of Deira.

662—Ethelwald of East Anglia dies. Succeeded by Aldulf, son of Egric (nephew of Hilda).

663—The Synod of Whitby.

664—1 May—eclipse. The yellow plague. Eorconbert of Kent dies. Succeeded by his son Egbert. Archbishop of Canterbury also dies in plague. Oswy of Northumbria and Egbert of Kent send to Rome for new archbishop. Alfrid, sub-king of Deira, dies. Egfrid succeeds him.

665—Cuthbert Prior of Lindisfarne.

669—The new Archbishop of Canterbury, Theodore of Tarsus, reaches Kent. Sets about ordering the Church throughout the Seven Kingdoms. Makes Wilfrid Bishop of York and the whole of Northumbria.

670—Oswy dies. Egfrid becomes King of Northumbria, Etheldreda Queen. Wulfhere overlord of Southern England. Theodore appoints penances for those who sacrifice to devils, foretell the future, eat food that has been offered in sacrifice, burn grain after a man is dead for the well-being of the living in the house, etc.

671—Lindsey conquered by Egfrid.

672—Chad dies. Ovin hears angelic singing. Etheldreda retires to monastery at Coldingham. Cenwahl of Wessex dies. Bede born.

673—Etheldreda flees from Coldingham.

Etheldreda begins to build the monastery at Ely. Wilfrid installs her as abbess. Egbert of Kent dies. Hlothere his brother succeeds him.

674—Wulfhere attacks Northumbria. He is defeated and killed by Egfrid. Another son of Penda, Ethelred, married to Egfrid's sister, becomes King of Mercia.

675—King of Sussex converted to Christianity.

676—Cuthbert becomes recluse on a small island of the Farne group. Ovin dies.

677—Egfrid divides the York diocese in revenge for Wilfrid's support of Etheldreda. Wilfrid goes to Rome to appeal.

678—Comet. Egfrid defeated by Ethelred (of Mercia) at the battle of Trent, but is not killed.

679—Ethelred of Mercia reclaims Lindsey. Etheldreda dies on 23 June. Wilfrid returns from Rome with papers to prove his right to York, but Egfrid declares them forgeries and flings him into prison. Council of Hatfield. Declaration of Faith against the monothelite heresy.

680—Hilda dies.

684-5—Eadric (son of Egbert of Kent) tries to wrest crown from his uncle Hlothere. Eadric is killed. Hlothere wounded. Chaos in Kent. Egfrid invades Ireland.

685—Egfrid is killed while invading Pictland. His half-brother Aldfrid succeeds him (son of Oswy by a former wife.) Cuthbert had had clairvoyant knowledge of Egfrid's defeat and death.

686—Wars in southern England. Wilfrid in exile from Northumbria establishes himself on the Isle of Wight. After Egfrid's death Theodore is reconciled to Wilfrid.

690—Theodore dies. Wihtred (grandson of Saxberga) restores order to Kent.

691—Wilfrid expelled again from Northumbria. Goes to Mercia and remains for eleven years under the protection of Ethelred.

693—17 October—translation of Etheldreda body from wooden coffin to stone one. Found to be uncorrupted. Saxberga Abbess of Ely.

699—Saxberga dies. Succeeded as Abbess of Ely by her daughter Eormengild, widow of Wulfhere.

709—Wilfrid dies.

870—Ely destroyed by Danes.

970—Ely restored.

974—The relics of Etheldreda's sister Withberga stolen from her shrine at East Dereham and placed with the relics of her two sisters, Etheldreda and Saxberga, and those of her niece Eormengild, at Ely.

Genealogies

The Royal House of Wuffingas: East Anglia

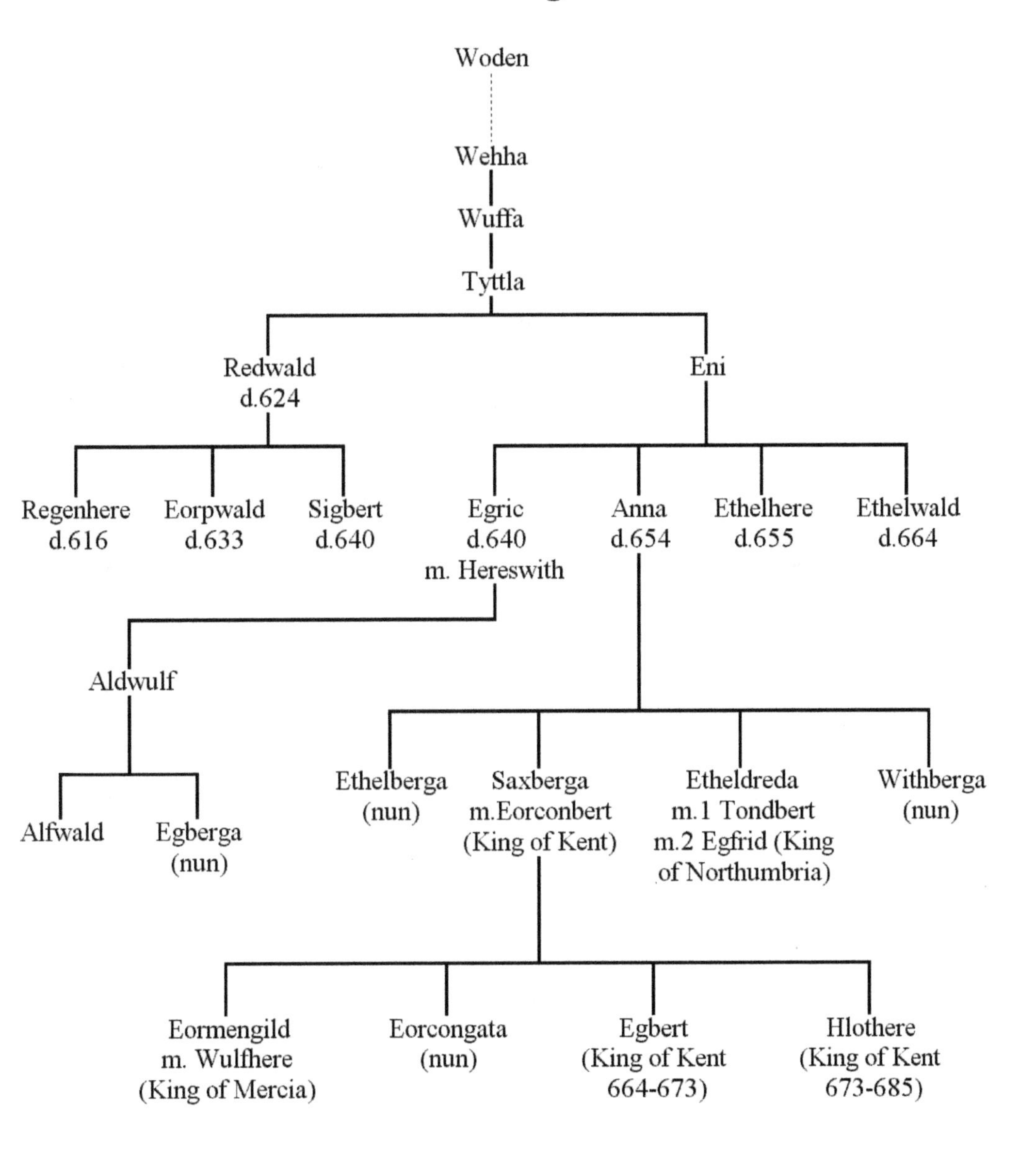

The Royal House of Mercia

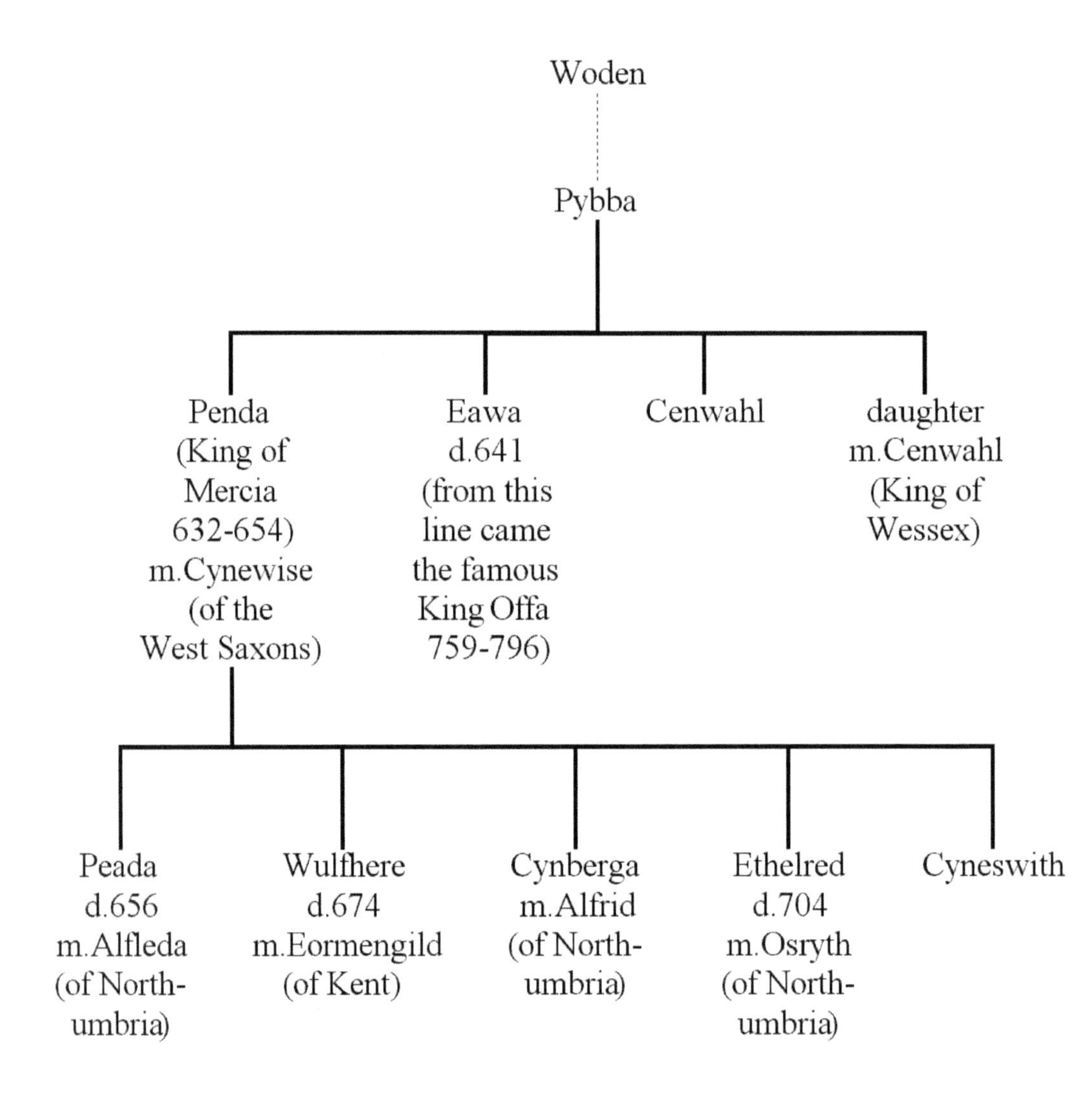

The Royal House of Kent

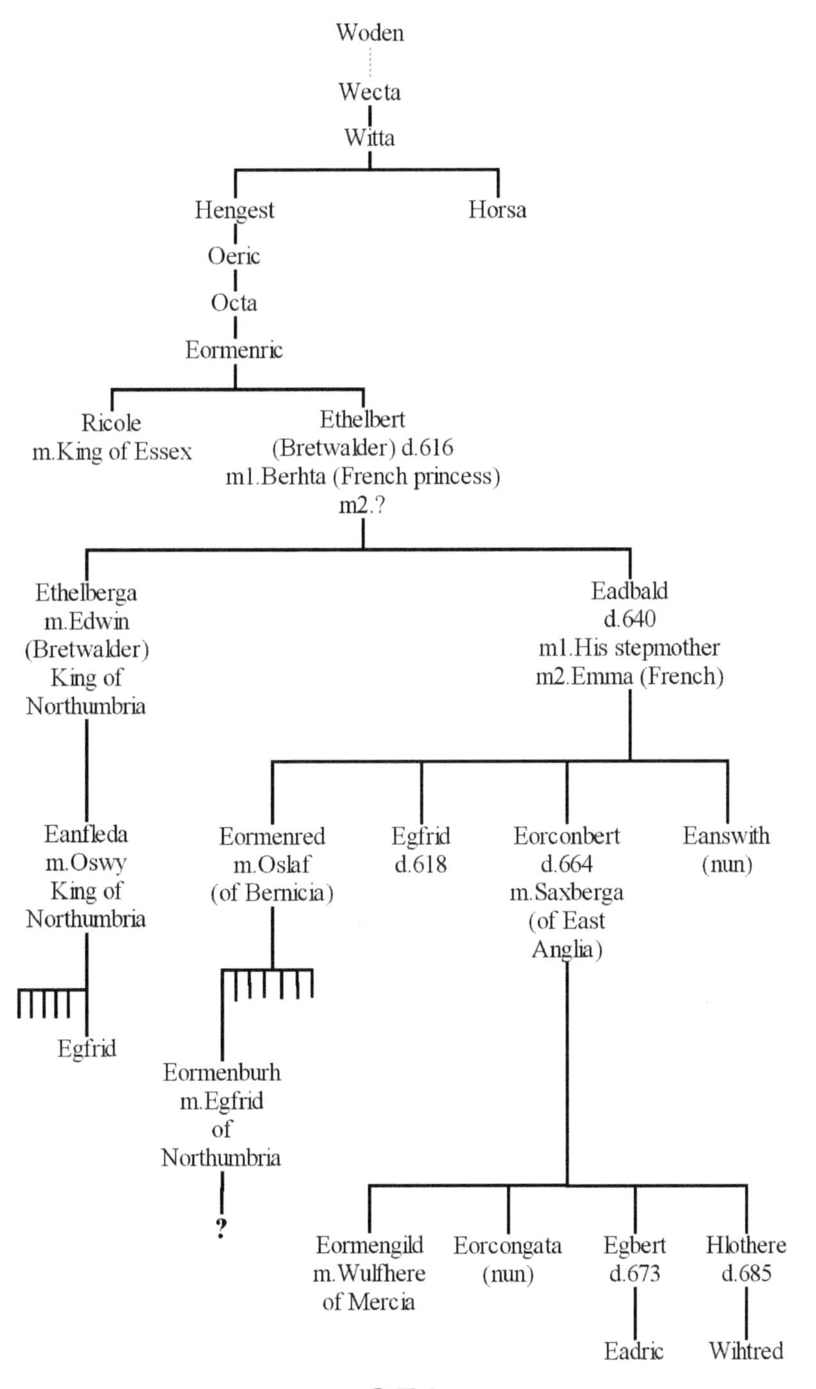

The Royal House of Bernicia

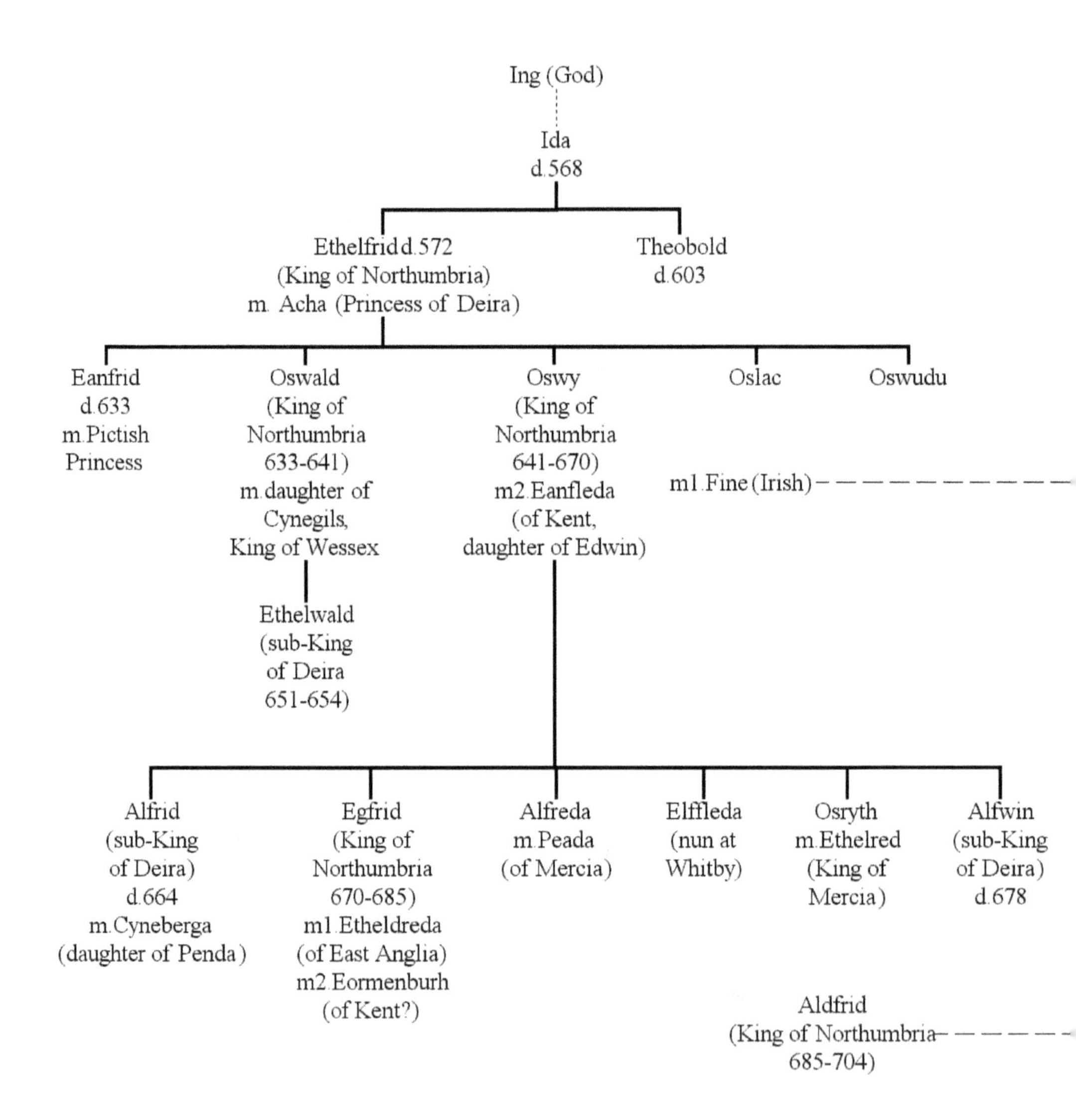

The Royal House of Deira

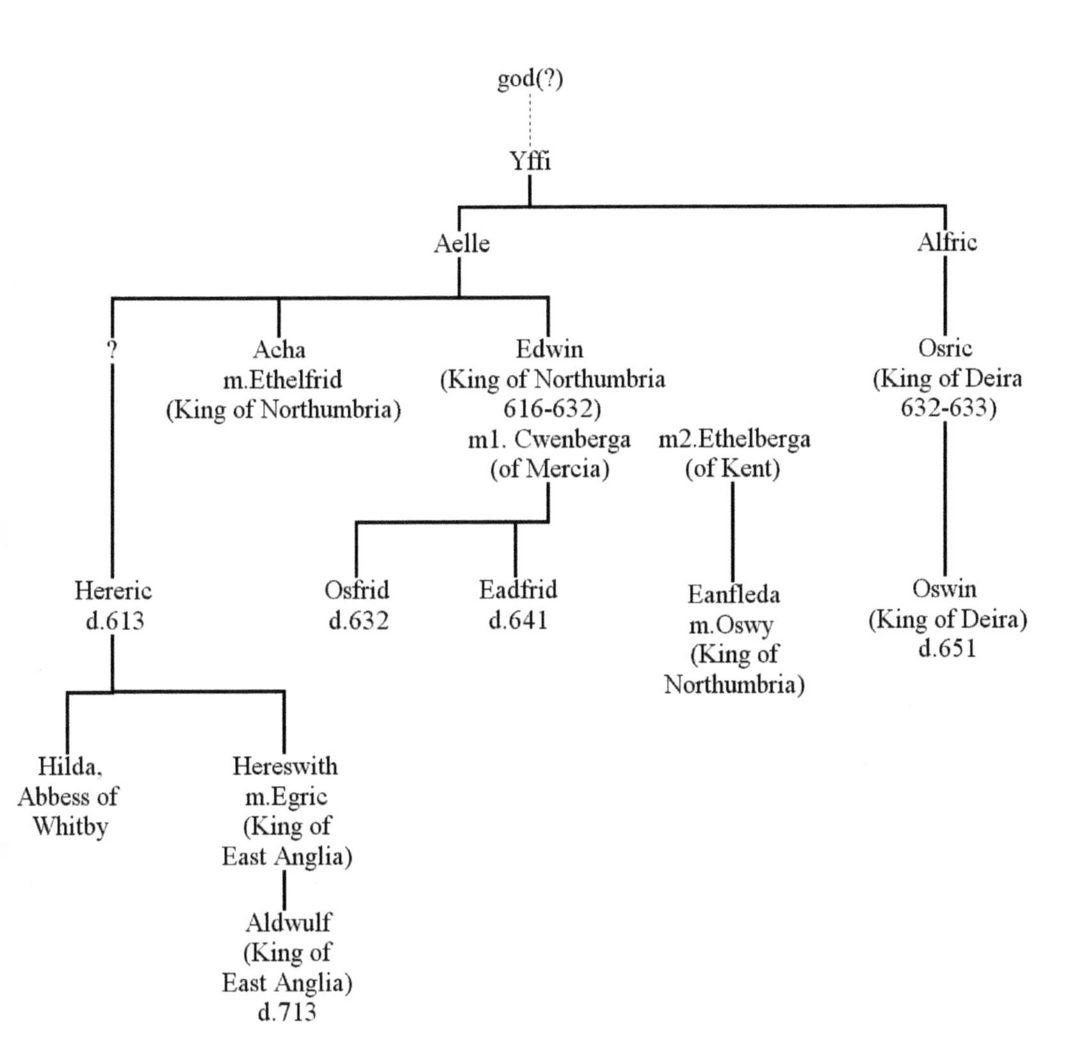

Names

Some differences in the spelling of names found among the authorities:

Etheldreda—Aethelthryth—Audrey

Saxberga—Seaxburgh—Sexberga

Egfrid—Ecgfrith

Eorconbert—Eorconberht

Ethelberga—Aethelburh

Ethelred—Aethelraed

Hlothere—Lothere

Eanfleda—Eanflaed

Redwald—Raedwald

Oswy—Oswiu

Sigbert—Sigeberht

Egric—Ecgric

Fursey—Fursa

Ethelwald—Aethelwald

Ovin—Owini

Cenwahl—Cenwalh

Place names

I have invariably used the place name that would be most familiar to the modern reader. In the list below, the present name is followed by the old name:

Coldingham—Coludi

Ely—Elge

Hexham—Hagulstad

Ripon—Inhrypum

Melrose—Mailros

Chelles—Cale

Whitby—Streanaeshalch

Bamburgh—Bebba

Iona—Hii

Lichfield—Lyccidfelth

Bury St. Edmunds—Beodricsworth

About the author

Moyra Caldecott was born in Pretoria, South Africa in 1927, and died in 2015 a few days before her 88th birthday. She moved to London in 1951 where she married Oliver Caldecott and raised three children. She earned degrees in English and Philosophy and an M.A. in English Literature.

Moyra Caldecott earned a reputation as a novelist who wrote as vividly about the adventures and experiences to be encountered in the inner realms of the human consciousness as she did about those in the outer physical world. To Moyra, reality is multi-dimensional.

Endnotes

1 Psalm 119.

2 Bede: A History of the English Church and People, iii.14, translation by Leo SherleyPrice, Penguin Classics, 1955.

3 Ibid. iii.19.

4 Ibid, iv.23.

5 Psalm 119 v.18.

6 Jeremiah 29.v.13.

7 Mark

8 Bede, op. cit., iii.17.

9 Isaiah 55.v.8

10 At Sutton Hoo, Suffolk. See magnificent grave goods in the British Museum.

11 From the fragment of an Anglo Saxon poem, The Ruin, translated and quoted by Michael Alexander in The Earliest English Poems, Penguin Classics, 1966.

12 Psalm 119 v.19

13 Bede, op.cit. iii.25.

14 Information taken from Mastering Herbalism by Paul Huson, Abacus, 1974.

15 Bede, op.cit., iv.2,3.

16 The Heresy of Eutyches.

17 From Beowulf, a verse translation by Michael Alexander, Penguin Classics, 1973.

18 Bede, op.cit., iv.24.

19 John 14.v.25-26.

20 Bede, op.cit.

21 ibid., iv.3.

22 The broken stump of Ovin's cross is still to be seen at Ely Cathedral.

23 Bede, op.cit., iv.22.

24 Psalm 119.

CPSIA information can be obtained
at www.ICGtesting.com
Printed in the USA
LVHW082236081020
668387LV00008B/1169